In Kelly's Corner

Roxie Rivera

Night Works Books

College Station, Texas

Roxie Rivera/Night Works Books
3515-B Longmire Dr. #103
College Station, Texas 77845
www.roxierivera.com

Cover Art Copyright © 2013 Melody Simmons/Ebook Indie Covers

In Kelly's Corner (Fighting Connollys #1)/Roxie Rivera. -- 1st ed.
ISBN 10: 1630420026
ISBN: 978-1-63042-002-4

DEDICATION

For my sweet Nyx, T-Rex tamer extraordinaire.

ACKNOWLEDGMENTS

I would like to thank Georgia Woods and Barbara Wilson from Taliesin Publishing Services for their editing services. It takes a lot of hands to bring a book to market and to make it the very best it can be!

CHAPTER ONE

"We're about to close up, Bee."

Startled by the coffee shop owner's voice, I tugged on the cord connected to my ear buds and glanced around the empty café. The lights were already dimmed, and he'd flipped up the chairs on the tables surrounding me. I offered an apologetic smile. "Sorry, Ron! I didn't realize it was so late."

"Oh, it's fine. You're one of my favorite and best customers." Ron drummed his fingers on the wooden chair across from me. He seemed hesitant to speak but finally worked up the nerve to say it. "Is everything okay? I noticed you've been spending more time here over the last couple of weeks. We just had that housewarming party for your new place so...?"

I brushed off his concern with a shrug. "I do some of my best work here. My brain seems to function better when I'm inhaling coffee fumes."

He laughed. "Maybe I should use that as part of my new marketing efforts to draw in the high-tech crowd."

"Make sure you emphasize the wicked fast Wi-Fi and

these super comfy chairs," I added while tucking my laptop and gear into my backpack.

"What are you working on tonight?"

"I'm troubleshooting some bugs in a program I built for a DJ friend of mine. She likes to interact with her fans and the audience while she's spinning, but it's hard to juggle social media while she works."

"I bet. That's a very hands-on job."

"Exactly. So I created a program that allows her to filter messages via hashtags and clip out the pertinent bits to build playlists." I drained the last of my lukewarm coffee. "She's trying it out at Faze tonight, but it's not working seamlessly."

"You'll get it figured it out," he said with a dismissive wave.

"I hope so."

"Bee, you built HomeFront at the kitchen table of your mom's house while you were still in high school. You created LookIt while you were a freshman at Rice. I'm pretty sure you can figure out some bugs in this new software."

I shot him an appreciative smile. "I might have to snap your pic and hang it in my workspace as a motivational tool."

He chuckled and combed his fingers through his blond hair. "Whatever it takes, right?"

"Yep," I murmured and slipped my arms through my backpack straps. When I reached for my chair, our hands bumped together. Ron quickly tugged his hand back. I'd noticed that he seemed to have an aversion to personal touch, so I didn't make a big deal out of it. Everyone had their quirks, and this one seemed to be his.

"Are you on your bike tonight?"

I nodded and dug the key to my bike chain from the

pocket of my jeans. "It's not a long ride now that I've moved into the new place."

He glanced toward the floor to ceiling windows lining the front of his downtown shop. "It's awfully late, Bee. You sure you don't want me to drive you? I'm happy to let you park your bike inside for the night."

"It's a tempting offer, but I'll pass. I need to burn off some energy anyway."

Ron seemed reluctant to let me go. "Well...if you're sure."

"I'm sure." I unclipped my bike helmet from my backpack strap and plopped it down onto my head. "I'll see you around, Ron."

"See you later, Busy Bee."

I smiled at his playful nickname and left the café. Outside in the humid night, I grimaced at the suffocating heat. Mid-May in Houston and the temperatures were already flirting with three digits. I shuddered to think what July would bring.

As I unlocked my bike and wound the chain around the handlebars, I wondered if it wasn't time to crack open that vacation folder tucked away in my desk. It wasn't just the heat I wanted to escape. The stress of my skyrocketing profile as a tech entrepreneur was finally starting to get to me.

A little nervously, I glanced around the dark but still busy street. One of the theaters up the block was just letting out, and the bars and restaurants lining either side of the avenue had steady streams of patrons moving through their doors. I don't know what I expected to see among the crowd. A boogeyman in black? A masked figure?

Shaking my head at my silliness, I inhaled a cleansing breath and hopped onto my bike. *There's no one there. You're just paranoid.*

I eased off the sidewalk and into the bike lane. Keeping an eye on the late-night traffic, I tried to focus on the cars and buses whizzing along beside me. My thoughts continually strayed to the weird vibe that had been following me around for the last few weeks.

At first, I had convinced myself it was merely the stress of preparing for finals, moving into my first real place, and entertaining an offer for my micro-blogging platform LookIt. I had even reluctantly conceded that years of pulling all-nighters to study or write code hadn't been kind to my body. All that caffeine and junk food? Not exactly good brain fuel.

Throw in all the normal coed partying and the occasional weekend hackathon, and I probably hadn't had a full eight hour stretch of sleep since high school. When I considered the fact that I had lost my mother and brother within the last four years? Well—it wasn't outside the realm of possibility that I was simply starting to mentally deteriorate from wear and tear and stress.

But, while I could brush off the strange sensation of being watched, there was no way I could ignore the bizarre phone calls and texts that couldn't be traced beyond the burner phones that had been used to send them. With my contacts in the tech world, there was very little information I couldn't get my hands on, but the phones were dead ends. They had all been purchased with cash and had been used at various places around the city, so I couldn't even create a geographical profile with cell phone tower pings.

Three days ago, I had started to receive disgusting photographs. They popped up in random places—tucked under the windshield wiper of my car, stuffed in my backpack—and made my skin crawl.

There was only one conclusion that made sense.

I had a stalker.

The very thought of some creep following me around and sending me snapshots of his dick made me want to puke. Ever since I had made a splash on the tech scene in high school with HomeFront—a real-time chat service for military families—I had experienced more than my fair share of weirdos. Most of them were harmless folks who lacked social skills and simply wanted to reach out to someone who interested or inspired them.

But this? No, this crap was in a different league altogether. It felt intensely personal, and it scared me.

More than once, I had considered calling Kelly. There wasn't a man on earth I trusted more than my brother's best friend. He had been a permanent fixture in my life for as long as I could remember. If anyone could protect me from this unknown menace, it was Kelly Connolly.

But the former Marine worked in private security for the Lone Star Group and had been bouncing in and out of the country since March while on a detail with a sheikh from Dubai. I had tried calling him a couple of times, but his phone went straight to voicemail. He hadn't returned my texts, either.

A twinge of hurt twisted in my chest at the way he had basically ignored me. There was no one to blame for that but me. A poorly timed attempt to kiss him on New Year's Eve had resulted in a quick rejection and such incredible embarrassment. Not surprisingly, Kelly shutting me down like that had strained our once easy relationship.

Whenever he was in Houston, Kelly made sure to stop by and see me, but our visits were growing shorter. He seemed unable to spend even half an hour in my presence.

And it hurt. Bad.

Even now, as I angled my handlebars to glide up onto the sidewalk, I couldn't ignore the gut-churning pain of unrequited love. Falling head over heels for your brother's ridiculously sexy friend? Definitely not my smartest move.

But it wasn't as if I had ever stood a chance. Kelly was...well...he was perfect, wasn't he? The bright green of his eyes had been my favorite color since I was old enough to have a driver's license. His boyish grin did crazy things to my belly, and that booming, raucous laugh of his made my heart race. I couldn't stop fantasizing about having his big, strong arms wrapped around me— or tumbling into bed with him.

Foolishly, I had let myself believe that I could be something more to him than just Jeb's kid sister. Clearly, I had been wrong. Now I was paying for that mistake. When I needed Kelly most, he wasn't there for me.

As I slowed to a coast near the building I had recently purchased, I experienced the strongest pang of loneliness at the idea of spending another night alone in my empty apartment. After living in a noisy dorm for two years and sharing a house with Coby and Hadley for another two years, adjusting to a newer, quieter space was proving incredibly difficult for me. I was having serious second thoughts about striking out on my own. I found myself wanting to crawl right back into the third bedroom at Coby and Hadley's place.

Hopping off my bike, I walked it the last few feet to the private entrance of my building. I had snapped it up in early February after the developer that had previously owned it was forced into bankruptcy after pleading guilty to a list of shady crimes. So far, only the top two floors were habitable. One I used as a living space and the other as a workspace. I hoped to have the rest of it renovated and operational as the headquarters for JBJ TechWorks, my company, by the end of the year. The floor I currently rented at Yuri Novakovsky's downtown skyscraper was nice enough, but we needed more space if we were going to continue growing.

After unlocking, entering and relocking the side entrance, I swiped my keycard near the RFID reader to access the elevator. I rolled my bike inside and punched the button for my floor. Leaning my head back against the cool metal, I tapped my finger against my bike seat while the elevator slowly climbed. The box bounced slightly as it reached its destination and dinged pleasantly.

I pushed my bike across the small private entryway to my front door. While I dug for my keys in the front pocket of my backpack, I noticed a strange brown residue on the door frame. Was it dirt? I couldn't tell and wasn't about to get close enough to sniff.

Holding the door open with my foot, I rolled my bike across the threshold and leaned it against the wall of my sparsely decorated space. I smacked on the light and took exactly three steps into the living room before freezing mid-stride.

There, sitting on my coffee table, was a hot pink gift box adorned with a bright white bow.

Adrenaline poured into my bloodstream as I realized someone had been in my home while I was gone. I was the only person who had a key to the front door or the access card for the elevator.

Panicked, I glanced around the open living space. Was my stalker still here?

Terrified, I frantically backed up to the door and escaped my apartment. I didn't bother waiting for the elevator. I rushed to the emergency stairwell and swiped my keycard through the reader there to unlock the door.

Taking the steps two and three at a time, I raced down the seven floors. It was a freaking miracle I didn't break my neck.

Bursting out the side entrance, I didn't even wait for the door to close behind me before sprinting to the sidewalk. My backpack bounced against my back as I desperately searched for people. A fast food joint on the next corner over beckoned me with its promise of safety.

Huffing and panting, I reached the brightly illuminated spot and sagged against the brick wall in utter relief. With shaking hands, I retrieved my cell phone from my backpack and started to dial 9-1-1. My finger hovered over the touchscreen, but I couldn't commit to calling the police.

During my freshman year, a girl in our dorm had been stalked by an ex-boyfriend who had followed her halfway across Texas just to harass her in Houston. The police had done absolutely nothing to help her, not until the creep had gotten close enough to abduct her from a grocery store parking lot. All the restraining orders in the world hadn't been enough to save her from seven horrifying hours of being held hostage at a rundown motel with that sicko.

Even though it made me feel awful, I had to consider the purchase offer for LookIt slowly working its way through the lawyers and accountants. There were so many people counting on that deal happening, especially the investors who had supported me from the beginning. Bad press like this? It could tank a shaky deal.

There was only one thing to do. I had to find Kelly.

* * *

The thumping, stretched beats of the trap track ricocheted off the walls of the night club and slammed into Kelly's brain in a way that made his ears ache. Rolling his aching neck, he moved around the packed dance floor of Faze and scanned the crowd for any signs of impending trouble. So far, the night had been quiet, but he never counted on it staying that way for long.

He hadn't pulled any bouncer shifts at the club since Yuri, the Russian billionaire owner, had finished the expansion of the space. It had taken Kelly almost an hour to get his bearings. He couldn't believe how many damned people were packed into the joint.

Apparently being the hottest nightspot in Houston wasn't enough. The Russian tycoon seemed determined to put Faze on the map as one of *the* clubs worldwide. Considering he'd already done it with his club in Paris and the one in Moscow, Kelly figured Yuri would push Faze onto that extremely elite list by the end of the year.

A couple of fanboys hanging around the DJ booth caught his eye. Cobalt's latest album was burning up the charts. Because there weren't many female DJs and electronic musicians operating at her level of notoriety, Coby garnered a lot of attention. Tonight, her devoted followers had come out in droves to hear her drop new tracks and mixes.

As Kelly angled in that direction, he studied the two guys pressed up against the booth. They weren't very old. Nineteen or twenty, close to Coby's age. In his many years a Marine and then working in private security, he had developed a good sense for reading people. These two were music lovers and maybe even wannabe artists, but they meant Coby no harm. Even so, Araceli, the general manager at the club, had a standing order that no one got close to the entertainers.

It took a flick of his fingers to send the two men back from the booth. He did it with a smile so as not to provoke an incident. The two guys nodded understandingly and did as directed without causing a scene. He was glad to see the pair weren't going to behave like dicks about it.

Behind her laptops and audio gear, Coby shifted her headphones and tapped her chest. Kelly understood the signal and reached into the pocket of the black blazer he was required to wear on duty to retrieve a couple of VIP after-party cards. He handed them to the guys and bent down to address them. "Stick around after we close. Coby will visit with you for a while."

"Thanks, man."

"Cool! Thanks."

Kelly nodded and continued his round. A familiar face coming through the front entrance caused his heart to stutter wildly in his chest. His reaction to spotting *her* irritated him. Of all the women in the world to have that effect on him, it had to be Beatrice Langston—the one woman he simply couldn't have.

There were few rules that Kelly followed without question but dating the baby sister of the best friend who had died in your arms? That was one line he couldn't cross—even if it ripped his damned heart out of his chest to see Bee with anyone else.

But she was alone tonight and looked tense and almost fearful. If she hadn't been on Yuri's list of VIPs, Big V, the club's head bouncer, never would have allowed her past the velvet rope in that casual getup. Among the sea of scantily clad women in curve-hugging dresses and criminally short miniskirts, Bee looked out of place in her vintage Rice University T-shirt and skinny jeans. Why the hell was she still wearing her backpack?

The sight of her so under-dressed and with that strange expression on her face tipped Kelly's internal alarm. Something wasn't right. Sticking to the shadowy edge of the club, he matched her weaving movements through the dancing throng. He caught up with her a few steps from the DJ booth and tapped her shoulder.

Startled by his touch, Bee pivoted toward him with her balled fist raised and ready to strike. His battle-hardened instincts were instantly activated. He closed his fingers around her smaller hand, slowing the momentum of her swing with his much stronger arm. "Bee!"

The sound of his voice and his friendly face must have finally registered. The panic in her dark eyes instantly fled. Her shoulders slumped with relief. "I've been looking *everywhere* for you!"

Concerned, he stepped closer to her. The urge to brush her wispy, dark bangs behind her ears and cup her sweet face overwhelmed him, but he shoved it aside. "What's wrong? Are you all right?"

She gulped and glanced around nervously. "I just didn't want to be alone tonight. I thought I'd come hang out with Coby." She offered him a stiff smile. "I need to troubleshoot that new software I built for her anyway."

Kelly wasn't fooled by her casual act. Where was the easy, flirtatious grin she always shot his way? Bee never missed a chance to push the boundaries of their relationship. What had her so scared tonight?

He slid his fingers under her chin and tipped her head. Unable to avoid his gaze, she swallowed hard again. He lowered his face so he didn't have to shout to be heard over the music. "The truth, Bee. What's wrong?"

She gripped his wrist. "Someone was in my apartment."

The words punched him right in the gut. "What!

When? Tonight?"

She nodded. "I came home from working late at the coffee shop, and there was a package in my living room."

Kelly's stomach dropped like a runaway elevator. Instantly on alert, he slipped his arm around her shoulders and dragged her closer. His practiced gaze scanned the club for anyone that looked out of place. Dipping his head, he asked, "Did you call the police?"

"No."

Incredulous, he gawked at her. "Why the hell not, Bee?"

Her lips tightened. "What are they going to do? Dust for prints? Tell me to get a restraining order against an anonymous stalker?"

His eyes narrowed. Frustration flared within his chest. "What stalker?"

She licked her lips and glanced away from him. No doubt she understood how upset he was at being in the dark about all of this craziness. "Someone has been following me and leaving sick photos for me to find."

He swore softly and tried not to grit his teeth. "And you didn't think I should know about all this?"

The light overhead shifted to a pop of yellow that illuminated her beautiful face. Her eyes flashed with anger. "Why do you think I've been calling and texting you?"

The realization that the calls he had been dodging put her in this incredibly unsafe situation made him feel like shit. "I'm sorry, Bee. I meant to call you back once the detail was over but—"

"You didn't."

His jaw clenched. "I didn't."

Before he could make a better apology, the bud tucked into his ear clicked. "Kelly? We need you up in the VIP section."

His lips settled into a frustrated line as Ryan's voice dinged his ear. He lifted his arm and spoke into the mic attached at his cuff. "Copy. On my way."

Grasping Bee's smaller hand, he tugged her over to the DJ booth where Coby watched them curiously. He clasped Bee's trim waist and lifted her petite weight without much effort at all. Her hands flew to his shoulders as he placed her on the other side of the short wall that acted as a barrier between the entertainment and the dancers. Her eyes were still wide at his manhandling when he pointed a finger at her. "Don't even think about leaving without me. You stay with Coby until we close. I'll come get you. Understood?"

She nodded. "Okay."

Satisfied that she would be safe, Kelly headed for the VIP section and tried to ignore how damn good it felt to hold Bee. He refused to acknowledge the way his heartbeat had sped up when their bodies had brushed together, her breasts so soft against his hard chest. He really didn't want to think about how badly he'd wanted to nuzzle her neck and inhale the sweet, bright apple scent that she favored. Remembering the short but sizzling kiss they had shared at New Year's sent heat rolling through his belly.

Stop it.

Jeb had entrusted him with Bee's care. If his friend were alive today, he would have kicked Kelly's ass up and down the street for the dirty thoughts racing through his head right now.

Up in the VIP section, he spotted Ryan watching a loud group of guys. He immediately recognized the men as professional baseball players. One of them had a nasty reputation for picking up—and roughing up—college girls exactly like the perky blonde one perched on his lap. How he'd gotten by Big V at the door perplexed Kelly. The giant bouncer and ex-Army sergeant never let assholes like that into the club.

Phoebe, the harried host of their table, smacked away the grabby hand of one of the ball players. Kelly's jaw tightened at the sight of a Faze employee having to defend herself against some prick who thought his high credit card limit and mediocre batting average gave him the right to abuse her.

Movement in the far corner of the VIP section caught Kelly's eye. Yuri stepped into view. He flashed an irritated glance at the offending party and gave a little jerk of his head. His message sent, Yuri slipped back into the ultra-private zone partitioned with gauzy curtains.

Kelly and Ryan didn't rely on their wrist mics and headsets to communicate. Like most of the private security agents on LSG payroll, they were both former military. Where Kelly had been a Marine, Ryan had been a corpsman in the Navy. He'd served alongside numerous Marine units during his many deployments so they were on the same page when it came to situations like this.

There were two ways this would play out—an easy ejection of the group from the club or an altercation. After the relative quiet of the night, Kelly had a sneaking suspicion punches were about to be thrown. Working for Yuri as a bodyguard, he'd learned that the billionaire had a fondness for getting things done quietly and with finesse. This was one time when he might have to step on Ryan's toes a bit to keep the situation calm.

"Look, guys, you were told to keep it down but it seems like your party is unable to comply. Management has asked that you settle your bill and head on out for the night." Ryan diplomatically offered the group a chance to save face and leave without a scene. "You crossed a line touching one of our employees."

"Come on, man! It was a love-tap. You can't expect us not to reach out and touch the merchandise when it's on display like that." The spokesman for the group had consumed enough alcohol to activate the stupid section of his brain. "Look, we'll leave her a nice tip, and it'll be fine."

"Oh, you're going to leave her a very nice tip—but you're all out of here. Now." Ryan leveled one of those icy glares. "Quietly."

The man closest to Ryan shot to his feet and purposely knocked into the bouncer. Kelly groaned inwardly and took a quick step forward to make his presence known. Like Ryan, he was taller and stockier than the athletes attempting to make a ruckus. "Is there a problem?"

"No." The smartest one in the group gently insinuated himself between his friend and Ryan. "We'll pay our tab and go. Can, uh, can you get our driver?"

Phoebe appeared from the sidelines of the almost dust-up with the small black folder holding the check. "He's already waiting out back."

While Ryan and the hothead remained in a staring match, Kelly carefully watched for any signs that things were about to kickoff. The guy paying the tab made an outraged sound when he saw the bill, but one look from Kelly prevented a protest. With a swipe of his pen, he settled the tab and handed back the check.

Kelly put a gentle hand on the shoulder of the young woman to prevent her from following the ball player with the bad reputation. He wouldn't let Bee leave with a man like that, and he sure as hell wasn't letting this woman either. "Not tonight, sweetheart."

She shot him a strange look. "But I—"

Kelly shook his head. "Believe me. You don't want what he's offering."

A rough hand shoved at his chest. "Mind your own fucking business."

Kelly carefully pushed the player's hand off his chest. "Don't touch me again."

"Or what?" He sneered and wavered on unsteady feet.

Kelly took one step forward and invaded the man's personal space. "Or this Marine is going to unleash the fucking beast that kept him alive through four tours in hell. One of us will be leaving in an ambulance. Understand?"

The drunk blanched and nodded shakily. He backed away slowly and didn't even try to make eye contact with the girl as his group beat a hasty retreat. Ryan shadowed them out the back exit while Phoebe started clearing away the table. The coed looked around, almost as if scoping out the joint for a better offer, before settling on him.

Flipping her hair, she licked her lips and smiled coyly. "So, soldier, you want to dance?"

His eye twitched at the soldier remark. She obviously didn't realize there was a world of difference between a soldier and a Marine. This didn't seem like the time to enlighten her. "No, thanks. I'm on shift."

She trailed one manicured finger down his chest and stopped right above his belt buckle. "Maybe later?"

Her touch didn't have the effect she intended. Instead of feeling good, it made his skin crawl. This woman was a knockout with that bombshell figure. There was a time when he would have craved the touch of a woman exactly like this. Now he found himself pulling away from her and trying to ease his rejection with a kind smile. "I'm flattered, but I'm taken."

Taken? Where the hell had that come from?

Undaunted, she shrugged. "I'm sure I'll see you around later."

"My answer won't change. You'd better find someone else to take you home. Be more careful this time."

While Ryan dealt with the aftermath of tossing the group, Kelly kept his eye on the VIP lounge. He moved closer to the balcony overlooking the dance floor below and allowed his gaze to drift to Bee. Standing next to Coby, she now wore a borrowed set of lime green headphones but kept the ear closest to her friend uncovered so they could talk as she tapped away at the laptop opened in front of her. The screen lit up her face with an ethereal bluish glow. Even in that safe spot, she seemed tense and nervous.

Yuri sidled up next to him at the balcony. "Does she ever stop working?"

Kelly snorted. "That question from you, huh?"

Yuri laughed. "Careful. You're starting to sound like Lena."

"I didn't see her tonight. Is she away on business?"

"No, she's having a night with her friends."

"You'll tell her I said hi?" Of all the security clients he'd ever guarded, Kelly had enjoyed Lena's detail the most.

"Absolutely," Yuri answered with a smile. Then, gesturing toward Bee with a bob of his head, he said, "Backing her might be the best business decision I made this decade. The advertising sales on LookIt have been phenomenal, and that cloud program for music that she's about to beta test will be huge. Have you seen this new program she's built for Coby so she can interact with her fans? Musicians will be all over it."

Kelly shook his head. "Tech isn't my thing."

17

Yuri studied him for an unnervingly long moment. "You should start brushing up on it. LookIt grabbed its twenty millionth user earlier this month. Bee and I have discussed the outlook of JBJ TechWorks. She's considering dropping out of Rice altogether to move forward with the expansion. Whatever she decides, she's going to need a strong supporter in her corner. Especially now that there's an offer on the table for LookIt," he added almost as afterthought.

Kelly's stomach clenched upon realizing he was *that* out of touch with Bee. "What offer?"

Yuri seemed surprised. "She didn't tell you?"

Guilt squeezed his chest like a vise. "I've been out of the country for the last few weeks. Dimitri convinced me to take a detail for a sheikh and his family. I've been bouncing between Houston and Dubai."

"Well, I'll let her give you the details. Personally, I think it's a smart move to slide LookIt under the umbrella of Insight."

Kelly's eyes widened fractionally at the mention of the multinational internet company. They were a massive force in the tech world and a company that had actually tried to hire Bee straight out of high school.

"Whether she agrees to sell her baby is another matter entirely. But," Yuri tapped Kelly's arm to draw his attention, "you need to convince her that it's time to hire round-the-clock protection. She might have been able to exist in that safe little bubble on campus, but once the news leaks about this deal or even how much advertising cash LookIt is drawing?" Yuri shook his head. "She's going to be an easy target."

Kelly's protective instinct ignited. "No one is going to hurt Bee."

"I said the same thing about Lena once. We both

know how that ended."

The sadness and guilt lacing the tycoon's voice reminded Kelly of the day a fellow bodyguard had tried to kill Yuri and Lena. His inability to see Jake as the threat still haunted him. "We both learned something from that experience."

"Yes, we did." Yuri clapped him on the back. "I need to go network and mingle, but I wanted to chat with you first. I hardly see you anymore." With a lopsided smile, the billionaire added, "I can't decide if that's a good or bad thing."

Kelly snorted with amusement as Yuri left to work his way through the VIP section. That giant man-beast Vasya trailed his boss. The Hulk-sized Russian spoke perfect English but he rarely uttered more than two words together in any language. Still, Kelly had enjoyed working with him. The guy took pride in a job well done, and that was something he really respected.

When Ryan returned to his usual post, Kelly moved back down to the main dance floor. Though he maintained focus on his job, he allowed his gaze to wander to Bee every now and then. As instructed, she remained with Coby, safe behind the barrier.

While he worked, Kelly couldn't stop thinking about how disappointed Jeb would be in him. He stretched his tight neck again and tried not to remember why he had put so much distance between himself and Bee. That kiss!

There weren't many people who could throw him off-kilter, but Bee was one of them. His mouth went dry as the memory of her soft lips pressed to his made his entire body buzz. His gut clenched as the image of her hurt face flashed before his eyes. Shutting her down and denying them both the one thing he wanted more than anything in the world had been one of the hardest things he'd ever

done—but it was for the best.
    Wasn't it?

CHAPTER TWO

Protected by the barrier and the wall of sound equipment, I allowed myself to relax enough to tackle the coding issues with Coby's program. Shoulder-to-shoulder with one of my best friends and under Kelly's watchful eye, I felt certain no one could touch me here. I still couldn't believe how damn lucky I was that Coby had messaged me to let me know that the green-eyed bodyguard was keeping Faze in line tonight. I had a feeling my guardian angel was looking out for me.

The lights were slowly brightening around the club as a way to gently force patrons out the doors. Coby had switched to music that wasn't very suitable for dancing as another clue that it was time to head home. I fished my cell phone from my pocket, swiped and unlocked the screen, and typed a quick message to test it in real-time.

"Well?" Coby bumped me with her hip. "Are you making any progress?"

"Yes. It's a temporary fix but I'm making notes so I can go back in tomorrow and rewrite this section."

"Dude, it's not that big of a deal. We're still in beta.

Don't stress over it."

"It's sort of my job to stress over these things. If I don't, then I'm like an architect who designs houses without doors. Sure, it looks really pretty from the street, but there's no way to get inside to see the really good stuff."

Coby gave me that look she had perfected from knowing me since we were in gymnastics together as little girls. "You know it's not a crime to take a day off, right?"

"Says the girl who has been living off energy drinks so she can finish her album and gear up for the festival season," I countered with a raised eyebrow.

Coby snorted and picked up one of those energy drinks that the bar staff had been supplying her with all evening. She swirled her wrist and swished the liquid around in the sweating can. "Maybe we should have gone with Hadley after all."

"The pictures from India are amazing," I agreed a bit enviously. "But we agreed that we were going to branch out more this year. We were going to try new things as individuals."

"Yet here we stand, hip to hip, at our favorite club doing what we've done every Friday night for the last year," Coby replied with a laugh. "I think Hadley is the only one of us sticking to the plan."

"That's because she's always been the bravest of us." I didn't have to mention that Hadley's heart problems were a big part of that courage.

"Don't look now," she said conspiratorially, "but KC is heading this way."

I didn't dare look up from my laptop screen. After the way Kelly had picked me up earlier, there was no way in hell I could wipe the yearning look from my face. I needed his help and didn't want to push him away again by making a jackass of myself.

"Bee." He said my name in that rough, rumbling voice of his. My tummy trembled wildly. "We need to talk. *Now*."

His gruff tone very nearly drew a *yes, sir* from my lips. Instead, I nodded and stepped around Coby. She surreptitiously reached out to give my hand a reassuring squeeze. Grateful for her support, I descended the stairs to the dance floor where Kelly awaited me.

When he held out his hand, I stared at it for a second before finally working up the nerve to place my palm against his. The rough heat of his fingers closing around mine blazed right up my arm and arced into my chest. I hated that every single touch affected me in this way, but I couldn't stop my reaction to Kelly.

He led me to one of the tables along the far wall. Choosing one of the sleek silver chairs, I avoided the sticky spill on the tabletop and rested my hands on my lap. Kelly sat close to me, too close, and made it impossible for me to avoid eye contact when he slid his arm along the back of my chair. Trapped between the table and his bigger body, there was no escape.

"Aren't you still on the clock?" I glanced at the small group of patrons hanging around the main floor.

"You let me worry about that." Tapping my shoulder, he said, "I want you to start from the beginning of this mess. Don't leave anything out. I need to know everything if I'm going to protect you. When did this start?"

Hearing Kelly say he was going to protect me eased the tight knot in my stomach. With a little sigh, I explained, "The first week of April, I had this weird feeling that I was being watched. I never saw anyone, but I had this creepy sensation following me around, you know? Then, the last week of April, the texts and phone calls started."

"What kind of texts?"

"They described what I was wearing or what I had for lunch, and were filled with compliments. They were specific enough that I knew they were legit and not simply someone trying to mess with me."

"Do you still have them? Dimitri keeps a couple of IT guys on the payroll at LSG."

I shot him an amused smile. "Kelly, come on. It's me you're talking to, remember? Jeez—I have friends who work at the NSA! And anyway, the messages came from burner phones bought with cash. The signals bounced off different towers around the city,"

"Even so, I want our guys to look at the messages." He rubbed his jaw. "When did this start to escalate?"

"Right before I sat for my finals, someone spoofed my LookIt page."

"Spoof?"

"Copied," I clarified. "Someone created a copy of my blog, but they filled it with some really filthy porn and other not so nice stuff. I caught it and took it down quickly, but it was a real pain in the ass, especially with that offer on the table."

The corners of his mouth turned down with irritation. "We'll talk about *that* later."

I bristled at his tone. "I've been wanting to talk to you about *that* for weeks."

"And we will talk about it," Kelly assured me, looking slightly chagrined, "but not until we've settled this. Now, what else has happened?"

"Three days ago, I began to find pictures."

"Find them where?"

"The first one was tucked under the windshield wiper

of my car. I found another one slipped inside my backpack."

"Do you leave your backpack unattended?"

"Sometimes," I admitted reluctantly. "When I'm working, it's usually out of my sight."

"And you're blasting music and engrossed in your code," he said knowingly and with a little frown. "What sort of pictures have you received?"

Embarrassment turned my ears hot. Glancing away from him, I said, "They're of body parts."

"Body parts? You mean dead bodies?"

"No," I quickly disabused him of the notion that someone was sending me chilling or gory messages. "Um…I mean…like *male* body parts."

Anger etched harsh lines into Kelly's handsome face. "Do you still have them?"

"They're in my backpack."

"I'll get them. You shouldn't have to look at them again."

I decided not to tell him that those images were burned into my retinas for life. The vein in his temple was already throbbing.

"And what about tonight, Bee? Tell me what happened."

"I was working late—"

"At that coffee place you like?"

"Yeah. I stayed there until Ron closed up, and then I rode my bike home to the—"

"You rode your bike that late at night?" Kelly interrupted, aghast. "Bee, you could have been hit by a car. You could have been grabbed by your stalker. You could have been—"

I held up my hand. "Yes, I know. Believe me. I know."

Kelly blew out a noisy breath. "So you get to your

apartment and?"

"I found a gift box wrapped in a white bow and freaked out, Kelly. I ran out of there and made it a couple of blocks before I finally stopped. I thought about calling 9-1-1, but then I thought of you..." I decided not to tell him exactly what I'd been thinking. "I had a message from Coby, and she said you were here, so I grabbed a cab and sweet-talked Big V at the front door."

Kelly stunned me by rubbing his thumb against the spot where my neck curved into my shoulder. His searing touch sent my heartbeat into overdrive. "I'm sorry, Bee."

I blinked with confusion. "For what? You aren't the one stalking me."

"No, but I promised Jeb I'd look out for you. I haven't done that. I should have been here for you when this started, not running around Dubai."

"Kelly, you have to work. I'm sure Jeb didn't intend for you to shadow me around the clock."

"Whether he intended it or not, it's going to happen."

"What do you mean?"

His thumb traced the fabric of my shirt. "In the morning, I'm taking you to see Dimitri and Lev so they can assess your situation and make recommendations for a full-time detail. I'm not sure how much money is on the table for the LookIt deal, but I'm going to assume it's enough to make you a huge target."

I met his questioning gaze and realized he was fishing for information. "It's a lot. Like—nine zeroes a lot."

Kelly's face slackened with surprise. Then, with a wide grin that made my heart swell, he said, "Bee, I'm so damn proud of you."

"Really?" It was the first time he'd ever said anything like that to me.

"Yes." He seemed incredulous that I would doubt him.

"How many other people in the world have accomplished what you have and done it all before they're even twenty-three?"

"In my field? More than you'd imagine."

He playfully chucked my chin. "You don't have to be so humble."

Even though I had some freak harassing me, I couldn't stop the silly smile that tugged at the corners of my mouth. It had been so long since we had shared a conversation like this, everything so easy and friendly.

As if realizing how good it was between us, Kelly let his fingertips drift along my jaw before inhaling a long breath. Sitting back, he said, "I'm going to wrap up here, and then we'll go home."

"Home? My home?"

Kelly stood and fixed his gaze on me. I couldn't read his face. "No. Mine."

Without another word, he pivoted on his heel and left me staring after him. Of all the ways I'd ever imagined Kelly asking me to go home with him, this sure as hell wasn't one of them.

*

Kelly forced his mind to the task at hand. Filling out shift reports for LSG wasn't the way he wanted to end this night, but it had to be done before he could get Bee out of here.

Big V sauntered up to the bar, leaned over, and snatched a bottle of water from the icy compartment there. "What happened up in the VIP?"

"Same shit, different night," Kelly replied while tapping away at his phone screen. Tomorrow, he would visit LSG headquarters to fill out the long shift report, but tonight the company only required some quick notes. He glanced at Big V and asked, "How did that third baseman get by you at the door? I thought he was on your never-again list?"

"He is," Big V growled. Then, with frustration in his voice, he gestured with a jerk of his chin toward the far side of the club's main dance floor. "The FNG was getting a taste of the door tonight. Obviously he needs some retraining."

Kelly glanced at the FNG—fucking new guy—in question. "He one of Lev's new hires?"

Big V nodded. "He's all right. He's still learning the ropes out front."

Kelly shrugged and went back to his typing. "Lev has good instincts when it comes to new hires. Dimitri trusts his intuition, and that's enough for me."

"What's the story with Bee?" Big V leaned his sizeable frame against the bar and sipped his water. In all the years Kelly had known Vincent Moretti, he had never seen the former Army sergeant drink anything harder. "She bailed out of that cab so fast I thought her ass was on fire."

Kelly frowned at the bouncer's description. "Did you notice anyone following her?"

"No. There were a line of cabs behind her, but I didn't notice anything out of the ordinary. Why?" He glanced at the DJ station where Bee chatted with Coby. "Is someone bothering her?"

Kelly nodded. "She thinks she has a stalker."

Big V ran his hand over his shaved head. "She thinks, or she's sure?"

"She's been receiving harassing texts and photos. Someone was in her apartment."

Big V narrowed his eyes. "She call the cops?"

Kelly shook his head. "She came to me."

He wasn't sure why that fact made his stomach do funny little flips. There was something primal and satisfying about the knowledge that Bee had thought only of him when she was frightened and needed help. She'd sought his protection over any other.

"Is it personal or business?"

Kelly shrugged and tapped the screen of his phone to submit the short report to LSG headquarters. "Knowing her situation? It could be both."

Big V finished off his water and tossed it into the recycling bin behind the bar. "You better watch your step, jarhead. Bee's going to be running around in Yuri's world soon. All that money? It's a powerful motivator for revenge and jealousy."

Kelly jerked forward as the sergeant whacked him a couple of times on the back. Big V's warning wasn't anything Kelly hadn't already been considering. With an offer worth a billion dollars or more on the table, Bee would have assholes crawling out of the woodwork to harass or harm her.

The very thought of it made his stomach churn. He glanced around the night club and suddenly felt very exposed. He needed to get Bee out of here and stow her some place safe until arrangements for round-the-clock security could be made.

He had never been happier to be in between clients. Though he trusted every man on the duty roster at LSG, he wanted to oversee Bee's detail personally. Of course, the prospect of being in such close proximity to her day and night didn't bode well for his intention to avoid his inappropriate desire for her. Earlier, he had crossed the line by touching her neck and jaw, but he hadn't been able to stop himself. It couldn't happen again.

Their gazes clashed across the mostly empty club. Bee shot him a bemused smile. Kelly lifted his hand and crooked two fingers in a come-hither motion. The gesture drew an irked expression from her, but she did as he asked, gathering up her things and bidding Coby a quick farewell before crossing the club to join him at the bar.

With his hand at the small of her back, he escorted her out of Faze and into the warm, muggy night. He constantly scanned their surroundings. Bee seemed to sense that he wasn't interested in chitchat. She moved quickly to match his pace and stayed close to his side.

Despite the many years it had been since he had last been faced with accidentally stepping on an IED while on patrol, Kelly couldn't shake the constant vigilance he used when placing every step. In the parking garage where he had stowed his truck, he paid special attention to the shadowy areas. Anyone sick enough to send Bee pictures of his dick would be cowardly enough to try to ambush them.

"In you go," Kelly instructed after unlocking the passenger side door of his truck. He waited for Bee to be safely tucked inside before walking around the truck and taking his seat.

"Can we stop for something to eat on the way home? I forgot to have dinner."

"Sure." He backed out of the space and started following the winding path down to the ground floor. "It'll have to be a drive-thru."

"That's fine. When do I get to go home again?"

"In the morning," Kelly decided. "We'll go with backup—just in case."

"Do you really think this creep is going to be hanging around there still?"

Kelly shrugged. "I'm not taking any chances with you."

His cell phone started to buzz in his pocket. If it was ringing this late, it definitely wasn't something he could ignore. He dug his headset out his pocket and snapped it up to his ear. "Hello?"

"Kelly, get your ass down to Fitzy's." Finn sounded breathless and angry. "We've got problems of the Albanian variety."

"Shit." He glanced at Bee and wondered what the hell he was going to do with her. "I'll see you soon."

She waited until he had tucked his headset back into his pocket before asking, "What's wrong, Kelly?"

He eased into the turn lane and waited for the light to turn green. "That was Finn. It sounds like Pop has gotten himself into a tricky spot again."

"Gambling?"

Frustration and anger welled within him. Grip tightening on the wheel, he asked, "What else?"

Bee fidgeted nervously with the strap of her backpack. "Maybe you should just drop me off at hotel or something. I don't want to get in the way."

"You're not leaving my sight."

"But—"

"This isn't up for discussion, Bee."

She huffed at him. "I'm starting to remember how infuriatingly stubborn you can be."

His lips slanted in a smile. "You sound like Jeb now."

"I'm not sure if that's a compliment or an insult."

"A compliment," he assured her. "Always a compliment."

"Should I stay in the truck?"

"Not a chance," Kelly said, unwilling to let her out of his sight for even as long as it took to extricate his father. "You'll come with me. Stay behind me but close. Don't say anything. Don't look at anyone."

"May I breathe?"

Kelly shot her a look. "None of the smartass routine either."

She rolled her eyes and settled back against the seat. "I guess all that practice will go to waste."

He laughed. "Somehow I doubt that."

As Kelly merged onto the interstate, he couldn't shake the feeling that Bee's problems with the stalker were about to be the least of his worries.

CHAPTER THREE

I wasn't sure what to expect as Kelly pulled into the parking lot of the rundown bar. His father's gambling addiction was well known and a constant source of trouble for their family.

A group of men at the far end of the lot caught my eye. Judging by the tense set of Kelly's jaw, he had noticed them as well. He killed the engine and unbuckled his seat belt. He leaned toward me, the alluring scent of his cologne filling my nose, and punched the button on the glove compartment.

My eyes widened when he retrieved a handgun and tucked it into the waistband of his jeans after checking to see if it was loaded and the safety in place. He flipped the bottom of his blazer over it. The dangerously sexy glint to his eyes sent a swarm of butterflies through my belly. There was something so incredibly enticing about his cool, commanding nature.

"Do you think you're going to need that?"

"No, but it never hurts to be prepared." Kelly flicked his fingers. "Let's go. Remember what I told you."

I glanced at the rowdy group that awaited us. "You won't hear a peep out of me."

Kelly reached out and tugged my ponytail. His teasing smile set me at ease. "I'll believe that when I see it."

We climbed out of the truck, but I hesitated, uncertain if this was the sort of neighborhood where I wanted to leave thousands of dollars of computer equipment unattended even for a few minutes. I grabbed my backpack and put it on while crossing the parking lot.

As we neared the arguing group, I spotted Kelly's older brothers, Finn and Jack, standing on either side of their father. They were facing off with a group of nine men who looked like big trouble. Mob trouble, if I had to guess.

"Kelly!" The man I assumed to be the leader of the group greeted my crush with a surprising smile. "I heard you were back in town."

"Besian." Kelly pushed me behind him and gave my hip a gentle pat. I didn't dare move from the spot. Jack, Kelly's oldest brother, glanced my way with some irritation. Feeling uncomfortable, I dropped my gaze to the pavement and tried to make myself as unnoticeable as possible. Intruding on this extremely private family matter was the absolute last way I wanted to spend my Friday night.

When Kelly shifted to the side, I finally got a good look at his dad and Finn. Both had busted up faces and hands. I winced as his father wiped at the blood seeping from his nose. Reaching back, I tugged on the zipper of a pouch on my backpack and retrieved a travel-sized package of tissues. I held it out to him and caught his attention.

His bleary-eyed gaze told me that he was drunk as a skunk again. When he recognized me, his red eyes widened with surprise. "Hey, kiddo."

"Hi, Mr. Connolly." Not taking offense to the kiddo remark, I pressed the tissues into his hand and gestured to my nose.

"Thanks." He fumbled with the package while Kelly took another step toward the man called Besian.

"I thought you were a fan of discretion, Besian." Kelly gestured to their very public surroundings. "What happened to keeping your business low profile?"

"What happened to men honoring their debts?" Besian neatly turned the question around on Kelly. "It's all about honor and loyalty with me."

"Sending five knee-breakers to a bar to attack two men is honorable?" Jack snarled angrily. He stood shoulder-to-shoulder with Kelly now.

"Nick was given ample opportunities to settle his debt. Let's not forget that your brother threw the first punch."

I glanced at Finn and then the group of gangsters. Finn might have lost his leg in war, but he was still quite a beast when it came to hand-to-hand combat. Five of the other group had battered faces. I counted four black eyes and two cracked noses. Honestly, I couldn't believe no one had called the cops for a brawl like the one that must have taken place here.

"Look, Kelly," the man said in his thickly accented English, "I let this account ride for a few months because your father was always a good customer for Afrim. When I took over Afrim's action after his murder, I kept the rates the same for the old-timers, but your dad has abused that privilege with his late and missed payments."

Kelly glanced at Jack. I couldn't tell what the two brothers were thinking but they seemed to be able to read each other's minds. Jack gave the tiniest nod. With tired resignation, Kelly began negotiating. "How do we bring his account current?"

I watched the way Kelly's older brothers deferred to him in this situation. Clearly Kelly had some sort of relationship with these bad guys. I wondered if Besian was someone he had met during his time as Yuri's private guard or from his friendship with Vivian Kalasnikov.

Vivian and my friend Hadley ran in some of the same artist circles, so I was aware of the up-and-coming painter. That husband of hers was rumored to be the Russian mob boss of Houston, but I wasn't sure if there was any truth to that. Considering the tight spot Kelly's dad was in, having friends in very interesting places might be useful.

"The time for bringing the account current is over," Besian replied with a slash of his hand. "I want the full balance paid by the end of the month."

"What's the damage?"

"Five hundred."

Both Jack and Finn stiffened with shock while Kelly made a choking sound. "Five hundred *large*?"

Besian gestured to the wall of muscle behind him. "You think I'd send this crew out for anything less?"

Jack whirled on their old man. "How the hell did you piss away half a million dollars?"

Nick dabbed at his still oozing nose. Rather indignant, he snapped, "It's not like it happened all in one night. I had a couple of bad runs. Tack on the interest and late fees..." He shrugged. "It adds up quick."

"Bad runs?" Jack looked like he was about to blow a freaking pupil and have a massive stroke. "Where the hell did you get the cash for the markers?"

Nick avoided his eldest son's glare. "I sold some things."

Kelly put a settling hand on his brother's arm. Their

gazes clashed as Jack shook it off, but it seemed to have reined him in a bit. Turning back to Besian, Kelly said, "We can't do that. Not by the end of May. We need more time."

"The timeline isn't up for negotiation. I have my own business interests to look after, Kelly. Your father settles his account by the end of May."

Or what? I didn't even want to think about what these men would do to Nick or his sons if the half a million wasn't repaid. "I can cover it."

The second the words left my mouth, I regretted them. Every eye snapped to me. Kelly pivoted slowly and pinned me with a withering stare. I suddenly remembered his instructions. I had promised to keep quiet, hadn't I?

"Do I know you?" Besian stepped to the side so he could get a better look at me. Snapping his fingers, he smiled. "Yeah. You're that computer genius that made Yuri even richer, right?"

I bristled at his description. "That's hardly the way I would frame our working relationship."

Besian's shoulders bounced dismissively. "Call it whatever you want. I'm only interested in getting my money."

"You're not getting it from her." Kelly's irritated glare skipped from me to Besian. "This is our debt to settle. She's not part of our family."

Kelly's remark shouldn't have hurt me the way it did, but I couldn't ignore the pang that pierced my chest. After losing my family to cancer and war, Kelly and my friends were all the family I had left. Now I understood exactly how he saw me. No wonder he'd found it so easy to ignore me since that stupid kiss.

"I wouldn't be so quick to turn down that offer," the gangster counseled wisely. "Where else are you going to come up with a half a million in two weeks?"

"We'll find a way."

Besian stared at him Kelly for a few seconds, almost as if he was mulling over something. Finally, he said, "Maybe we can work out a deal that helps all of us."

I didn't like the sound of this possibility at all. Any deal that this guy would offer probably had some gnarly fucking strings attached.

"Let's hear it," Jack said.

"Paulie broke his leg last night in a rollover. I'm in the market for a new fighter. The tournament is the first weekend in June. Two nights and it's done." Besian slid his hands out in front of him. "We wipe the slate clean."

I blinked and tried to wrap my head around the offer the gangster had just made. Fighter? What kind of fighter?

"No fucking way," Finn interjected forcefully. "Those fights are brutal. Men die in that cage."

Suddenly, I understood. This wasn't sanctioned mixed-martial arts or boxing. They were talking about the underground fights that happened at the old meatpacking plant. I'd learned about them after starting college. A guy I had dated had shown me a video on his phone from one of the invite-only fights he'd attended with some of the guys from his frat. I'd nearly vomited watching half a minute of the bloody brawl.

My panicked gaze jumped to Kelly. Their dad had a reputation as a fighter from his younger days. It was the reason Connolly Fitness had been so successful. The business had taken a downturn while the boys were away at war, but Jack was turning things around now.

Jack made a living instructing others in self-defense and Krav Maga. But Jack couldn't fight anymore. His unit had come under heavy fire in Iraq. An explosion had caused a head injury that forced him out of the corps. As far as I knew, he had been warned to keep any hits to his head to a minimum or he risked serious injury. It was one of the reasons he didn't spar with his students.

And Finn? He'd lost his leg when his convoy had been hit by an IED. The men who fought in those bare-knuckle matches needed all their limbs in working order to survive. He simply couldn't compete against some of the freakishly built men who fought on that circuit.

That left only Kelly—and I would be damned before I let him go into the cage.

"Give us forty-eight hours," Kelly replied, ignoring his brother's outburst. "We'll give you an answer."

"Twenty-four," Besian countered before backing away with his men. "You know where to find me."

The tension eased, and I glanced nervously between the Connolly brothers and their father. Nick swayed on his feet. Whether it was from the hits he'd taken or the alcoholic bender he'd clearly been on, I couldn't tell. From the looks of his rumpled shirt and stained jeans, he hadn't showered or changed in days. Was it the stress and guilt of his gambling debts that made him drink?

Jack exhaled roughly. "Let's go, Dad."

Kelly reached out and tapped Finn's shoulder. "You okay to drive, man?"

"I didn't drink!" Finn snapped at his brother. "I came here to drag Pops out of there."

Kelly held up his hand. "Cool it, bro. I meant your head. Looks like you took a good smack."

Finn brushed away Kelly's hand before his younger brother could check the bruise forming on his jaw. "I'm fine. I'll see you at the house." His expression softened as he smiled at me. "It's good to see you again, Bee."

"You're about to see more of her." Kelly put his hand against my back. "She's coming home with me tonight."

Finn's expression was almost comical. "Uh, Kelly, you think that's a good idea? I mean, *tonight*?"

Kelly made an annoyed sound. "Not like that, Finn. She's in trouble. We're going to keep an eye on her until I can get her security situation sorted out tomorrow."

"Oh. Well. Then I guess I'll see you both back at the house." Finn didn't push for any more details before heading to his truck.

Kelly gave me a gentle push forward but refused to meet my questioning gaze. "So…you're living with Finn and Jack?"

"I've been traveling so much it didn't make sense to keep my place. Jack lets me rent a bedroom from him."

Before I could ask how the arrangement was working, we reached Kelly's truck. I quickly climbed into my seat and waited for him. As he crossed in front of the vehicle, I caught the clenched set of his jaw and realized he was upset. With me? With his dad? I figured he would tell me soon enough.

Buckled into his seat, Kelly jammed the key in the ignition and started the engine. He didn't make any attempt to back out of the parking space. Instead, he exhaled loudly. "What did I tell you, Bee?"

I swallowed nervously. "Look, what was I supposed to do, Kelly?"

He darted an irritated glance my way. "You were supposed to be quiet." Gripping the wheel, he asked, "Do you have any idea what you've just done?"

"I offered to help a friend in trouble."

"No," he countered roughly. "You just announced to the Albanian mafia that you can get your hands on half a million dollars without breaking a sweat. The next time one of those assholes is short on his pickups or makes a bum side deal, your face is going to be the first one that pops into his head. They're going to be thinking that some young, sweet thing like you will be easy to blackmail or strong arm or kidnap for ransom." With a ragged sigh, he added, "Jesus, Bee! How the hell am I supposed to keep you safe from a stalker if you're walking around advertising your net worth to lowlifes? For someone so damn smart, you just made a really dumb move. "

His outburst shocked me. In all the time I'd known Kelly, he'd never once raised his voice with me. Within the cab of his truck, his normally deep voice seemed so much louder. Feeling stupid and embarrassed, I hastily averted my gaze to the window and blinked rapidly to clear the tears burning my eyes.

I heard the snap of Kelly's seatbelt unlatching. A second later, his big hands were grasping my shoulders and gently turning me toward him. With the weight of my naïve misstep heavy on my shoulders, I hurriedly apologized. "I'm sorry. I didn't realize—"

"No." Kelly touched my lips with his fingertip. "God, Bee, don't apologize to me. Not after I just acted like the biggest jackass to you." The moonlight and the parking lot lamps highlighted the pain and regret etched into his handsome face. He cupped my cheek and brushed the tears from my skin with the rough pad of his thumb. "I'm sorry, Bee. I'm so damn sorry."

When he touched his forehead to mine, the spark of contact arced through me like lightning. "I'm upset and angry and stressed—but that doesn't excuse the way I spoke to you."

With trembling fingers, I stroked his cheek, the slight stubble there rasping my fingertips. "It's all right."

"It's not all right. You don't have any idea how the underworld works. You were just being kind."

Relishing this moment of intimacy, I trailed my

fingertips down his cheek to follow the curve of his jaw. "Please take the money, Kelly. Those men looked so dangerous. I don't want you or your brothers or your dad to get hurt."

Kelly clasped my hand. My heart flip-flopped in my chest when he pressed his mouth to my palm. Tugging away from me, he ended our sweet moment. "No. This is our mess. We'll clean it up."

"But—"

"Bee," he eyed me carefully, "if you give us half a million dollars, Besian and his crew will do one of two things. They'll either tack on more interest and fees to squeeze more money out of you or they'll give Pop a bigger line of credit. The next time it will be two or three million that he owes—and then what? I'm supposed to come to you with my hat in my hand and beg for charity?"

"It wouldn't be charity, Kelly. You're my friend."

"Friends don't abuse one another in that way." He shook his head and put his truck in reverse. "Jack, Finn, and I will figure out something else."

I studied him as we pulled out of the parking lot and onto the street. "You're not seriously considering fighting for that Besian guy." He didn't answer me immediately so I pushed harder. "Kelly?"

"I've fought in the cage before," he admitted finally. "When I first left the corps and I was pissed off all the time," he amended. "It felt good to beat the shit out of some other guy, and I made a good chunk of money doing it."

I gaped at him as his revelation hit me. If I was being totally honest, it didn't really surprise me. When Kelly came home alive and Jeb came back in a box, he was so incredibly angry. I could totally see him seeking out a venue like that to blow off steam.

"That was then, Kelly. This is now. You're an employee of a very well-respected private security firm. What the hell is your boss going to say when you come into work all busted-up?"

He didn't have an answer for that. "You don't know what men like Besian are capable of, Bee. Taking a few hits in the ring to clear our family's debt is nothing compared to what those men will do."

"And what happens if you get hurt in the ring, Kelly? I've seen those fights. I know what happens there. What if you become badly injured?"

He glanced at me as we passed through an intersection. "When did you see one of the cage matches?"

"Do you remember Cade?"

The irritated expression on his face told me he did. "The frat guy you dated your freshman year?"

"Yes. He showed me a video on his phone." My gut lurched as I considered all the horrible ways this could end. "Kelly, please don't do this. Just let me help you."

"No."

"Why not?"

"Because it isn't right."

"Oh my God! Who cares about what is right or wrong, Kelly? The Albanian mob owns your dad. They're trying to extort you into risking your life." I glared at him. "Is this because I'm a girl and you're a guy? Would you take the money if I was a man?"

"What? Your gender has nothing to do with this."

"So it's not about some dumb male pride thing?"

He rolled his shoulders. "Pride isn't dumb, Bee. Honor. Loyalty. Pride. They'll take a man far in this world."

"No, they're going to take you to an early grave. I've already lost Jeb. I'm not going to lose you too!"

He reached across the center console and took my hand. He gave it a reassuring squeeze. "I'm not going anywhere, Bee."

Staring at our entwined hands, I expected him to let go, but he held tight as he deftly navigated the dark streets. I wasn't brave enough to believe we were charting a new course in our friendship, but I couldn't stop the glimmer of hope burning within me.

We were on the cusp of something exciting and real— and I'd be damned if a loan shark mobster was going to threaten that. I'd move heaven and earth before I let Kelly step into that cage.

I just prayed he would forgive me.

* * *

It was after four in the morning when Kelly made his way downstairs to the kitchen. Bee had been safely tucked away in his bed and was already passed out from exhaustion. Before she'd put her head on the pillow, she had switched on the bedside lamp. He refused to let her feel embarrassed for needing a night light. Discovering someone had broken into her home had shattered her sense of personal safety. If she needed the lamp, that was perfectly fine.

Remembering the way she looked as she climbed into bed, Kelly experienced a wave of need. The door to his room had been ajar just enough to let him catch a glimpse of her in only her T-shirt and panties. He didn't know that any woman had ever made such a simple getup look so damn sexy.

He'd be a bald-faced liar if he said that he didn't like the way she looked in his bed. The urge to slide in with her and spoon up against the curve of her bottom had nearly overwhelmed him.

Fighting the lust she inspired in him, Kelly rubbed the back of his neck and stretched his aching shoulders. Though he'd grown accustomed to his insomnia, he still had nights where it grated on his nerves. Like tonight.

Still feeling guilty over his awful outburst in the truck, Kelly hoped he could keep his temper under control while his father laid out the ugly facts of his gambling debts. He refused to let any more of the traits he'd inherited from his old man show tonight. He didn't know if he would ever forgive himself for allowing Bee to glimpse the darkness that came from his father's blood.

In the kitchen, he found Finn and Jack seated on either side of their father. The old man was sucking down coffee and sobering up some. Kelly doubted they were going to like anything he had to say, but they needed everything laid out on the table to avoid making a rash decision.

"What's the story with Bee?" Jack leveled a knowing stare his way. "I thought you said you were giving her some space after New Year's?"

Kelly wished he'd never confided in his brothers about that kiss. After the initial taunting had passed, they had both tried to convince him to give it a go with her. Neither of them seemed to understand the various angles of his predicament.

Grabbing the carafe, Kelly poured a cup of coffee and moved to the table. He reached for the sugar. "Some shithead is stalking her."

Jack's gaze flicked to the ceiling and concern etched hard lines into his face. "Stalking her how?"

"Until earlier tonight, it was just texts, emails, and disgusting photos. When she came home, someone had broken into her apartment and left her a box."

"A box?" Finn sat forward. "What was in it?"

Kelly sipped the hot coffee and enjoyed the soothing burn. "She didn't stick around to find out. I'm having Dimitri and Lev meet us at her place in a few hours."

"Ordinarily, I'd recommend going to the cops in a situation like this," Jack said, "but with Bee's profile?" He shook his head. "I've had clients come into the gym to learn self-defense because the restraining orders aren't working. She needs dedicated security and private investigators who cater only to her needs."

"Agreed." Kelly dumped more sugar in his coffee. When he reached for a fourth scoop, Jack frowned at him and moved the bowl out of the way.

"You're going to give yourself diabetes if you keep eating like this."

Kelly rolled his eyes but didn't try to jerk the bowl back. Instead, he leaned back in his chair and eyed their father. "Well, Pop, what's the real story here?"

Their old man wiped both hands down his face and cleared his throat. "Afrim always kept me on a tight leash when it came to my credit. After that Russian loon stuffed Afrim in a trunk last Christmas, Besian took over his action. He extended my line." His shoulders rounded with defeat. "I couldn't say no. Before I knew it, I was in *deep*."

Kelly wanted to lash out in anger but the pathetic old man sitting across from him only inspired sympathy. He couldn't imagine being so lost to his demons that he'd risk the lives of everyone he loved. "So what are we going to do?"

The harsh expression on Jack's face warned that he

was about five seconds away from losing it. "What we always fucking do! We'll have to clean up his mess yet again."

Finn drummed his fingers on the tabletop. "I have some cash stowed away. It's not hardly enough, but it will make a dent."

"I should be receiving my payout for that sheikh's contract before the end of next week." Kelly ran his finger around the rim of his cup. "Even after taxes, it's a good sized chunk."

Jack sighed loudly. "Most of my cash is tied up in the gym. I've sunk everything into it. I might be able to get a loan against the building but with Pop's credit..."

Kelly didn't hear whatever Jack said next. Their father furiously rubbed that spot on his wrist where his watch normally sat. No doubt he'd hocked the damn thing again to buy booze or lottery tickets. It was his father's tell—that rubbing motion—that made Kelly perk right up. "What haven't you told us, Pop?"

Finn and Jack snapped their attention to the old man. Tension soared around the table as they waited for their father to finally work up the damned courage to come clean. He sucked down the rest of his coffee before admitting in a rush, "The building is already mortgaged."

"What?" Jack hissed the word. "We're on the note together after the refinance. There's no way you could have—"

"I used the building as collateral for a loan from Hagen."

Kelly damn near fell out of his chair at the revelation that their father owed money to Houston's most notorious loan shark. The Albanian crew was bad enough, but Hagen had a certain reputation around town.

Jack jumped out of his chair, knocking it over in the

process, and stormed out of the kitchen. Kelly heard the back door open and close as Jack sought silence and privacy on the patio. He figured that was better than the alternative of Jack wringing their father's neck.

Finn flopped back in his seat and shoved his empty coffee cup across the table. "How much do you owe Hagen?"

"The full value of the building plus interest and late fees," their dad reluctantly said. "I took out the loan to clear the Albanian debt but—"

"But you hit a hot streak, right?" Kelly asked acidly. "Except it wasn't so hot, was it? Now you owe two loan sharks, and we're fucked."

He stood up, fixed the chair Jack had knocked over and crossed the kitchen to stare out the window into the backyard. Jack paced angrily back and forth across the flagstone pavers. Kelly couldn't even imagine what his oldest brother was feeling. Jack had sacrificed so much to scrape together the money to renovate the family gym. He'd been busting his ass to build up a thriving clientele and working his contacts for training contracts like the one with Dimitri. Every employee of LSG trained and conditioned at Connolly Fitness and Fighting.

What would happen if they lost the gym to Hagen? Jack would lose everything. Finn would be out of a job. Their father would be on the streets. Not that he would survive very long if the Albanian debt went unpaid. There were plenty of men in Besian's crew who would be only too willing to snuff out that problem.

For the briefest moment, Kelly considered accepting Bee's offer. She would happily give him the money to settle the family debts. It was the easiest, cleanest way to do it.

But he would never be able to look her in the eye

again if there was money between them like that. She would never throw the debt in his face, but he would remember what it felt like to accept her charity.

And he couldn't do it. Maybe she was right. His damnable pride might put him in an early grave after all.

"I'll fight." He pivoted slowly to face the kitchen and discovered Jack hovering in the doorway there. "We'll pool our money and bet on me to clear the debt with Hagen."

"I don't like it." Finn tapped his hand against the table. "It's too dangerous. The Albanian's guy—Paulie—was a good fighter, but he's nowhere near as good as the men the Russians have fighting for them."

"Sergei will kill you." Jack didn't even mince words. "The bastard is nearly seven feet tall and outweighs you by fifty pounds. We've all watched him fight before, and we all know that he's a fucking beast. I'm a good trainer, but I'm not Ivan Markovic. Ivan survived years in that cage, and he has skills to offer his fighters that I don't."

Kelly didn't disagree with that assessment. "Pop used to fight underground. He trained me when I fought there a few years ago. He can train me again."

Their father lifted his shamed head. "Kelly, son..."

Jack scoffed. "You want to put your life in the hands of an old drunk?"

"Why aren't we discussing the obvious option?" Finn interjected carefully. "What about Bee's offer?"

"No." Jack and Kelly spoke in unison.

"No," Jack growled again. "We aren't dragging Bee into this nightmare. She's got too much going for her to have the taint of mobs and loan sharks following her for the rest of her life."

"She worked hard for that money," Kelly added. "I won't have her throw it away like this." He thought of the deal on the table. "She's entertaining an offer on her business. One whiff of the Albanian mob could tank it."

Finn twirled a sugar spoon between his fingers. "You'll need more than Pop, Kelly. If you're going to win, I mean. You'll have to find a coach who's been in the ring sometime this century."

Kelly rubbed his face between his hands. "We'll figure it out tomorrow. Right now, I need a shower and a nap."

Jack sighed heavily. "Yeah. Okay." His vicious gaze turned toward their father. "You can stay until you're sobered up, but then I want you out of here. Don't show your face around the gym either. Understand?"

The old man nodded stiffly. "Yes."

Finn, always the most sympathetic and gentle of them, helped their father out of his chair. "Come on, Pop. You can stay in my room. I've got some clothes you can borrow."

Feeling the weight of the world on his shoulders, Kelly headed back upstairs. He slipped into his room to grab a clean pair of shorts before ducking into the bathroom he shared with Finn. After showering, he returned to his bedroom and slowly sank down into the low, wide chair in the corner. The comfortable plushness of his favorite chair cradled his tired, aching body.

He propped his feet on the edge of his bed and watched Bee sleep. The sheet had slipped down a little and revealed a tantalizing glimpse of skin between the top of her pink and white striped undies and the bottom of her shirt. He tried to ignore the throbbing ache in his cock as his body reacted naturally to the sight of her sexy curves.

But it wasn't simply the natural reaction to a beautiful woman that left him feeling so unsettled. Ever since Bee had blindsided him with that New Year's Eve kiss, he'd been fighting a losing battle. Until the moment their lips first touched, he had been able to pretend that the flutter in his stomach every time she was near wasn't real. Her kiss had demolished the wall he'd erected between them.

Even now, simply watching her sleep, he felt his resolve slipping. Twice tonight, he'd flirted with danger. While interrogating her at the club, he'd indulged his desire to touch her soft skin. Later, in the truck, when he'd been overcome with guilt for snapping at her, he'd opened himself up to sharing some intimacy with her.

Now that he knew what it felt like to touch her so tenderly, Kelly accepted there was no going back. It was time to face the facts. When guarding clients, he always insisted in total honesty from the protectee. He would expect the same from Bee—but she should expect the same from him. Guarding her wouldn't be just another job to him and his emotions would be tangled up in it.

Because he would be protecting the woman he had loved since he was twenty-four years old.

Kelly still remembered the first moment he had recognized Bee not as the slightly strange and always silly little sister of his best friend, but as a woman. Every summer Jolene Langston hosted a huge Fourth of July bash at their house on Lake Conroe. It was the first time in a couple of years that both Kelly and Jeb hadn't been deployed or on duty. It was also the summer Bee's mother learned she had Stage IV ovarian cancer, but that day everyone had been blissfully ignorant of the fate that awaited Jolene.

Stuck in Afghanistan while his mother fought the cancer ravaging her body and Bee tried to hold it all together, Jeb had slipped into a shell that Kelly simply hadn't been able to penetrate. Those final months of Jeb's life, before he'd been killed in action, had been strained and tense. For the first time since meeting as four-year-olds, Kelly and Jeb hadn't been able to connect. Something had gotten between them, and Kelly still didn't know what it was.

"Kelly?"

Lost in his thoughts, he hadn't noticed her waking. Dropping his feet to the floor, he sat forward in his chair. "What's wrong? Are you okay?"

A bemused smile curved her mouth. "Yes. Are you?"

"Sure."

"It's late. Why aren't you sleeping?"

"I was thinking."

"About?"

"You." He didn't even try to deny it.

Her tired eyes widened. "Me?"

"You," he said with a sigh and pushed out of his chair. Standing next to his bed, he gestured toward the wall. "Scoot over, Bee."

She didn't hesitate to follow his order. He eyed the space she'd created for him and wondered if he was really about to cross this line. The mischievous smile that brightened her sleepy face convinced him it was time to throw caution to the wind. When he slid in beside her, she moved even farther away and hugged the very edge of the mattress.

Chuckling, he clamped his arm around her waist and dragged her against him. "Come here."

"Kelly." She spoke breathlessly but didn't fight him. "What are you doing?"

"I don't know," he admitted, "but it sure as hell feels right."

Brushing black strands of hair from her face, he shifted Bee in his arms until her cheek rested against his chest. She tentatively hooked her leg across his. Running his hand up and down her back, he said, "I was thinking about the last Fourth of July barbecue your mom hosted."

"Oh." Sadness colored her voice. "That was one of the last times our family was together."

"I know," he said softly, thinking of the torment Jeb had suffered while deployed in Afghanistan during his mother's valiant fight for her life. Wanting to remind Bee of happier times, he asked, "Do you remember that box of sparklers we burned through?"

"Of course," she replied with a little laugh. "Why?"

"No reason." He wasn't brave enough to tell her that playing tic-tac-toe in the twilight had been the moment when he'd first started to fall for her. It had been a blessed relief to do something so incredibly innocent after months of enduring the hard slog of war.

Soon, he promised himself, but not tonight. For now, he was content to hold her. Giving her arm a squeeze, he murmured, "Go to sleep, Bee. We have to be up in a few hours."

Knowing Bee, she probably had a thousand questions racing through her brilliant mind but she didn't ask them. Maybe she understood that this was one of those moments where talking wasn't necessary.

When her hand hesitantly lifted to his chest, he caught it before she could draw it back to her side. Lifting her fingertips, he kissed each one and then settled her smaller hand against his shoulder. The sensation of her warm, lush body curled up against his affected him in ways he couldn't quite articulate.

For the first time in years, sleep came easily and swiftly. There were no nightmares of bullets whizzing by his head or explosions rocking convoys. No, tonight, he dreamed only of the incandescent bursts of white phosphorous lighting up Bee's sweet face—and it was good.

CHAPTER FOUR

I nervously tugged at the bottom of the borrowed Connolly Fitness tee Kelly had left on the bed for me and descended the stairs. The sounds of male voices drew me toward the kitchen where I discovered Finn and Kelly making breakfast. I assumed Jack had already gone to the gym but didn't dare ask about their father.

Finn spotted me first. "Morning, Bee."

"Good morning, Finn." I noticed the way Kelly kept his back to me as he fiddled with something on the counter. Toast, I thought, by the smell.

"Sorry you only got a few hours of sleep," Kelly said over his shoulder. "Once we get everything squared away with LSG, we'll get you stowed somewhere safe, and you can nap."

I shrugged and reached for the carton of orange juice on the table. A glass had been set out for me, so I filled it halfway. "I'm used to running on no sleep. My schedule has been hectic these last few years."

"You still juggling college and the business?" Finn asked as he slid into a seat and motioned toward another one for me.

"Sort of," I said before taking a sip of the cold juice. "I part-timed the last two semesters, and I'm thinking of leaving altogether."

"Is that so?" Kelly didn't sound very pleased by my decision. When he turned toward me, I glanced at the plate in his hand. He'd smeared a bagel with chocolate hazelnut spread and topped it with sliced bananas. Remembering my favorite breakfast combination somehow seemed more special than it really was.

"Thanks." I accepted the plate with a smile.

He gave a little shrug before sitting down with his bagel and eggs liberally covered with green salsa. "How many hours of college do you have left?"

"I don't know." He shot me a look, and I rolled my eyes. "Like thirty."

"You're too close to quit."

I took a bite of my bagel rather than engage in an argument with him. It was way too early and neither of us had gotten enough sleep for a discussion that intense. "Are we going to my apartment soon?"

Finn smiled behind his coffee cup at the way I had deftly avoided a morning tiff with his younger brother. Kelly stabbed at his eggs and nodded. "Lev and Dimitri will be meeting us at your place. I also called the police department to see if they could send out an officer to take a report so everything is documented."

"For?"

"A restraining order or arrest," he said. "We'll figure out who this creep is eventually. When we do, I want him arrested and thrown in jail. Dimitri is bringing one of LSG's techs to sweep your place"

"Techs?"

"LSG has added more support staff to help the agents

in the field," he explained. "Dimitri wants to be able to provide full-service protection for all of his clients. It's easy enough to work side-by-side with the police here, but in some of the areas where we protect clients, it's not that simple."

As Kelly and Finn launched into a debate about the most corrupt countries, I polished off my yummy bagel and orange juice. Finn took my plate and cup and tucked them into the dishwasher along with his and Kelly's. He bid us a quick farewell before grabbing his backpack and darting out the door.

Alone with Kelly, I waited for him to finish wiping up the counter. "So—your dad?"

He spared me a glance. "He was gone when I came downstairs."

"Gone where?"

He shrugged. "Hell if know. I don't really care."

"Kelly," I admonished. "He's your father."

His green eyes narrowed. "Bee, there's a lot of things I'm willing to let you chastise me for, but this isn't one of them. You don't know the score with our old man. He's a sad, pathetic drunk now, but he used to be a mean old bastard who liked to knock all of us around. This shit with the loan sharks is the last straw."

I had always suspected Nick Connolly was an abusive parent. Jeb used to make remarks that made me question what sort of upbringing Kelly and his brothers endured. In some ways, the Connolly brothers' aloof natures made sense when viewed within that context.

As far as I knew, none of them had ever been involved in a serious long-term relationship. At thirty-three, thirty-one and almost twenty-nine that was quite an accomplishment, all things considered. Most men would have had at least one long-term girlfriend by those ages.

"I'm sorry, Kelly. I didn't mean to step on your toes."

He came around the island and slid his hand along the nape of my neck. Lowering his head, he kissed my forehead. The touch of his lips against my skin branded me as his. I wasn't sure what had brought on this change in his demeanor toward me, but I prayed the gentle sweetness he had been showing me since last night wasn't going to end anytime soon.

"You didn't, Bee. You're probably right. I should care where he is, but right now you're my top priority. After you, it's saving the gym and everything Jack and Finn have worked to build."

Frowning, I pulled back enough to look at him. "What's wrong with the gym?"

He brushed his thumb across my cheek. "Dad took a loan against the building from Hagen."

"The loan shark?"

"How do you know about him?"

"When LookIt exploded overnight, I needed funding fast to expand JBJ TechWorks or else the whole damn thing was going to collapse. A friend on campus who did a lot of poker playing told me that Hagen could advance big sums of cash for competitive interest rates, but I decided to aim big."

"So you marched into Yuri's office and asked for a million bucks, right?"

"Well…it was quite a bit more than that, but basically, yes." I chewed my lip as I considered this new bit of information about their father's second outstanding debt. "Kelly, please reconsider my offer. If it's the charity angle that bothers you, we can set up a payment plan or something."

He tugged away from me and ended the connection between us. "It's not up for discussion, Bee. We've decided to handle this our way."

Frustration boiled in my gut. "Your way requires you getting the crap knocked out of you in a warehouse."

"It's the best way." He tentatively reached out to caress my face. My eyelids drifted together as his fingers glided along my cheek. "I'm not dragging you into this. Your reputation has to remain spotless, Bee."

I decided not to push the issue with him, but I swore then and there that I would find a way to save his family's gym and his father's life that didn't require Kelly to risk permanent injury or death. He was going to be furious with me, but I didn't care. I wasn't going to stand on the sidelines while the man I'd loved for so long killed himself to restore his family's honor.

"We should go."

On the drive to my building, we didn't talk much beyond agreeing on a radio station. It wasn't an uncomfortable silence by any means. The easiness between us this morning reminded me of the time before that kiss. I wasn't sure what had happened last night to make Kelly lower his fences. When he'd climbed into bed with me, I had been nearly delirious with excitement. The way he held me and stroked my back until I fell asleep had been absolute perfection.

The ball remained firmly in his court, and I had no intention of asking him what the hell was going on between us. I wanted so much more with him, but I'd waited this long for even the chance to try. I could wait a little longer for him to make up his mind.

When we reached my building, Lev and Dimitri were waiting at the side entrance. The tall, blond Russian was a friend of Yuri's and a man I recognized on sight. I stopped by his wife's bakery once or twice a month and often saw him there. He was a familiar face at Faze too.

The other man I didn't know at all. Kelly had told me that Lev was a former Israeli commando who specialized in counter-terrorism. I wasn't quite sure what a man with that sort of expertise could do to help me, but I trusted that they had their own system for sizing up their potential clients.

After a round of introductions, I unzipped my backpack and retrieved my keycard. Before I had even gotten close to the door, Dimitri asked, "Who else has a keycard?"

"No one else has one. There's an extra in my safe that I planned to give to Kelly the next time I saw him."

Lev jotted something down in a notebook he produced from the pocket of his cargo pants. "We'll have someone follow up with the security firm you're using. We need to know where every key is. Spike, our tech guy, is running a few minutes late, but when he gets here, we'll have him run diagnostics on everything."

I didn't tell Lev I could access those records myself. He would likely want their own man to pull them anyway. Once inside the building, we headed for the elevator. I noticed the way the men kept their hands close to their sides and didn't touch anything. Probably because they wanted to get good prints later when the police officer Kelly had requested arrived on the scene.

"How many floors?" Dimitri asked.

"Eight," I answered.

"There is no one else in the building but you?"

"Just me," I confirmed. "I had planned to look over the construction bids to get the renovations started, but I think I should postpone for a while."

Kelly's hand landed on my shoulder. "You can't let this stalker prevent you from living, Bee. That's what he wants. You'll have to modify your life so we can keep you safe, but don't stop your long-term plans."

I caught Lev's interested gaze at Kelly's hand touching my shoulder. Something about the twitch in his cheek told me that he didn't approve of the idea of Kelly mixing business and friendship.

When we reached my floor, I led them to the still ajar front door. Kelly carefully stepped in front of me, putting his body between mine and the door. Dimitri shielded me from the side closest to the fire exit I had used to rush out of the building. Lev entered my apartment first and spent a few moments inside.

"All clear."

Kelly reached back and found my hand, dragging me along with him. We stopped in the middle of the living area. Lev picked up my bike—apparently it had fallen over when I'd run out of the building—and leaned it against the wall. "You left in a hurry," he rightly deduced.

"You could say that," I murmured, unable to look away from the menacing pink box.

A buzz startled me. Kelly's soothing hand rubbed my back and I managed to get my racing heart under control. Pivoting back toward the door, I glanced at the screen mounted on the wall and then at Dimitri who confirmed the man was friendly. I pressed the intercom button. "Yes?"

"It's Spike Carson with Lone Star Group."

"Come on up." I hit the button to let him inside and punched in the code to unlock the elevator for him.

"We'll need to pull your security camera feeds," Dimitri said. "Hopefully they caught something."

"Hopefully," I agreed and stepped away from the door. Not long after, the technician appeared on my doorstep. He immediately came to the box that had been left for me and started talking with Lev about the safety of it. After digging in one of the bags he'd brought up with him, he carefully swabbed the box. Glancing at Kelly, I asked, "Is he swabbing for explosives?"

"Yes. We can't be too careful."

Thankfully the box tested negative for explosives and chemical residues. Kelly stepped forward when Carson was done and snatched a latex glove from the opened kit. He pulled it on and jerked on the big, white bow. He lifted the lid on the box and peered inside. Instantly, his jaw locked as the harshest expression I had ever seen crossed his face.

As if fighting to control his temper, he asked, "Bee, do you do your own laundry?"

His question confused me. "Yes. Why?"

"You do it here?"

"Yes."

Kelly lobbed a look Dimitri's way. The ruggedly handsome Russian crossed the distance between them and peered into the box. His reaction mirrored Kelly's. In fact, he looked pissed. "Miss Langston, have you noticed any missing laundry?"

"Missing laundry? I..." My voice trailed off as a better picture started to form. "Last week I thought I was missing some clothes, but I just decided they must have gotten lost in the move or left behind at my old place." Suddenly, a terrible thought struck me. "Wait. Are my panties in that box?"

Kelly jammed the lid back on the box. "Yes."

My stomach churned. "Just my panties?"

Kelly looked like he wanted to lie but he didn't. "Not exactly."

"What does that mean?"

His jaw worked back and forth. "It means we're going to need to have the contents DNA tested."

Sickened by the realization that some creep had used my stolen undies to masturbate, I dropped into the nearest chair. I felt so incredibly violated. Then another, even more terrifying thought hit me. "My underwear didn't go missing until after I had moved in here. That means this freak was here, what, ten days ago?" I tried to remember exactly when I'd noticed them gone. "Oh my God! How many times has he been here?"

Kelly glanced around the apartment with a critical eye. "You can't stay here anymore."

"No, she absolutely cannot," Lev agreed. "We'll need to find a safer, more secure place for her."

"I have an idea. Let me make a call." Dimitri dug his phone out of his pocket and moved to the far side of the room. A few moments later, he started speaking in Russian.

Lev sat down across from me. "We need to begin your threat assessment."

"My what?"

"It's a way of cataloguing the threats that may exist against you," Lev explained. "So, obviously, something like that," he gestured to the box, "suggests a boyfriend or lover. Let's talk about your dating history?"

"Um...okay."

"Have you recently had a breakup?"

"No."

"Were any of your past breakups violent or messy or awkward?"

"No."

"Were any of your boyfriends possessive or jealous? Did anyone try to abuse you? Verbally or physically," he added.

"No." I could feel Kelly's intent gaze on me. Could this be any weirder?

"And, if you'll excuse me," Lev offered an apologetic smile, "have you ever had a lover who behaved inappropriately in bed?"

"Inappropriately?" Did he mean, like, rough sex? Spanking? Bondage? Deciding it didn't really matter what he meant, I hurriedly answered, "No."

Lev smiled kindly. "It's all right, Miss Langston. You don't have to be embarrassed."

Face on fire, I avoided Kelly's curious stare. "Nothing inappropriate has ever occurred in my bed. I sleep alone. *Always.*"

"Oh. I see." Lev seemed a little surprised. Perhaps he didn't come across many members of the V-Club my age. "Well. Then we'll skip those questions. What about admirers?"

Still refusing to look at Kelly, I said, "Well...I mean...I get the occasional weird messages on my blog or via email but never anything that was strange enough for me to seek police protection. This whole mess came out of left field, you know?"

"Let's talk business." Lev directed the interview in a different direction. "What do you do?"

"The press calls me an internet entrepreneur, but I'm a web developer and programmer at heart. I've designed software and various applications in social media. Some have done extremely well, and some flopped right out of the gate."

"You designed a secure chat software for the military?"

"I did."

"Some people can be touchy about military applications, even the ones with the most innocent uses. Have you ever received any hate mail or threats about working for the US government?"

"First, I don't work for the government. I designed

HomeFront independently and licensed the rights to it to the DOD. Secondly, yes, of course, I've received some nasty-grams from unhinged jerks, but that was years ago. They were all cranks. I haven't heard a peep out of them since then."

"Do you make a lot of money doing this?"

"I'm starting to, yes."

"How much?"

"That's a complicated question."

"Ten million? Fifty million?'"

"More than the first but currently much less than the latter," I answered a bit cryptically. "If you're talking liquid assets I could get my hands on in a week or less, I mean. If you're talking the current valuation of LookIt and the amount I personally stand to bank if I sell the platform to Insight, then you could easily quadruple that top figure."

The expression on Kelly's face changed to one I couldn't read. Before I could contemplate what he might be thinking now that the numbers were on the table, Lev continued with his barrage of questions.

"Insight is that internet search engine, right?"

"They started as a search engine but they now own pieces of various social media platforms, news organizations and digital media companies."

"And what is LookIt?"

"It's a blogging platform."

He shot me a bemused smile. "And why is it called LookIt? Is this an American expression I'm unfamiliar with?"

"It's something my brother used to say," I explained. "Whenever he got annoyed with me or thought I needed a lecture, he'd say, 'Look it, Bee…'"

"I see." Lev scribbled on his pad. "And your company

is called?"

"JBJ TechWorks."

"Your company currently has how many employees?"

"We have twenty-one, including me, in the Houston office here, but we also outsource on a contract basis with various providers for tech support for the users of the blogging platform."

Lev made more notes. "And of the twenty people in your office, how many of them are against the possibility of selling to Insight?"

"None."

Lev's eyebrows arched. "None?"

"They stand to make a lot of money if the sale goes through," I explained. "They've all been incredibly encouraging. Most of them have been with me since I put out a call for help during a hackathon I held over Spring Break a few years back. They want this as badly as I do."

Lev frowned. "A what-athon?"

"Hackathon," I supplied. "It's when a group of coders get together to tackle a project."

"I see." His pen scribbled some more. "You compensate your employees well?"

"Sure. We don't have the outrageous perks some of the startups in Silicon Valley offer, but it's still very nice."

"What about ex-employees?"

Two names came to mind. "I'm currently being sued by Richard Hawkins. He was hired to be the COO of JBJ TechWorks, but he didn't work out so well. The guy had all the right qualifications to push a startup into the stratosphere—but he was extremely difficult. It wasn't a good fit, so I let him go after seven or eight months."

"Why is he suing you?"

"He started a new company and poached some of my employees. One of them is a guy named Trevor Cohen who stole a project from me and used it as the basis for one of their products. When we rolled out the original product in beta, Richard sued us so I countersued. Now he's brought a second suit against me for more compensation based on the employment contract between us." I waved my hand. "It's a whole complicated thing."

"When was the last time you spoke to either of them?"

"It's been awhile since I've spoken to Trevor or Richard. We communicate through lawyers."

"And is this Richard Hawkins actually owed further compensation?"

"Absolutely not," I said forcefully. "He feels that his connections at Insight are what brought interest to LookIt—but that's not true. The deal they offered wasn't even thrown onto the table until nine months *after* he left. He received a generous severance package. Believe me. He made out just fine on that deal."

"Regardless of what did or didn't happen, he may feel wronged. People do stupid things when they're feeling vengeful."

I considered the gross gift box. "I don't think Richard is that sort of guy. I mean—okay—maybe I could believe that he had Trevor spoof my site but breaking into my home to steal my undies to...*you know*?" I shook my head. "That's not him."

"You would be surprised at what some men will do." Lev tucked his notebook back into his pocket. "We'll need some time to come up with a proper protection plan, but I would *strongly* suggest you take on full-time guards. You need a minimum of two men working around the clock to secure and protect your person. We may need to add a third or fourth body when you're traveling or going out in the evenings."

I glanced at Kelly for some guidance. He nodded in agreement. "All right. Let's do that."

"I'll assign two of my men to start today. If you don't like them, we'll go through the roster until we find men who fit with your personality."

"You only need to find one other man," I interjected. "Kelly can be one of them and then you can pick someone else."

Lev cast a quick look Kelly's way. "I don't think that's a good idea."

"Why not?"

"He's personally involved with you. I don't allow the guards to cross that line. It's not safe for the clients."

I didn't insult Lev by denying what he could see so clearly and bit my tongue at the thought of correcting his assumptions as to just how close we were. When I dared to meet Kelly's gaze, I was surprised by the calm expression. He hadn't spoken since Lev began his interrogation but now he seemed ready to say something.

"Dimitri?" he addressed his boss.

"Yeah?" The Russian pocketed his phone.

"I'm formally requesting a leave of absence."

Dimitri's face registered surprise. "Excuse me?"

"I'm not leaving Bee alone until this creep is in jail. I fully understood the rules when I joined the private security side of the firm. I won't ask you to bend them for me." Kelly slid his hand out in front of him. "I have some personal issues that have crept up in the last twenty-four hours. It's better if I take some time."

Dimitri crossed his bulky arms and sighed. "I can't stop you from taking time. I wish you'd reconsider. I could use you on the active roster, especially with Benny due any day."

Kelly's hard stance softened. "Of course, I'll do

whatever I can to help when your baby comes, but right now, I need to worry about my own family." His gaze landed on me. "All of it."

Butterflies swarmed in my chest at the way he'd included me as part of his family. After that comment last night, I had seriously doubted where I fit into Kelly's life. Had he said that to keep those mobsters from thinking they could squeeze me for cash? As protective as Kelly was of me, it made sense. I liked that possibility more.

Lev stood up. "Rather than taking complete leave, why don't we let you run the detail? I thought I'd put Sully and Winn on this one. You draw up the rotation and comb through her schedule. You can act as the contact point between the police department and Lone Star."

Kelly didn't mull over the offer. He accepted immediately. "Works for me."

The counter-terrorism expert lifted a warning finger. "The first report from Sully or Winn that you're making work difficult, and I'll pull my support for this arrangement."

"Understood."

"Now that's settled," Dimitri said, "I spoke with Yuri. He's incredibly concerned for Bee and has offered up his penthouse suite downtown. He and Lena never use it, so it's completely vacant. It's ideally located because Bee's company is only a few floors down. It's also a fortress." He turned to me. "Would you be willing to stay there for a while?"

"Sure." Even though I was certain money and the success of the Insight deal had entered his mind, I knew Yuri's kindness had motivated his desire to help me. "I'm lucky to have such good friends."

"That's Yuri for you," Dimitri replied. "All right. Get her to the penthouse, Kelly. We'll send Sully and Winn that way. I'll drop by later this afternoon with a contract."

I had no doubt this was going to be one pricey little venture, but my safety was worth it. "I'll need to have my lawyer look at it."

"Perfectly fine with me," Dimitri assured me. "I want you to be comfortable with anything you sign."

"We'll need to see everything you've received from this stalker," Lev said. "Texts, emails, photos—give it to Spike."

"What about the police?"

"I'll handle that," Kelly assured me. "It's not uncommon for us to act as a go-between for clients." He gestured toward the back of my apartment. "Let's get you packed and get the hell out of here."

As I hurried to gather the things I would need for my stay at the penthouse, I experienced the strongest wave of revulsion. I actually shivered, and Kelly reached out to caress my arm. "Are you okay?"

Hugging an armful of clothes to my chest, I said, "I can't stop thinking about what this creep has done in my house. If he did *that* to my undies, what has he done in my bed? Ugh. What if he's, like, touched my toothbrush?"

Kelly got a strange look on his face. "Don't take anything that can't be washed. Leave anything that can be replaced. Make me a list and after Winn and Sully have you squared away at the penthouse, I'll go out and personally pick up the things you want."

With Kelly's help, I packed my suitcases and gathered up all of my tech equipment. Dimitri helped him carry it out to the truck while I talked to the police officer who had arrived. Spike turned over the box of soiled panties to the police but I had a feeling he'd already taken the samples he needed to run his tests.

Leaving my apartment, I wondered when or if I would

ever come back. It would be hard to ever feel comfortable in my private space again after knowing that someone had broken in multiple times without me even realizing it.

"Do you think he was watching me?" I asked as he drove away from my building. "What if he put in cameras or something? He could have been watching me shower or get dressed."

"If there are hidden cameras, Spike and Lev will find them." Kelly's grip tightened on the wheel. "When we find this guy—"

"You'll let the authorities deal with it," I interjected calmly. "The last thing you need is to be thrown in jail for beating up some loser."

"I won't get caught."

"No, you probably wouldn't," I agreed softly. "But I would prefer it if you leave it to the police."

"And if they won't do anything?"

I didn't even want to think about that. "Tell me about Sully and Winn."

"They're good guys. Sully was Delta and Winn was British Special Forces."

"Wow. Are all of the guards that caliber of soldier?"

"Yes." He reached over to tap my thigh. "You'll be in good hands, Bee."

I clasped his big paw and relished the feel of his warm fingers interlaced with mine. "I already am."

CHAPTER FIVE

Later that afternoon, Kelly studied the schedule Bee had written down while she negotiated her contract in another room of the penthouse with Dimitri, Yuri and her lawyer. Yuri had been waiting for them when they arrived and had worked his billionaire magic to ensure the kitchen was stocked and the rooms in perfect order. Kelly could read the genuine concern on Yuri's face. This wasn't simply about protecting an investment. It was about protecting a friend.

"Does this girl ever sleep?" Sully scratched his head as he glanced at the schedule in front of them. "Most of these days are eighteen hours long, Kelly."

"I can read," he replied testily. Truthfully, he had been a bit shocked to see how packed her days were. He'd known that most successful tech startups required a shit-ton of work, but he feared Bee was pushing herself too hard. No wonder she had mentioned dropping out of college. Even those two part-time semesters must have been incredibly difficult for her to complete.

He was probably the last man on the planet who

should lecture anyone about getting some rest, but he was really worried about Bee. She meant too much to him to stand by and watch her work herself to the point of exhaustion.

"So what's the story with you two?"

Kelly didn't even glance up from the schedule as he started jotting notes in the margin. Those morning stops at her favorite coffee spot had to go. They were much too predictable. "She's my best friend's sister."

"And?" Sully continued to fish for information.

"And what?"

"Is she seeing anyone?"

Kelly's glared at the former Spec-Ops man. His reputation as a lothario was well-known around LSG headquarters. "I'll have your balls in a vise if you put one fucking hand on her."

"Whoa." Sully laughed and held up his hands. "Calm down, Kelly. Shit!" With a leer, he added, "I can think of a dozen different ways I might have fun with our hot little protectee without using a single hand."

Kelly didn't find the joke even the slightest bit funny. "You realize I'm the one drawing up the duty rotation, right? Because I'm sure Winn would love the dayshift."

"Come on!" Sully gave him a good-natured smack. "I'm just messing with you. It doesn't take twelve years in black ops to read the situation between the two of you." Reaching for one of the printed penthouse floor plans, he asked, "So what does her brother think about his best friend robbing that cradle?"

Kelly's teeth clenched but he tried to remember that Sully had no idea about Jeb. "There's less than six years between us. That's hardly cradle robbing."

"Touchy," Sully said with a laugh. "And big brother?"

"No idea," Kelly replied honestly. "He's been dead for

four years."

Sully's smile faded. "Shit. Kelly, I didn't realize—"

"It's fine."

"It's not." Somberly, he asked, "How?"

"Firefight," he answered, his ears starting to buzz as those awful memories washed over him. He could almost smell Jeb's hot blood and feel the slick fluid spilling onto his hands as he had desperately tried to stop the bleeding. Shaking himself from the gruesome vision of it, he added, "2010 was a bad year to be in Afghanistan."

"Yeah, it was." Sully's tone convinced Kelly he had been there too. Maybe they'd crossed paths there without even knowing it. "When did it happen?"

"July." Unwilling to travel down that path of memories any longer, he cleared his throat. "Did you and Winn decide on your accommodations?"

"We sure did." Sully took the hint. "We left the room next door to the master suite for you. We assumed you'd be, uh, bunking with the protectee and might like the buffer."

Kelly let the assumption slide. The fact was—he hadn't quite decided where he would be sleeping either. He'd be a damned liar if he said those few hours of sleep he'd snatched earlier that morning hadn't been some of the best he'd had in years. Bee's body heat called to him even now. It had been a long while since he had looked forward to bedtime.

What would happen once they were under the covers together? Well—Kelly didn't have that answer. He figured it was best to leave that decision up to Bee. He'd made the first move this morning. Now it was her turn to make one.

"Kelly?" Dimitri popped his head into the kitchen. "May I speak with you?"

"I'll be right there." He tapped the floor plan in front of Sully. "Draw up the escape routes. Bee needs to memorize the various ways out of here in case of fire, etc."

"On it."

Leaving Sully occupied, Kelly left the kitchen and found Dimitri on the rooftop terrace. The gorgeously decorated and intensely private area was instantly his favorite spot in the entire penthouse. He joined his boss near the railing. "What's up?"

"Bee asked to have authorization for two extra guards. If you feel like you need them, call Lev and he'll arrange it. I'd like a status report every morning and evening."

"Done."

Stepping closer, Dimitri reminded Kelly of just how damn tall he was. "This personal business you wanted to take leave for? Would it have anything to do with a certain Albanian mob boss?"

Caught, Kelly rubbed the back of his neck. "Yuri?"

Dimitri shook his head. "Nikolai."

Kelly's eyes widened. "Kalasnikov?"

"The one and only," Dimitri replied. "He likes to keep an eye on you."

"On me? Why?"

"You're one of Vivian's friends. He's very careful when it comes to the company she keeps." Dimitri's shoulders bounced. "I think he may have been under the impression that you and Vivian were...closer once upon a time."

Kelly didn't often experience fear, but the thought of a man like Nikolai harboring jealousies toward him? The Russian mob boss was not the sort of man Kelly needed as an enemy. "Vivi and I never crossed that line. From the first day I met her, I knew that there would only ever be one man in her life—and he's her husband now."

Dimitri waved his hand. "You don't need to worry. Nikolai can be...overprotective...when it comes to Vivi, but he's not the type to fly into a jealous rage over imagined slights. Besides, one look at you with Bee, and no man could ever imagine there was anyone else for you."

Kelly shifted uncomfortably. "I'd prefer not to discuss my private life."

"What you and Bee do is your own business. It's not against the company policy for a man to be in love." He clapped his hand on Kelly's shoulder. "I'm more concerned about the precarious position you find yourself in with Besian. Can you honestly say that you're able to dedicate your full attention to Bee's safety when you have the Albanian mob breathing down your neck?"

"It's about to be handled."

"How? You're going to take Paulie's place and fight for Besian?"

Kelly frowned. "Jesus, Dimitri. Is there anything you don't already know? Let me guess. You also know what I had for breakfast?"

His icy stare served as a reminder of how Dimitri had gotten where he was today. "Knowing you? Bagel. Eggs. Probably hot sauce."

Neatly put in his place, Kelly sighed. "Look, I don't have any other choice. The debt is huge and it's got to be settled."

Dimitri studied him. "You're a good fighter, Kelly. You impressed me the times I watched you in that cage. It's one of the reasons I approached you to work for Front Door when I was just getting the security company off the ground."

"I know."

"Have you ever seen Nikolai's man in the cage?"

Kelly nodded reluctantly. "I've watched Sergei fight a few times."

"Then you know that he will tear your fucking head off to win."

"I know he'll try."

Dimitri shook his head. "This isn't the time for bravado, Kelly. This is a time to be serious." He hesitated. "Maybe you and I could work out a loan—"

"No," Kelly cut him off before he could finish the offer. "No more debts for the Connolly family."

"Kelly, please, it wouldn't—"

"Would you take a loan from me, or would you find a way to make it work on your own terms?"

Dimitri didn't answer him. Instead, he exhaled roughly and reached into his back pocket to retrieve his wallet and a pen. He tugged an LSG business card from a sleeve and neatly printed a name and address on the back. "Go see him. He's expecting you."

Kelly took the card and turned it over to read the information written on the back. "Alexei?"

"He used to fight with Ivan. He's the only man who ever came close to beating Vanya. He's your best bet."

"How the hell am I supposed to convince a Russian trainer to help me get ready to fight against Nikolai's champion?"

"It's been arranged." Dimitri tucked his wallet into place. "Alexei owes Kolya a favor, and Vivian made sure her husband called it in when she heard about your situation."

Kolya? Oh. Nikolai. "I suppose I owe her a big thanks."

"After Alexei gets finished with you, you may have other ideas." Dimitri clapped him on the back. "Good luck, Kelly."

"Thanks, D. For everything," he added sincerely. "You've always been a great friend to me."

"As your friend, I'm telling you to be careful with this girl. I know what losing her brother did to you. If something happens to her—"

"Nothing is going to happen to her."

"You forget that I've been where you are with Benny. She and I barely survived that attack on her bakery, but we did it together. You have no idea how many times I've replayed that night, wishing that I'd taken the time to properly educate Benny on self-defense and firing a weapon. Don't make my mistake. Give Bee the skills to save herself."

His advice given, Dimitri left Kelly to contemplate his options. He fingered the card his boss had given him. While Jack was a damn good coach and trainer, he wasn't comparable to Ivan Markovic. If this guy Alexei had fought with Ivan, he would know the man's tricks. Since Kelly really hoped to survive his time in the cage, he figured Alexei was his best chance.

Back in the penthouse, he discovered Bee sitting at the kitchen island between Sully and Winn. The two guards were talking her through the emergency exit plan and giving her safety pointers. Certain she was in good hands, he waited until Bee had successfully repeated the four routes five different times before asking her about that shopping list.

"Here." She handed it over to him. "There are a couple of other things I'll need but you can only get them at the salon I use. I hoped I might be able to run over there on Monday."

"We'll make it work." Kelly didn't want her to feel like a prisoner in the penthouse. "When was the last time you fired a weapon?"

Her gaze flicked to a spot just beside him as she rolled back through her memories. "The weekend we buried Mom. Jeb took me out to a range, and we went through dozens of boxes of ammunition. It actually felt kind of good to blow holes in targets."

He could empathize with that feeling. "Tomorrow, we're going to take you down to the range and get you comfortable with loading, clearing jams, and firing. I'm also going to talk to Jack about getting you into some self-defense classes. Have you ever taken one?"

She seemed a bit dazed by his plan. "No. Well—they have these, like, two hour courses on campus every semester. I went to one my freshman year. We learned a lot of useful stuff, but it was very basic."

"I can show you some moves, sweetheart," Sully offered with a sly smile. "I'm a master when it comes to hands-on training."

Kelly had never wanted to wring a man's neck more. He started to question his ability to work in close-quarters with Sully but Bee simply rolled her eyes. "I could have sworn Mr. Stepanov assured me that you men had all undergone sexual harassment training. Maybe you need to sit through another course?"

Sully's playful grin melted. Kelly could tell that Bee was joking but the other man didn't know her well. "No, ma'am."

"*Mmmhmm*," she murmured. She motioned to Winn who had remained stoic and silent, his usual operating style. "This one I really like. Would you mind being the guard who accompanies me to work and meetings? I think I'll actually be able to get work done with you. That one?" She gestured to Sully. "I have a feeling he'd be chasing skirts up and down the office floor."

Winn actually allowed the barest hint of a smile to

crack his stony façade. "Yes, ma'am. I would be more than happy to escort you to business meetings."

"Fantastic."

Glad to see that Bee could handle these two, especially Sully and his smart mouth, Kelly relaxed some. "I'm going to head out and take care of your shopping. If you need anything, text me."

Bee shadowed him to the front door. She started to step close to him, but a glance over her shoulder stopped her. He grasped her hand and tugged her forward. She dropped her voice to a whisper. "Is this okay?"

He trailed his finger down her cheek. Since giving himself permission to touch her, he couldn't get enough of her silky skin. "You tell me, sugar."

Her eyes sparkled with mischief. "It's perfectly fine with me. In fact, please, continue." She gestured behind them with her head. "I meant Sully and Winn. Is it going to be a problem?"

"No. They understand the dynamics of the situation."

"Okay." She drew a shape on his forearm. "Will you be gone long?"

He understood what she was asking. "I have to make a couple of stops."

"You'll be safe?"

"I can handle myself." Unable to help himself, Kelly leaned down and pecked her cheek. "Do exactly what they tell you." Thinking of Sully's outrageous flirtation, he hastily amended, "Do whatever Winn tells you. You can use your best judgment with Sully."

She snorted and whacked his arm. "You seem to forget that my big brother was a Marine. I've got this."

Convinced that she did, he reluctantly left the penthouse and took the private elevator down to the parking garage. He sat in the blasting A/C for a few minutes while he tried to decide where to go first. The business card with Alexei's name on it was burning a hole in his pocket. He figured that getting his training situation squared away was more important than seeking out the Albanian mob boss who held his father's loan.

He tapped the address into the GPS and left the parking garage. The drive took him to one of the mega luxury car dealerships along I-45. Sitting in the parking lot there, he thought he must have been in the wrong place. He whipped out his phone and punched in the name of the dealership.

Skimming the information, he learned Alexei Sarnov owned a string of high-end dealerships around Houston as well as a trucking service. Kelly wasn't at all surprised about the trucking company part. A man who could have trucks available at a moment's notice was probably very useful to someone like Nikolai. Even the men who had gone legit seemed to have kept at least one of their fingers submerged in the dirty waters of the underworld.

Sliding out of his truck, Kelly crossed the parking lot. He had barely set a foot upon the sidewalk when a young man in a neatly pressed suit hurried over to greet him. Before the guy got any ideas about making a sale, he explained, "I'm here to see Alexei."

The younger man looked him up and down with a scrutinizing eye. "You must be the Connolly guy we're supposed to send to the main office."

"Yeah. That's me."

"Come on."

Kelly followed the salesman into the sleek building. With all the glass lining the front, he shuddered to imagine what the electricity bills were like to keep this joint so damn cold. It sure felt good to escape the muggy heat, though. Unlike the other prospective buyers who were offered water bottles and snacks and taken to cushy seats before they had their wallets emptied by the credit *experts*, Kelly was simply led through the sales floor to a set of stairs that led to offices overlooking the bullpen of car salesmen.

The younger guy hesitated, almost as if frightened to disturb his boss. That was enough of a clue for Kelly. His timid knock was answered by an aggressive looking man in his early forties. He wore a crisply tailored suit and stark white shirt. The neck was unbuttoned enough for Kelly to spot the bluish tint of prison tattoos.

Alexei didn't even look at Kelly as he growled at his employee in Russian. The man paled and nodded and scurried away from the door. Finally deigning to acknowledge Kelly's presence, Alexei asked, "Did you understand any of that?"

"No. Russian isn't a language I speak."

Alexei made a grumbling noise that communicated his distaste before gesturing for him to enter the office. "I told him that if he approaches his sales as weakly as he does his knocks, he'll be out of a job by the end of the month."

"I see you're a fan of positive motivation," Kelly dryly replied.

Alexei actually laughed. "You might be all right after all, Mr. Connolly."

"Kelly," he corrected. "If you're going to be screaming in my face, we should be on a first name basis."

Alexei leaned back against his desk. "You realize that training you puts me in an awkward position with my friends, yes?"

"I can imagine."

"And you also understand that I'm only doing this as a favor to a friend?"

"I do."

He inhaled a long breath. "Nikolai tells me you've fought before and that you have talent. We're on an incredibly tight schedule here. There's no time to properly condition you or teach you the finer points of surviving in a cage match." Alexei tilted his head. "You look like you're in good shape. Nikolai says you're a Marine?"

"I'm working in private security now."

"With Dimitri?"

"Yeah."

Alexei made that humming sound again as he studied Kelly from head to toe. "I'm going to be upfront with you. I'm not sure anyone can beat Sergei. You look like you might have a good chance, but it will be very close." As if to encourage Kelly, he added, "I'm reasonably certain he won't cripple you."

"Wow. Thanks."

Alexei shrugged. "I make it a point to tell the truth."

Kelly motioned to the bullpen behind him. "You own a car dealership."

With a quirk of a smile, Alexei amended, "Whenever possible." Stretching out his legs, Alexei said, "We'll have to start tonight if you're going to be ready. I would have recommended we head to Ivan's warehouse but..."

"My family owns a gym. Connolly Fitness."

"Yes, I know it." Alexei pushed up the cuff of his jacket to see his watch. "Does six work for you?"

He didn't want to be away from Bee again in the evening but there was nothing else to be done about it. Alexei's remark about being crippled wasn't lost on him. Sergei wouldn't hesitate to put the hurt on him if it meant walking away with the victory. He needed to get into the ring and get working. "Sure."

"I'll have a set of instructions for you tonight. We'll

need to watch your diet and your sleep." His eyes narrowed. "No drugs. No alcohol."

"Not a problem," Kelly assured him.

"Try to keep the extra-curricular activities to a minimum."

Kelly got the message. He wasn't about to make a promise he couldn't keep, not with his own personal temptress in such close quarters. "I'll try."

"Fair enough." Alexei shoved off his desk. "I'll see you this evening."

"Thank you for helping me." Kelly extended his hand. "I know you're sticking your neck out for me."

Alexei considered his hand for a moment before gripping it tightly. "I've been where you are. Family can be...messy." Still holding Kelly's hand, he squeezed harder. "But if you even think about taking a dive to play the sharks against each other, Sergei crippling you will be the least of your worries."

"If I took a dive, I'd deserve it." Kelly had considered that Besian or Hagen might try to force him to throw one of his tournament rounds to satisfy the debt. It was the one thing he absolutely wouldn't do.

Alexei seemed satisfied by Kelly's reply and released his hand. Pivoting on his heel, Kelly left the dealership and drove straight to the social club where Besian liked to hold court. Like Alexei, the Albanian mob boss was expecting him.

"Kelly!" Besian grinned widely from behind his desk.

Not in the mood for chitchat, Kelly asked, "What are your terms?"

"Would it kill you to be friendly?" Kicking back in his chair, Besian tucked his hands behind his head. When it was clear that Kelly wasn't going to attempt friendly banter, he rolled his eyes and sighed. "If you make it into the final round, I'll consider seventy percent of the debt cleared. Win it and we're even."

"Ninety percent," Kelly insisted. "You're asking me to take multiple beatings. I know you'll have action on my fights. If I make it into the final round, I want ninety percent of the debt cleared."

"Eighty," Besian countered.

"Eighty-five," Kelly replied.

Besian seemed to mull it over and shrugged. "Yeah. Okay. You make into the final round and I'll wipe eighty-five percent of the debt. I'll want the remaining fifteen percent within seven days."

Kelly figured this was the fairest deal they were going to get. "Agreed. I want Pop's account closed. No more credit with you or your underground casinos, or the bookies."

"Done." Besian leaned forward and picked up a pen. "I hear Alexei is going to help you."

Kelly wondered how these criminal types shared information so quickly. He suddenly wished he had a network like theirs. "He's agreed to train me for the tournament."

"Then you should have no problem making it to the final round," Besian said as he scribbled something on a slip of paper. "The tournament is capped at sixteen men. There will be two fights the first night and two fights the second. We'll have the bracket out next Wednesday. I can say with some confidence that you won't be facing off with Sergei that first night."

Kelly's jaw tightened. "Is this tournament fixed?"

Besian snorted and tossed down his pen. "You say fixed like it's a bad thing. No." He met Kelly's glare. "The brackets try to match fighters against equal partners. You're not in Sergei's league. If you survive the first night, you'll get your chance with him." The mobster turned loan shark made a face. "I hope Dimitri's company provides good health insurance."

Ignoring the subtle insult, Kelly asked, "Are we finished?"

Besian waved toward the door. "Go."

He'd just stepped into the hallway when the mobster called out, "If you decide that you want to get a loan on the gym, come back and see me. I'm sure we can work something out to save it from Hagen."

The reminder of their precarious position with Houston's most infamous money man hit Kelly like a brick to the face. How they were going to square that one remained a mystery. Placing bets on his fights was one way to make the money, but would it be enough?

Sitting in his truck, Kelly called his eldest brother. He expected to leave a voicemail, but Jack answered after two rings, sounding a bit out of breath. No doubt he'd sprinted to his phone while in the middle of a class or training session. "Well?"

"I met with Besian. He's agreed to clear eighty-five percent of the debt if I make it to the final round. The tournament is sixteen men. Two fights on Friday and two on Saturday."

"Jesus, Kelly." Jack's anguish came through loud and clear. "That's a fuck load of punishment, little bro."

Kelly ran his fingers along the curve of his steering wheel. "I've survived worse. You've survived worse. Finn has survived worse. It's two nights and we're done."

"I don't like it."

"I know you don't."

"What are we doing about training?"

"Yeah...about that."

"What?"

"So Vivian's husband found out that I was in a bind and he called in a favor for me."

"Vivian? Wait. The painter who married the Russian mob boss? The guy who owns Samovar?"

"Nikolai," Kelly supplied his name. "He hooked me up with Alexei—"

"Sarnov?" Jack interrupted. "Alexei Sarnov?"

"Yeah. You know him?"

"I know of him. He's a damn good fighter. He still does some training down at the Warehouse. You know, Ivan Markovic's joint." Jack hesitated. "His help won't come cheap."

"I got the feeling his help is free."

"Shit. That must be one hell of a favor he owes Nikolai."

"Apparently," Kelly agreed. "He wants to start training this evening. We're meeting at six at the gym."

"I'll make sure there's an empty space for the two of you."

"Thanks. Now—what are we going to do about Hagen?"

"I arranged a meeting for tomorrow afternoon. We'll feel him out and see what he's thinking."

Kelly had a feeling they weren't going to like what Hagen was thinking.

"How is Bee?"

"She's safe."

Jack didn't ask him to elaborate. "Good. I assume you won't be home tonight?"

"I'll run by to grab a bag, but I'm sticking close to her until we get this stalker."

"Yeah. I bet you'll be sticking *real* close to her."

"Are we going to do the playground taunting now?"

"Let me get Finn. We'll do a Kelly and Bee K-I-S-S-I-

N-G in a tree duet for you."

Kelly laughed. "I'm hanging up now."

"Be safe, bro."

"Always."

With his personal business in order, Kelly drove to the nearest big box store to pick up everything on Bee's list. He had never shopped for a woman before, so he was glad she had been specific about the brands she wanted. A couple of times she didn't note the fragrance she liked, so he had to resort to strange measures to get it right.

Glancing around, he sniffed the soap and antiperspirant until he found the ones that smelled right. He prayed no one would come around the corner. They would probably report him to management for being a soap-sniffing freak.

As he pushed his cart down the aisle of shaving supplies, Kelly considered what it said about his feelings toward Bee that he had memorized her scent profile. The threat against her had shaken him up enough that abiding by some unspoken rule of friendship no longer seemed important. The twenty years of friendship he'd shared with Jeb had been the greatest of his life. Never again would he have a friend like that.

But right now the possibility of creating something real and intimate and lifelong with Bee hovered just before him. He'd put his life on hold for the last four years—and he was done. It was time to live.

Back at the penthouse, he used the private elevator to access the top floor of Yuri's skyscraper. He wasn't surprised to be greeted by Winn the second he stepped off the elevator into the reception hall of the luxurious suite. The highly decorated soldier had obviously seen the security feed of Kelly entering the elevator from the parking lot, but he wasn't taking any chances. Kelly liked him all the more for it.

"She's in her room." Winn held open the door since Kelly's hands were full. "We ordered a late lunch. There's a sandwich and salad in the refrigerator for you."

"Thanks." He crossed the living area and glanced at Sully who was fiddling with a book of Sudoku puzzles. They nodded at each other before he disappeared out of sight. When he reached the master suite, he knocked twice. "Bee?"

"Yeah?"

Taking her response as permission, he opened the door—and lost his grip on the bags. They tumbled to the floor amid Bee's gasp of surprise. Unable to stop himself, Kelly raked his needy gaze along her very naked and incredibly nubile form. The dampness of her hair told him she'd just had a shower. The foot propped on the bed and the tiny bottle of complimentary lotion filled in the blanks.

Finally shaking herself from the shock of being discovered in this precarious position, Bee reached for the towel but Kelly stopped her with one gruffly spoken word. "No."

Closing the door behind him, he pushed aside the bags with the toe of his boot and flipped the lock. Bee slowly lowered her petite leg. She bit her lower lip and eyed him like prey keeping a wary eye on a prowling jungle cat. Not wanting to push her too fast, too soon, he said, "Tell me to leave, Bee."

She didn't even hesitate. Holding out her hand, she said, "Stay."

So he did.

CHAPTER SIX

My belly trembled violently as Kelly strode toward me. Wondering from where this surge of bravery emanated, I counted the steps until he could touch me. Standing there as naked as the day I'd been born, there was no way for me to hide the way he affected me. One look at my breasts and their puckered peaks, and Kelly would have no doubts about how much I wanted him.

He came so close to me that I had to tilt my head back to gaze into those bright green eyes of his. The scent of him, that masculine mix that made everything feminine in me go crazy with desire, surrounded me. I could feel the throbbing heat of him and wanted nothing more than to burrow against his wide, sculpted chest.

Kelly traced my collarbone with his long, thick finger. "I've never kissed you properly."

I laughed nervously and gestured to my naked body. "I think we're going about this whole thing backwards."

His sexy mouth slanted with amusement. "Seems rather fitting considering the way the two of us have gone about everything else in our lives." He dragged his finger across my lower lip. "I want to kiss you, but I need you to be sure, Bee. I've been able to hold back and stay away from you, but once I taste you? All bets are off."

Showing him I was ready, I rose on tiptoes and sought his descending mouth. Ever the alpha male, Kelly refused to let me have control over our first real kiss. I let him have this small victory, certain there would be plenty of times for me to play the aggressor in the future.

Gently, he cupped the back of my neck and brushed his lips against mine. My heart thudded in my chest, and my knees wobbled as he lovingly claimed my mouth. I clung to his arms, gripping the thin cotton of his T-shirt, and closed my eyes as a joyous chorus erupted in my head. *Finally!*

Our chaste and sweet kiss quickly transformed into a hungry, needful thing. Instead of stooping down to kiss me, Kelly slipped his hand around my waist and dragged me back toward the bed. Not once breaking contact with my mouth, he sat on the mattress and tugged me between his thighs.

His rough, strong hands glided over my skin. Like a spark to dry tender, passion ignited within me. The burning flames of it licked at my core and made my clitoris pulse. I squeezed my thighs together, but it was no use. The ache there couldn't be assuaged.

Kelly's tongue flirted with mine. Whimpering, I wound my arms around his neck and relished the feel of his brawny arms enveloping me. He drew me against his heat and stabbed his tongue between my lips, tasting me and taking what he had so long denied himself.

He palmed my soft flesh and rubbed his thumb over my dusky pink nipple. "I used to dream about this."

His confession surprised me. My voice sounded husky as I asked, "When?"

"Over there."

Afghanistan or Iraq? I didn't dare ask lest the moment be ruined by dredging up the horrific memories of his seemingly never-ending deployments.

He pressed a noisy kiss to the swell of my breast. "I used to imagine the way your skin would feel. I wondered how you would taste and what sounds you would make if I did something like this."

When his tongue started to trace my nipple, I almost crumpled to the floor. My poor legs shook so badly that it was only Kelly's supporting arm keeping me upright. Clutching his shoulders, I exhaled a shuddery breath. "*Kelly*."

He made a happy noise. "Yeah. That's about how I imagined it."

As he began the sensual torment of my breasts with his mouth, I asked, "What made you stop?" At his confused look, I clarified, "Imaging us like this, I mean."

"Who said I did?" He pinched my nipple between his fingertips. The bright arc of pressure traveled right to my clit in the most delicious way. "It started over there, after the last barbecue, and never stopped."

Placing my hand along his jaw, I commanded his attention. Even though it embarrassed me to bring up that spectacularly awkward rejection, I had to know why. "So why did you push me away on New Year's Eve?"

He drew a shape on my chest that felt suspiciously like a K. "You can't imagine how guilty I felt when Jeb was alive. The way I felt about you then?" He shook his head. "It's not right. You're not supposed to have those kinds of thoughts about your best friend's sister. I think Jeb knew that I liked you way more than I should have. He started pulling away from me on that last deployment. I couldn't reach him."

Kelly talking about guilt made me think of Jeb and the secrets he had carried to the grave. My brother's guilt over his double-life had spilled over into his friendship with Kelly and ruined the support system he had so desperately needed as our mother lost her battle with cancer.

Even now, all these years later, I had to bite my tongue. I'd sworn to Jeb that I would never tell anyone his secrets. The lies between Kelly and me made me uneasy. If anyone deserved to know the truth...

"When you kissed me at New Year's, all that guilt came rushing to the surface. I reacted badly." He captured my mouth so tenderly. "It was wrong of me. I should have been man enough to own my feelings."

"You're owning them now. That's enough for me." Not wanting our naughty interlude to be distracted by discussions of the past, I dragged it back on course with a playfully provocative question. "What else did you imagine us doing?"

With all the skill of a seasoned lover, Kelly expertly scooped me up and flipped me right back onto the bed. The movement made his incredibly muscled arms flex in the most deliciously enticing way. His short sleeves bunched up to reveal even more of the heavy tribally influenced tattoos emblazoned on his skin.

Placing his knees on either side of my thighs, Kelly pinned me beneath him on the bed. I grew lightheaded as he kissed me into submission. There was no doubt who was in charge here. With my lack of experience, I happily placed my trust in him, certain that whatever Kelly had planned for us would feel so good.

"You're so damn beautiful," he murmured, his caressing hands gliding over my breasts and along the slope of my belly.

"Let me see you." I breathlessly pleaded for him to remove his shirt. Smiling indulgently, he let me drag his shirt up high enough to bare his navel before taking over for me. In one swift movement, he ripped it over his head and tossed it behind him.

Our mouths crashed together as the years of pent-up passion exploded between us. I couldn't get enough of his hot, sexy body. The light smattering of hair on his chiseled chest fascinated me. I'd spent so much time dating men who were more comfortable in cubicles than on the battlefield that I'd never experienced the thrill of being completely at the mercy of such a delightfully beastly man.

Kelly showed his incredible strength by sliding his hand under my back and dragging me up another foot or so on the bed. Still straddling me, he nuzzled his nose against my cheek and coaxed me to turn my face. When he nipped at the curve of my neck, I gasped and bucked against him. "Kelly!"

He chuckled softly and continued to lick and suck that sensitive spot. I worried he might mark me but then decided I wouldn't mind carrying around the reminder of our tryst. Though I'm sure his grazing teeth left a red trail on my skin, he wasn't harsh enough to leave a lasting sign.

Sliding onto his side, Kelly kept his leg crooked across mine as our tongues started a dance as old as time. The erotic coupling of our mouths mimicked the movements I desperately hoped would soon be happening between other parts of our super-heated bodies. His roaming hands stoked the fire deep in my core, and my thighs clenched.

"Tell me what you want, Bee." His eyes were dark with desire.

I gulped nervously but found the courage to say, "I

want you to touch me."

"Where?" He teased his lips across mine.

My face was on fire now. "You know where."

He caressed my hip. "Here?"

A smile tugged at the corners of my mouth as I stared up into his teasing face. "Um...a little lower."

His hand moved to my thigh, bypassing the place where I wanted to feel his touch most. "Here?"

"You're getting warmer."

He walked his fingertips up my thigh. "Am I getting closer?"

I parted my thighs and encouraged his curious hand. "Yes."

When he cupped my bare pussy, I thought I would die from the sheer excitement of having him touching me so intimately. I tried to avert my gaze as he brushed his knuckles up and down the seam of my sex but Kelly wouldn't allow it. He silently demanded I lock eyes with him. With one look, he shattered the embarrassment holding me back from enjoying what he offered.

With the softest touch, he parted my pink folds and exposed the aching bud of my clitoris to his fingertip. I bit back a groan as he carefully strummed the little pearl hidden there. Though I'd never shied away from exploring my body, my own touch had never felt like this.

Every nerve ending in my body seemed electrified. I practically buzzed as the white-hot pulses of bliss arced through me. Kelly savored my mouth while manipulating my clit, rubbing small, slow circles around it until I started to dig my toes into the duvet. Emboldened by the heat inflaming me, I nibbled his lower lip and sucked the tip of his tongue. Kelly growled and stabbed his tongue against mine.

Overcome with lust, I reached down and jerked on the

button and zipper of his jeans. The moment I had them undone, I slid my hand beneath the denim and followed the outline of his rock-hard cock under his boxer briefs. I had always suspected Kelly had a big dick, and he certainly didn't disappoint.

Groping him through the cotton, I drew a low, needful groan from his throat. "Touch me," he ordered. "Take out my cock and touch me, Bee."

Hearing him speak so roughly made the slick heat between my thighs grow even damper. Kelly seemed curious to see how he affected me because his fingers abandoned my clitoris and gently probed my wet depths. I arched my back as he penetrated me with one finger, easing it inside me so gently and with such care.

With one finger buried inside me, Kelly worked his thumb across my throbbing clit. Hands trembling, I managed to finally free his cock from its fabric prison. I used both hands to stroke and fondle him. Marveling at the steely hardness of him, I worked my hand up and down his shaft.

"Harder," he urged and pumped his hips. "I'm not made of glass. You can be rough with me."

I gulped at his frank instruction but followed his advice. My fingers tightened around his cock. Using more pressure, I stroked him faster. The rumbling groan that vibrated through his chest assured me I was doing everything just right. He pumped his hips, pressing the blunt crown of his penis against my palm in search of more stimulation.

Our tongues dueled wildly now. Kelly's skilled hand masterfully manipulated me. Deep inside my belly, that shuddering pulse began to build. The coil tightened and tightened while the panicky flutters moved like vibrating fingers through my core and into my chest. Tearing my mouth away from his, I cried out his name as the first spasm of ecstasy ripped through me. "Kelly."

"That's it, sweetheart." His excited breaths tickled my throat as that wicked hand of his made me buck and rock my hips. He buried his face in the crook of my neck and kept rubbing my clit until I seriously saw stars. The blissful sensations crashing over me were so good my stroking hand fumbled and lost its grip.

Kelly didn't seem to mind. If anything, he seemed so wrapped up in giving me pleasure that nothing else mattered. He made me come and come until I just couldn't take anymore and reached down to force his torturous hand to stop. He curved his hand over my pussy in a protective, possessive gesture and made love to my mouth with such sensual eroticism that it left me boneless and limp.

His cock throbbed against my thigh, reminding me that he hadn't yet found his release. Wanting to see him come undone, I shoved on his shoulders and coaxed him onto his back. Straddling his thigh, I tugged his jeans down even lower, dragging his boxers with them. Using both hands on him now, I leaned down to capture his mouth while caressing his shaft.

"Bee." He growled against my mouth, the rough sound eliciting excited shivers from me. To know that I could have so much power over a man like Kelly did wild things to my heart. It stuttered in my chest as I watched his face with awe. When I flicked my tongue against his lips, he groaned and tangled his hand in my hair, pulling me down for a kiss that left me dizzy.

His harsh, quick breaths heralded his climax. My clit throbbed incessantly as I waited for him to come, the very act of touching him like this arousing me to the point of desperation. Proving he could read me like a damn book, Kelly slipped his hand between my thighs and found my aching clit.

Hips rising off the bed, he thrust his cock against my hands and grunted softly. As the first spurt of his blazing seed hit my belly, I followed him over the edge, tumbling head-first into the wicked sea of ecstasy with him. Panting and shuddering together, I milked his cock for the very last drop, gliding my hand up and down his hard, quivering shaft until he fell back to the mattress.

Reaching for me, Kelly pulled me on top of him and hugged me tightly to his chest. His lips drifted across my forehead. Still breathing heavily, he started to laugh. The rich, baritone sound filled the room and made me smile. "What's so funny?"

"What the hell were we waiting for, Bee?" He wiped a hand down his face. "We could have been having this much fun together for years."

I traced one of the tattoos on his chest. "I was starting to wonder what it was going to take to make you see me."

"I've been *seeing* you that way since you were in high school, Bee."

That revelation surprised me a bit. I began to understand the guilty feelings he'd harbored. "When that barbecue happened, the one with the sparklers, I was already eighteen and a high school graduate, Kelly. It wouldn't have been illegal or skeevy. You were, what, twenty-three?"

"I was twenty-four. Illegal and unethical aren't the same thing." He skimmed his fingertips along my arm. "You were so young and had so much potential. The last thing you needed was some Marine boyfriend holding you back while you were at college."

"You're not holding me back now."

Kelly didn't reply immediately. Eventually, he said,

"I'm not so sure about that, Bee."

I rose up on my elbow so I could peer down into his face. "Why would you say something like that?"

He pushed wayward strands of hair behind my ear. "Bee, I barely finished high school. If it hadn't been for Jeb, I never would have made it through chemistry or physics. College degree or not, you're already a certified genius."

I rolled my eyes. "I don't care about your high school transcripts, Kelly. I care about *you*."

"And I care about you," he murmured. "That's why I have to be realistic. What the hell can a washed-up Marine like me offer a girl like you? I don't know anything about writing code or making billion-dollar business deals."

"Kelly, I can hire people to help me with those things. Lawyers, programmers, minions—they can all be had for the right price."

"Minions, huh?"

"They're extremely useful." Tapping his chin, I added seriously, "The one thing I can't buy is love and support. I need someone in my corner who cares about *me*. Not the company or the money or the notoriety. Just me."

Kelly dragged me down for a soulful kiss. "I care about you, Bee. Only you."

"I know." Trying to suppress the giddiness threatening to overwhelm me, I snuggled up against Kelly. Here inside this master suite, we could pretend we were just like any other couple. Unfortunately, it was impossible to ignore the very real threat of my crazy stalker, two loan sharks, and the Albanian mob. "How did your meetings go?"

"As well as could be expected," he said, playing with my hair. "Besian agreed to terms we can accept.

Tomorrow we're meeting with Hagen."

The urge to offer him money again was strong, but I smothered it. "Do you think you can win this tournament?"

"Honestly?"

I glanced up at him in time to catch the barest hint of fear reflected in his eyes. "Yes."

"No."

"Oh."

"Sergei is unbeatable. There's a reason Nikolai Kalasnikov trusts Sergei to guard and protect Vivi." Kelly wound my hair around his scarred finger. "Everyone else? I can beat. It'll be hard but I'll win those rounds. Unless some unexpected fluke puts Sergei down, he'll be in the final. If I make it that far, the odds are highly against me."

I couldn't imagine what kind of balls it took for Kelly to walk into a cage knowing that he was probably going to get the living shit beat out of him. The thought of him being badly hurt made me want to vomit. I couldn't let him do this. I really couldn't. There had to be a way I could make everything okay that wouldn't require him risking his life.

"One of the Russians is going to train me."

I perked up at that bit of information. "How did you swing that? I figured they all stuck together."

"They do. Vivi persuaded Nikolai to pull some strings to help me. I owe her a huge thank you over this one."

The mention of the hauntingly beautiful artist caused my gut to twist with jealousy. "You're lucky to have a friend like that."

Kelly must have heard something in my voice that made him curious because he shifted our position so that we were both on our sides and staring eye-to-eye. His eyebrow quirked at an odd angle. "Are you jealous of

Vivi?"

"No."

Kelly grinned. "Yes, you are."

"No, I'm not." Irritated that he could read me so easily, I tried to squirm away from him, but there was no escaping his strong hands. Kelly held me in place and forced me to meet his intense gaze.

"You are a terrible liar."

"I wouldn't know. I've never had much practice."

"You better ask Yuri for pointers because you're going to have to learn how to bluff in high-stakes meetings, Bee." Slanting his head, he studied my face. "Why in the world are you jealous of Vivian?"

Like a petulant child, I pouted. "You took her out for dinner and dancing."

"Bee, those were group activities. We have friends in common. It was never a one-on-one thing."

"You've never taken me out like that. When I tried to kiss you and you shut me down, I thought maybe it was because of her. She'd just been kidnapped and all that so I thought—"

"I see." Kelly nuzzled my neck in that way he had discovered made me tremble with need. "You have nothing to be jealous about, Bee. Sure, I think she's beautiful—but we're only friends. That's it."

I swallowed hard as he sucked on my neck and grazed his teeth over the spot before laving it with his tongue to ease the small hurt. "Just friends, huh?"

"Just friends," he whispered and then skimmed his lips along my breast. "You can rest assured I've never done anything like this with her."

"Why not?"

As his hand slid along my inner thigh, Kelly turned that piercing gaze of his on me. "You know why."

I inhaled a shaky breath when he gently probed my slick folds. "Tell me."

With a lascivious grin, he murmured, "I think I'd rather show you..."

CHAPTER SEVEN

Kelly considered himself to be in excellent shape, especially with Lev's physical fitness requirements for all LSG guards and Jack's training regimen, but—God help him—Alexei was going to kill him.

Slinging sweat from his eyes, Kelly rubbed the back of his sparring gloves across his forehead and hopped from foot to foot, keeping his weight properly shifted as he awaited his partner's next strike. Alexei had brought four fighters with him, men he trained on the side at Ivan's warehouse, and they were whipping his ass.

The first mock fight had gone well, with Kelly winning it easily. Alexei seemed to have used it as a rubric. The rounds had gotten more intense and more brutally violent. The Russian trainer had insisted on proper sparring equipment so at least he was being spared the worst of it. Even with his shin guards and helmet, Kelly would be sporting bruises tomorrow.

Alexei had been rotating his men out halfway through every round. Facing a fresh foe every few minutes forced Kelly to exert himself in ways he hadn't since the long, hard slog of war. The former fighter's point wasn't lost on Kelly. If he couldn't win multiple sparring rounds in the safety of the ring, he was going to get his damn neck snapped by Sergei.

If he was lucky.

From the corner of the sparring mat, Alexei's voice boomed at him. He snapped directions in Russian but Kelly couldn't understand them. Uncertain if Alexei was speaking to him or the guy throwing punches, he glanced to his left—and gave his opponent just enough of an opening to land a killer fucking kick right to his thigh. It knocked him off balance and the blast of pain radiated right into his stomach. Before he could recover, his opponent hooked his foot around Kelly's ankle and took him down to the mat.

Stopping the round, Alexei stormed onto the mat in utter disgust. "What did I say? Huh?"

Kelly pushed aside the guy trying to put him in a hold, shoved to his feet, and spit out his mouth guard. "I can't fucking understand you. Speak. English."

Alexei smacked Kelly's face with such speed and force that his head snapped back. He heard his brothers' gasps of outrage from the sidelines, but they didn't intervene. "Did you understand that?"

Getting up in Alexei's face, Kelly pushed down the rage and frustration boiling in his gut. Through gritted teeth, he answered, "Yes."

"Are you pissed at me?"

"Yes."

"Do you want to hit me?"

"Yes."

"Good." With a growl, Alexei shoved him back into the center of the ring. "Pretend he's me—and watch that leg."

Rolling his neck, Kelly shoved his mouth guard into place. Jack clapped two wooden blocks together, signaling they could go at each other again. Alexei continued to shout pointers from the sidelines, but he did it in English most of the time. The remainder of the sparring session went fairly well, but by the time Kelly finished his cool down, he feared his jelly-like legs were going to collapse at any moment.

"Get cleaned up," Alexei ordered. "Come join us when you're done."

Dragging ass, Kelly made his way to the men's locker room and showered the sweat from his ragged body. Every muscle in his body ached as he dried off and got dressed. The knowledge that tomorrow morning would feel even worse and the next morning after that ten times as bad as this made his chest tighten.

"Suck it the fuck up, man," he hissed to himself. He'd survived so much worse than this. Explosions, firefights, the Taliban, Iraqi insurgents—he'd beat them all. He'd get through this. Three weeks of training. Two nights of bloody battle. He could do this.

Because he didn't have a choice. His father's life, the gym, Jack and Finn's livelihoods—they all rested on his shoulders.

Leaving the locker room, he found Alexei talking seriously with Jack. He joined the pair just as Alexei asked if Jack had any sledgehammers.

"Sledgehammers?" Jack glanced around his gym. "This look like a Home Depot to you?"

Alexei actually laughed. "I'll bring my own—and tires too."

"Tires?"

The Russian nodded. "It's an old training technique but a good one." He glanced at Kelly. "How are you feeling?"

"I'll live."

Alexei considered him for a moment. "You're not bad."

Kelly figured that was the best compliment he was going to get from the trainer. "Thanks."

"Your defensive techniques are shit." Alexei practically sneered the words. "You take too much punishment. You're too focused on powerful hits and kicks. You need to think about stamina. That's the only way you survive four fights in two nights, understand?"

Kelly was starting to get it. He trusted that Alexei knew what he was talking about so he nodded. "I understand."

"If you can't knock a man out in the first minute, you've got to change tactics. You have to wear them down. Look for those openings. Then? Strike!" He slammed his fist into his palm. "Tomorrow we work on take-downs, okay?"

"Yeah."

"I want you here at five in the morning. Jack and I have agreed on your morning conditioning and strength training regimen. I gave your other brother," he gestured to his leg, "the rules of nutrition I want you to follow. You've got to eat clean. You need to fuel your body."

"Okay."

"I'll be here at six tomorrow evening to start our night session. All right?"

"Yeah."

Alexei clapped his back a few times. "You're a good fighter, Kelly."

His final compliment paid, Alexei left the gym. Jack grasped the back of Kelly's neck and massaged his tense muscles. Concern darkened his face. "You sure you want to do this, bro?"

"I've done it before," he reminded his oldest brother.

"That was different. You were fighting one guy a night, maybe two in a month. This is four guys in two nights. The money in the pot is huge. Every mobster and criminal in Houston has a piece of this action. These guys are fucking animals who are out for blood."

Exasperated, Kelly shook off Jack's hand. "What the hell else are we going to do? Huh? You want to stand by and let the Albanians kill Pop? Or maybe you'd like to take on the mob? And all this?" He gestured to the building. "It's gone if we don't win enough cash to pay back whatever the hell Hagen wants."

"I'd rather go bankrupt and live in a fucking box on the street than watch my baby brother get killed."

Irritated, Kelly chafed under his worrying. "Don't be so melodramatic. No one is going to die. Not me, at least. Am I going to get hurt? Yes. I'll be lucky to make it through the first night without breaking something—but I'll heal."

Jack turned his back and sifted his fingers through his black hair. Kelly noticed Finn standing nearby, watching them and mashing that cinnamon gum he liked between his teeth. Finn had always been the calmest of them. He liked to watch and listen, and had more patience than any man Kelly had ever met. It was one of the reasons Finn had excelled as a sniper.

"You two about done?" Finn strode toward them. "Because Kelly needs to go home and rest, and you've got to be up here before five to get the gym open for him."

Jack narrowed his eyes at Finn. "Yes, Mother."

Finn shot him the finger. "Get the keys and lock up. I'm beat."

"I don't know how the two of you work together

without killing each other," Kelly remarked.

"I pray. A lot," Finn added with a smile. He motioned to the entrance across the gym. "How is Bee handling her new living situation?"

Kelly lifted the strap of his gym bag a little higher on his shoulder. "She's adjusting well. I don't think she even realizes how much danger she's in yet."

"She's always been sort of—"

"Watch it," Kelly warned as his brother searched for the right word to describe his sweet Bee.

"Idealistic," Finn offered. "She's a dreamer, Kelly. I won't say that she's naïve. God knows she's seen more than her fair share of death and sadness and the cruelty of this world—but she's also lived inside an insulated bubble for years. Even now, she's being protected and coddled."

"Coddled? Some fucking asshole broke into her house, stole her panties, and jacked off on them! You can call it coddling if you like, but I'm not about to let a psycho like that get close to her."

Finn held up a hand. "All right. It was a bad choice of word."

"You're damn right it was."

"What are you two arguing about now?" Jack had caught up with them in the parking lot.

"Nothing," Kelly said with a wave of his hand. "We're fine."

Jack glanced from one brother to the next and finally shrugged. "Go home and take some anti-inflammatories. If you feel like you need to ice, do that. I'll see you in the morning. You might want to go easy on breakfast—unless you plan to mop my floors after your workout."

"I'll take it under advisement." Before he broke away from his brothers, Finn reached out and patted his arm. He accepted the silent apology with a nod. "I'll see you guys later."

Sitting in his truck, he didn't immediately leave the parking lot. He dug his phone out of his gym bag and swiped the screen. There were no messages or missed calls, which he took as a good sign. Because he had the LookIt app on his phone and followed Bee, he received a notification any time she posted. He tapped the icon and waited for the page to load.

Kelly grinned the moment the image appeared on his screen. Bee had framed her smiling, beautiful face with her fingers in the shape of a heart. There was no caption to the photo or even a line of text accompanying the post, but it had already drawn nearly nine thousand likes and hundreds of comments. He checked the time stamp. It had only been live for a few hours.

Though he enjoyed her secret message to him, Kelly begrudgingly admitted that Finn might have been right in his assessment of her and the current situation. Had she even considered that her stalker might believe this message was meant for him? He hated the thought of laying down the law with her, but it had to be done.

When he reached the penthouse, his muscles protested every single step. Sully greeted him at the door this time. Despite being off the clock and already in his pajama bottoms and T-shirt, the man was armed and ready for anything that might come across the threshold.

"You need me to carry you?" Sully leaned against the wall and seemed to delight in the agony Kelly experienced.

He lobbed a one-fingered salute the other man's way. "Where's Winn?"

"He's in the kitchen going over the dossiers Spike sent over." Sully locked the door and reactivated the alarm. "Bee left some ibuprofen for you and had the restaurant on the ground floor send up fifty pounds of ice before they closed for the night. It's stowed in the second freezer in the kitchen."

Touched by her consideration, he decided to thank her very nicely later. "She still awake?"

"No idea. She came in about an hour ago to get something to eat and then disappeared back into her room. She was on her phone, so I didn't ask about her plans for the night."

"Who was she talking to?"

"Someone named Haley?" He shrugged. "I only heard snippets of the conversation."

"Hadley," he corrected. "It's one of her friends."

"The DJ?"

He shook his head. "That's Coby."

Sully made a face. "Who names their daughter Coby?"

"It's Jacob, actually. She's named after her dad. He was a SEAL."

"No shit?"

"Yeah."

"Was?"

"He was killed over there. 2005," added. "Iraq."

Sully looked a bit surprised. "I might have known him."

"I never met him, but I gather he was a damn good operator." He gestured to the kitchen. "I'm going to talk to Winn and then hit the sheets."

To his credit, Sully didn't crack any jokes. In the kitchen, he found Winn seated at the island. Sheets of paper, neatly stacked and already labeled with brightly colored notes, surrounded him. The quiet Brit didn't even glance up as Kelly entered the kitchen and dropped his bag near the door. "You need help putting together some ice packs?"

"I've got it, but thanks for the offer." Snatching up the bottle of ibuprofen, he twisted off the cap and shook a couple tablets into his palm. "Anything interesting in the dossiers?"

"That depends on your definition of interesting, I suppose. I'm sorting these into three stacks according to their threat rating—red, yellow, green. I want to triage these for Spike so he has less work to do."

"Let me get situated, and I'll help."

Winn pointed to the corner. "There are plastic bags in that drawer."

"Thanks." He found the zip-top bags and filled two with ice. Grabbing two dishtowels and a bottle of sports drink, he eased onto a stool opposite Winn. He draped a towel over his thigh and another across his sore shoulder, and covered them with the ice bags.

"Did you know that Bee's company only has six male employees?"

"I did." He tossed back the ibuprofen with a long drink of the berry-flavored fluid. "She was part of a symposium earlier this year about encouraging women to enter STEM-related studies and careers. There are a series of articles posted online. It's good reading."

Winn tapped his pen against his notepad. "The men who work at the company aren't likely stalker candidates. There are a handful of ex-employees who fit the bill, that Trevor and Richard among them." He handed over a stack of folders. "These aren't complete yet, but Spike has sent over what he has."

As Kelly flipped through the pages of information Spike had collected, he marveled at the man's ability to scour publicly available databases and the internet. Without a legal warrant, there were barriers to what he could find, but somehow Spike always managed to come through for the team. The rumors around LSG pegged Spike as a former intelligence officer, maybe even CIA. Seeing Spike's handiwork first-hand, Kelly had to wonder if those rumors weren't based in reality.

"She had a high-turnover two years ago," Winn mentioned. "I flagged the employee names that coincided with that time so Spike can dig deeper."

Kelly scratched his chin. "That's around the time she moved into the offices downstairs. Yuri convinced her that it was time to stop operating out of coffee shops and dorm rooms, so she took the twelfth floor."

"She started to see phenomenal growth after that. It was clearly a good business move."

"Yes, it was." Kelly reached for the copies of the text messages and photos she had received. He turned the erection snapshots face down because they infuriated him. Reading through the messages, he started to get a strange feeling. "Winn, you notice anything odd about these texts?"

Winn finished making his note, peeled off the sticky sheet, and slapped it onto a file. "I had a distinct feeling they were written by two different people."

"So do I," Kelly murmured. He separated the messages into two stacks. "These read as threats, and these read almost like...love letters. He's telling her how beautiful she is in her dress and how the green ribbon in her hair makes her brown eyes pop."

"He sounds like he's totally obsessed with her." Winn tapped the threatening stack. "This guy sounds angry. *'Without me, you'd have nothing.'* It's an entirely different tone."

"Agreed." Picking up the photos, Kelly flicked through them. He ignored the creep's dick that was front and center in each snapshot, and studied the backgrounds.

"Look at the way he's framing his junk."

"I'd rather not."

Kelly slid the photos across the island to Winn. He reached for his cell phone and brought up the photo of Bee using her fingers to form a heart. Showing his screen to Winn, he said, "See the way Bee communicated with me?"

Winn's reddish eyebrow lifted toward his hairline. "Yes."

"Now look at the way her stalker is presenting himself to her. It's almost as if he's making an offering. It's...reverent."

"It's fucking disgusting." Winn flipped over the photos. "But I see point."

Kelly studied the information in front of them. "What if we have two stalkers? One of them is probably an ex-employee or someone she's crossed paths with during her rise to fame."

"The other one, the one who is infatuated with her, is the one we should be worried about the most."

Kelly conferred with Winn's assessment. The man had broken into Bee's home at least twice and had left behind his semen without any fear. He was following her around and getting close enough to make remarks about changing her perfume. The knowledge that one of her stalkers had been within sniffing distance of Bee spurred Kelly's protective instincts into overdrive. If he'd gotten *that* close, he could have snatched her.

"After my morning workout, I'll call Dimitri and fill him in on these new developments. We need to adjust our strategy if we're looking for two very different men."

"What time are you heading out in the morning?"

"I'll try to be out of here by a quarter past four. I'll be back before eight."

"Don't rush." Winn gathered up the photos. "She's in good hands, Kelly. We're taking good care of her for you."

"I appreciate it." Feeling guilty, he awkwardly added, "I realize this situation isn't ideal—"

"Kelly, there isn't a man on the duty roster at LSG who hasn't had to step into that gray world you're in right now. We've all been there—and some of us have done much worse than fight in an underground tournament."

He wondered what Winn might have done that put that haunted look on his face, but he didn't ask. Something told him it wasn't a story he would enjoy hearing or Winn would like to tell.

After draining the bottle of sports drink and tossing it into the recycling bin, he grabbed his bag and made the trek to the master suite. When he stepped inside, he discovered Bee sprawled on her side, fast asleep. She had two laptops opened on the bed and the TV blaring in the background. Her cell phone rested on the pillow next to her. Two empty soda cans and a bag of half-eaten crunchy cheese puffs sat on the bedside table.

Normally, that sort of untidiness would drive him crazy, but Bee had a way of making it seem cute. He'd watched her work on numerous occasions. She seemed to disappear into her own world where nothing and no one could reach her.

Here, in the safety of the penthouse, it was perfectly fine for her to get lost in her lines of code. How easy would it be for her stalker to sneak up on her in a coffee shop or restaurant while she worked? He shuddered at the idea of how many times that exact scenario might have already happened.

Leaning over her, he stroked her soft cheek and pressed a tender kiss to her temple. He closed her two laptops and placed them in a chair before moving her phone to the bedside table. He picked up the trash and carried it into the bathroom.

By the time he'd brushed his teeth and stripped down to his boxer briefs, Kelly was dead on his feet. He flipped off the lamps and slipped into bed next to Bee. The movement woke her, and she bolted upright. Reaching out, he dragged her against his chest and patted her hip. "Easy, sweetheart. It's me."

Curling up against him, she pressed featherlight kisses against his jaw and idly caressed his chest. "I tried to wait up for you, but I guess I was more tired than I thought."

"You've had a rough couple of days."

"So have you," she murmured against his neck. "How was your training session?"

"Brutal. How is Hadley?"

"She's having the time of her life, apparently. She's in China now. Beijing," she said. "The pictures are so incredible."

He detected the hint of envy in her voice. Wanting her to know that he considered their fledging relationship a long-term thing, he threaded his fingers through her hair and said, "Why don't we go on vacation after this whole thing settles down?"

"Really?"

"Really."

"I'd like that." Her hand moved gently along his stomach to the very top of his underwear before gliding back up his chest. She seemed oblivious to the effect her touch had on him. After their afternoon of heavy petting, he'd whetted his appetite for Bee. His dick ached to be buried in her snug, wet pussy but he didn't think they were ready for that step—yet. Even so, he couldn't turn off the biological signals that were diverting blood to his throbbing cock.

"I keep a dream vacation folder in my desk filled with photos and brochures."

He tried to think of anything but the way her fingertips felt as they grazed the sensitive patch of skin just below his navel. "That's very analog of you."

"Even a girl in the digital world needs a break from a computer screen once in a while."

As if feeling adventurous, Bee let her hand slide lower. He held his breath, but there was no way to stop the automatic twitch of his cock as her hand drifted dangerously close to the hard-on straining against his boxer briefs. He knew the moment she felt the evidence of his arousal. Her breathing hitched, and she gave him a playful squeeze.

"Looks like one of us isn't that tired," she teased.

Kelly laughed softly. "Sugar, I could be knocking on death's door, and your touch would make me hard."

"Just my touch?" She peppered ticklish kisses down his chest while sneaking her hand under the elastic band of his of his boxer-briefs. When she wrapped her fingers around his shaft, Kelly didn't even try to stifle his groan of enjoyment. Her silky, warm digits felt so fucking good as they stroked up and down his hard length.

She flipped back the covers and kissed her way down his chest and abdomen. Tugging on the waistband, she freed his cock and shocked him by placing a kiss right on the tip of it. Before she could proceed, he shielded himself with his hand. "You don't have to—"

"I want to," she said, almost breathlessly. "Please? I've been thinking about it since you left. I want to try. With you."

Hearing her practically beg to suck his cock snapped his control. Voice husky with need, he commanded,

"Turn on the light. I want to see you."

She happily complied and was back at his side before he'd even adjusted to the sudden brightness in the room. Grasping the bottom of her camisole, he pulled it over her head and threw it aside. His hands moved over naked skin, memorizing the feel of her perky breasts and the smooth plane of her belly. He jerked on her tiny shorts and dragged them down her thighs. "Take these off."

She followed his gruff order, falling to her side and wiggling out of them before kicking them off to the floor. He smiled at her eagerness and gave her plump bottom a playful smack. "Come here, sugar."

Bee fell into his waiting arms and let him kiss her until she was moaning and arching into him. When he tried to take the aggressor's role, she shoved him down and wagged a finger in his face. "This is my turn to play."

"I have a better idea." He sat up and nipped at her lower lip. "Let's both play."

She eyed him almost warily. "What do you have in mind?"

"Straddle me," he ordered, "but face my feet."

She considered his instruction. "But then my...*you know*...would be..."

He grinned wolfishly and claimed her mouth in a sensual, promising kiss. "Exactly. Now—come here."

She giggled as he manhandled her, pulling her onto him and twisting her around into just the right position. He could feel her trembling with excitement and nervousness as he hauled her parted thighs higher up on his chest. Nuzzling his face between them, he sought out the pink bud hidden there and flicked his tongue against it.

"Oh. My. God." Bee tried to wriggle out of his grasp but he held firmly to her hips and kept her right where he wanted her. Her short nails scratched at his legs when he lapped at her clit. "Kelly!"

He chuckled against her sweet pussy and continued his sensual assault on the most sensitive part of her. She recovered from the shock of his tongue fluttering over her swollen clitoris and began to explore his cock. She painted his shaft with saliva before sucking just the crown of him into her mouth. He groaned at the amazing sensation and fought the urge to pump up into at that hot, wet alcove.

Balls buzzing and gut clenching, he relished the velvety rasp of her tongue against his cock. What she lacked in skill, she more than made up for in enthusiasm. She drove him fucking wild with her passionate moans. The humming vibrations rattled through his shaft and amplified the wicked sensation of her tight lips.

Loving the taste of her, Kelly attacked her clit with a steady circling rhythm. He could feel her thighs clenching, her knees digging into his sides as she chased her climax. Gripping her hips, he craned his neck and attacked her pussy. Hell bent on making her come first, he suckled her clit, drawing on the pink pearl and fluttering his tongue over it until she pulled away from his cock with a muffled howl.

"Yes!" She came hard, rocking and thrusting back against his mouth. "Oh! *Oh*!"

He loved the way she let loose with him. He wanted her to feel free to explore the sensual side of herself, to enjoy the blossoming eroticism that their time together was awakening.

She was still shaking with the aftershocks of her climax when she wrapped her lips around him again and began sucking him in earnest. Lazily tonguing her, he let go of the stranglehold on his own release. Just as his groin tightened and those electric jolts began, he tried to pull free from her mouth. "Wait. Bee, you don't need to—oh, fuck! *Fuck!*"

She stunned him by swallowing him as deep as she could and hungrily groaning. There was no way he could hold back now. The top of his head felt as if it might blow off. At the first blast of his semen against her tongue, she made a surprised sound but didn't pull back. She responded with enthusiasm and drank him down with such eagerness.

Totally spent, he sagged against the mattress while she licked him clean. Overcome with exhaustion, Kelly watched her flick off the lamp. He grasped her hand as she cuddled up against him. They shared a few passionate, sleepy kisses before settling down to sleep.

Despite his tiredness, Kelly managed to stay awake longer than Bee. Stroking her arm and petting her silky hair, he allowed himself to dream about the future. For so many years, he'd been living day to day, maybe week to week. Holding Bee, Kelly wondered what it would be like to have her in his arms every night.

Once they caught her stalkers—and they would—he would have to make a decision. He could get used to this. Going back into the field wouldn't be an option. How could he guard a protectee when he would be constantly thinking of Bee?

He was still mulling over thoughts of his future when he finally succumbed to the lull of sleep. Sometime later, the most annoying ringtone ripped him out of his dreams. He sat up and glanced around the dark room to get his bearings. It was just before four. His alarm would go off soon, but it wasn't his phone ringing.

Reaching over, he gently shook Bee. "Sugar, it's your phone."

She mumbled something and slapped at his hand. He gave her another shake. "Bee. Wake up. Your phone."

Groaning, she rolled over and smacked at the bedside table until she located her phone. Answering groggily, she greeted, "Hello? Hari? Do you know what time it—what? When? Shit. Okay. Okay. Call everyone and get them in as quickly as possible. I'll be down in a few minutes."

Instantly alert, Kelly braced for the worst as she hung up, flicked on the lamp and scrambled from bed. "What's wrong, baby?"

Rubbing her face, she said, "Someone has attacked the site. It's very bad." Rushing to the bathroom, she grumbled, "I'm in deep shit."

Exhaling roughly, Kelly threw his legs over the edge of the mattress and shoved into a standing position. His instincts told him this day was only going to get worse.

CHAPTER EIGHT

"How bad is it?"

I glanced up from the lines of code on my computer screen to see Yuri standing in the doorway of my office. Sighing, I flopped back in my chair and gestured for him to come in and sit with me. Not that he needed the invitation, of course. He owned the building and merely leased me this space.

"It's bad, but we had certain failsafe protocols in place. We estimate approximately twenty percent of our users were hacked."

Yuri settled into the chair. "Lena said this attack was exchanging certain words in your users' blogs with profanity and racist remarks. Is that it?"

"Porn." I cringed at the thought of some of the hardcore filth popping up on unsuspecting users' screens. "The program switched out photographs users had posted with some really awful stuff."

Yuri stretched out his legs. "Lena is coming to see you in half an hour or so. She's bringing Ty with her. You know him, yes?"

"I do." As far as anyone knew, we were merely acquaintances who ran in the same social circles, but that wasn't the real extent of our relationship. Of course, that was a secret I'd sworn to keep and one I wasn't about to reveal to Yuri.

"It's important that you get out in front of this in a meaningful way. Lena and Ty are very good at crisis PR. They'll find a way to spin this positively. Insight is still vetting your company before they make their final offer and you need to be seen taking this seriously."

"Do you think they will still make an offer after something like this?"

Yuri shrugged. "You said yourself that it only affected twenty percent of your users. The fact that you had safeguards in place to protect the other eighty percent speaks highly of your security capabilities. Do you know how these hackers were able to manipulate your platform?"

"It's someone with knowledge of our inner workings. It's definitely personal."

"Your stalker?"

"That's a complicated issue. Kelly and my guards now think I may have two stalkers. One of them thinks I'm, like, his girlfriend or something. The other one seems to be motivated by anger toward me."

"Because you fired him?"

"Maybe?" I toyed with the notepad on my desk. "There were a couple of guys early on in the business that I had to let go under less than amicable circumstances."

"Yes," he growled. "Richard and Trevor." With a shake of his head, he murmured, "We never know what ghosts from our past may return to haunt us, Beatrice."

Was he thinking of the crazy personal assistant and bodyguard who had tried to kill him and Lena?

"How is Kelly?"

His change of topic caught me off guard. "Okay, I guess. He should be back from his morning training session any minute now."

"So he's really going through with it?" Yuri's displeasure was evident.

"I offered him money, but he refused it. He and his brothers had some sort of Connolly family powwow where they decided it was more honorable to let Kelly risk his life than to take my money."

Yuri stared at me for a moment. "Do you love him?"

"You know I do." I was pretty sure Yuri had figured that out the first time he saw us together.

"I love my Yelena more than anything in the world—but my God—that woman can be maddeningly stubborn sometimes. It's easier to act first and ask penance later."

"What are you saying, Yuri? Are you suggesting I go behind his back?"

"I'm suggesting you think long and hard about what you want with Kelly and what you're willing to do to protect him. You can't build a life together if he's killed on some filthy warehouse floor."

"Do men really die in those fights?"

"Yes. I haven't seen one go that far in years, not since Moscow, but it's not uncommon. When Ivan fought, he always showed restraint. He was always careful to only put down his opponent but not injure him irrevocably. He fought with honor. His man—Sergei—will fight with honor. The others?" Yuri inhaled slowly. "I do not know."

If he was trying to frighten me, he succeeded. "He'll never forgive me."

"If he loves you, he will." Yuri rose from the chair and buttoned his suit jacket. "Let me know how the meeting with Lena and Ty goes. If you need anything from me, don't hesitate to ask."

"Thanks."

No sooner had Yuri left my office than Amita Chatterjee, programmer extraordinaire and the woman who taught me everything I knew about coding, popped her head into my office. "I found something you need to see."

Her tone told me it was something I wasn't going to like. As I left my office, Sully shadowed me. Just as I'd expected, he had been flirting up a storm with every single woman on the floor. Not that any of them seemed to mind receiving attention from the wickedly sexy former Delta operator.

"What did you find?" I followed her around the desk and leaned forward on my elbows.

"Does this look familiar?" Amita tapped her screen.

I read the lines of code she had isolated. "Son. Of. A. Bitch."

"Yep. I was digging through the malicious code, and the moment I saw his signature, I knew this was all about ReadIt."

I dropped my head into my hands and smothered the scream of frustration threatening to erupt from my throat. "You know, I should have listened to you about hiring Trevor. You were so right."

"You know what they say, kid. Age and wisdom and all that."

"Thanks for not rubbing it in, Amita."

"I wouldn't dream of it." She patted my back. "What do you want me to do?"

"We'll have the site cleaned up by midnight, so would you mind digging out all these little signed bits of code for me? Knowing Trevor, he's left me some pernicious message."

Amita laughed. "Pernicious, huh? Is that our word of the day?"

Smiling, I pushed off her desk. "I'm taking a meeting with Lena and Ty soon. Would you like to join us?"

"Sure."

"Great. I'll call you when they get here."

Crossing the wide open office floor, I caught sight of Kelly and Ron coming through the main entrance. The sight of the two men took me by surprise. Seeing the delivery boxes filled with piping hot coffee and pastries they both carried, I nearly did cartwheels. Hands on hips, I admitted, "I can't decide who I'm happier to see."

Kelly leaned forward and pecked my cheek. His lips brushed my ear, and he whispered naughtily, "I'll have to remind you who put that big smile on your face last night."

"Behave. We're in public." I patted his hard chest. "Did you arrange this?"

Kelly shook his head. "No. I found Ron downstairs and pitched in to help him.

I stepped toward Ron. "How did you know I needed my coffee fix?"

"The XSS attack is all over the tech blogs. I figured you might need a little extra caffeine this morning."

I threw my arms around him and gave Ron the biggest hug before noisily smooching his cheek. "You're the best. Like—seriously. Today you just might be my savior."

Face aflame, he looked so uncomfortable, and I silently cursed myself for forgetting that he didn't like to be touched. To his credit, he tried to play it off with a smile. "Well, I don't know about that."

"I do. Let's drop most of this in the kitchen and take the rest to my office."

We segued into the kitchen, picked out what we wanted, and headed to my office where Winn and Sully waited.

"We should make this delivery a regular thing, Ron." I noticed the way the scent of coffee and the promise of free pastries was pulling people from their desks. "But you have to bring those sprinkle cookies I love so much."

"The ones I brought to the housewarming party?"

"Yes!"

"Not a problem. I'll be here bright and early tomorrow."

"Fantastic."

Once inside my office, I leaned back against my desk and sipped the hot coffee loaded with creamer and sugar, just the way I loved it. Winn and Sully were spreading out files atop the long table at the far side of my office. I used it for brainstorming sessions and smaller meetings. Today, it seemed to be the space they'd claimed as their command center.

Ron wandered over and earned an annoyed look from Winn. Not easily daunted, he scanned the table. His face lit up with recognition. "Hey! This guy? He was in the coffee shop four or five times over the last few weeks."

When he held up the photo, I nearly choked on my coffee. My reaction didn't go unnoticed. Kelly frowned. "Baby, what is it?"

Swallowing my mouthful of steaming hot coffee, I explained, "Right before you showed up, Amita pulled me into her office to show me some of this malicious code she's isolated. Most programmers leave a signature when they want their work to be recognized. The one left on this shit-storm belongs to Trevor Cohen." I pointed to the picture Ron held. "That guy."

Kelly snatched the photo from Ron's hand. "What's

the story, Bee?"

"He's extremely talented. I met him at a hackathon right after I'd first launched LookIt in beta among a small group of friends. When I got funding from Yuri to go big, I needed more hands on deck, you know? So I approached Trevor, and he accepted my offer." I took another sip of coffee. "Amita pegged him as trouble from the first moment she met him. She begged me not to hire him, but I thought I could handle him. Clearly, I couldn't."

"What was the problem?" Winn asked.

"He had that *brogrammer* mentality. Everything was a joke or a game. He didn't like having tasks delegated to him, especially by women. He spent all his time working on an app that he called ReadIt instead of working on the projects assigned to him."

"ReadIt?" Kelly's brow furrowed. "What's that?"

"It was a bookmarking app that never went beyond beta," Ron answered. At Kelly's strange look, he held up his hands. "Sorry."

"Don't mind him, Ron. He's grumpy this morning."

"Maybe he needs more coffee," Ron suggested.

Smiling at my friend's remark, I continued with my tale of woe. "When I decided it was time to let Trevor go, he wanted to take ReadIt with him, but he couldn't. His employment contract didn't allow him to claim ownership of anything he built on my time."

"That's harsh," Sully commented.

"He built that app on *my* framework while I was paying him to do another job. He used my computers, my office space, and my temps to do his coding." Realizing I sounded overly defensive, I reined it in a bit. "Look, I made sure that he was compensated for his product. Frankly, he was overpaid. It was buggy as fuck and never worked. He accused me of sabotaging him—and then he took ReadIt and built an identical product for Richard. Hence the lawsuit."

Kelly turned to Ron. "You said he was in your shop multiple times? Did he say anything?"

"I assumed he was a contractor." Ron winced. "He asked about your new building, Bee. I thought he was thinking of bidding on the renovation project. I told him he could find you at the coffee shop in the evenings."

"It's all right, Ron."

"No, it's not." Kelly spoke through gritted teeth. "You told a man that he could find a single woman who rides her bike after dark back to an empty building how to find her and stalk her."

"Kelly!" Aghast at his tone, I gaped at him.

"Bee," Winn carefully interjected, "Kelly has a point. I'm sure your friend didn't mean to put you in harm's way, but that doesn't change the facts. You said yourself that you started finding photos in your backpack after you'd been to the coffee shop. What if this Trevor fellow was able to hide in the background and slip them into your bag?"

"Well..."

"I'm sorry, Bee." Ron looked so guilty. "I should have been more careful."

"It's fine, Ron. Really," I added before Kelly could interrupt with some rude remark. "I share way more blame in this mess. I'm the one who didn't pay attention to my bag. I'm the ditz who rides her bike at night and lives alone in a big, empty building."

"You are not a ditz." Ron scowled at Kelly and Winn. "Don't let these guys make you feel guilty for living your life. You have every right to do what you please."

Kelly narrowed his eyes at Ron. "Don't you have a

coffee shop to run?"

"Kelly!"

Ron waved his hand. "It's okay, Bee. He's right. I need to get back."

After shooting Kelly an ugly look, I walked Ron out of my office. "I'm really sorry about that. Kelly can be a bit testy."

Ron glanced back toward my office. "He cares about you."

"Yes. Very much," I said. "That doesn't excuse his rudeness."

"I've taken worse from customers." Smiling at me, he said, "I'll be here in the morning with your coffee delivery."

"I'll make sure to put my Rottweiler on a leash."

With a laugh, he waved and pivoted on his heel. When I re-entered my office, Kelly offered a contrite smile, but I glared at him. "Dimitri swore that you guys had taken sensitivity training, and that you were skilled in handling the public with finesse."

Kelly's jaw tightened. "I could have handled it better."

I arched one eyebrow. "You think?"

"Come on, Bee. Don't make me grovel."

"If you're going to make him grovel, let me get my camera," Sully said, already digging in the front pocket of his jeans. "We'll use it for our company Christmas card."

The wisecracking guard killed the tension with his funny remark. Kelly sent a smoldering look my way that promised he would make this up to me. I planned to wrangle a huge apology to Ron from him first.

"So," Kelly crossed his arms, "Trevor Cohen, huh? Looks like we have our prime candidate for the stalker sending you threatening messages."

"Why doesn't that make me feel any safer?"

He held out his hand, silently bidding me to join him. I let him drag me into his protective embrace. He brushed a tender kiss to the crown of my head. "We'll deal with this Trevor asshole as quickly as possible. Then we focus on stalker number two."

He made it sound so simple and easy. Sully and Winn's confident expressions encouraged me. If the three of them concurred, that had to be a good sign. I trusted these incredibly skilled men knew what they were doing.

While the trio stood around the table strategizing, I returned to my desk with my coffee. Hourly updates on the crisis were popping into my inbox, so I triaged the messages waiting for me.

A certain email address caught my eye. Certain I was hallucinating, I read and reread the name of the sender. I gulped nervously and sneaked a stealth glance at Kelly, Sully and Winn. With their heads together, the three men had their backs to me and were totally unaware of my panicked state.

Trying to convince myself this was just some stupid spam email with a spoofed address, I clicked on the message. My stomach pitched violently as I skimmed the email. Somehow that rat bastard Trevor had hacked into Jeb's old email account and gained access to thousands of his messages—and very private photos.

ReadIt and weep, bitch! I know all your brother's dirty secrets now. If you don't want me to share them, I suggest you pick up your phone and make me a deal. Seven days—or these go live!

The message had been written under a snapshot of my brother, cuffed and collared, wearing lacy panties, fishnets, and heels while kneeling at the feet of his Master.

With a click of my shaking, clammy finger, I closed out of the window and stared at the ominous message still fouling up my inbox. I thought I had deleted every single photo in the account, but obviously I'd been wrong.

Regret punched me right in the stomach. Why the hell hadn't I closed Jeb's email account? At first, I had left it open so I could receive and reply to messages from his friends and fellow Marines. Later, I hadn't been able to close it because of sentimentality.

I tried to ignore the gut-churning terror ripping at my belly as I spared another glance toward Kelly. He remained blissfully oblivious to my personal hell. The weight of Jeb's secret life weighed so heavily on me. The things he had done—and the people he had done them with—were not the types of things that anyone wanted publicized.

It wasn't embarrassment or disgust that kept me from acknowledging publicly who Jeb had been. He was my brother and I loved him—all of him, even the fetishes and kinks that he had indulged in secret and on the side for years and years. The pain and anguish his unorthodox desires had caused him had been so great. He'd never been able to fully mesh his life as a heroic Marine with the man who enjoyed wearing women's clothing or following his Dominant lover around on a leash.

As far as I knew, Jeb's secret sexual life was the only thing he had ever kept from Kelly. Sometimes I wondered if Kelly hadn't suspected that Jeb was...different. If he had any suspicions, he'd always kept them to himself. Of course, Jeb had been extremely good at keeping his two lives separated from each other. Maybe Kelly truly didn't know.

I couldn't let him find out like this. Fury burned hot in my chest at the idea of that asshole Trevor blackmailing me like this. If he'd been able to access and recover this photo, he may have been able to find others where Jeb's lovers' faces were visible. A couple of internet searches would yield him even more blackmail material.

His Master—his longtime lover—was still in the Marine Corps. I hadn't spoken to Peter in years, not since a few months after Jeb's funeral, but I didn't know how I could avoid him now. He had to be warned, just in case I couldn't get Trevor to stop his threats.

"Bee?" Kelly's concerned voice cut through my troubled thoughts.

I tore my gaze away from my screen. "What?"

Kelly uncrossed his arms and gestured to the door. "Lena and Ty are here."

"Oh." I popped out of my chair and hurried to greet my guests. The duo of PR experts hovered just inside the doorway.

Dapper as always, Ty wore a two-button blazer in the softest dove gray layered over a plaid shirt. He'd paired the ensemble with dark jeans. Beside him, Lena looked so incredibly beautiful in her exquisitely tailored dress. The bright pinkish orange color popped against her warm brown skin. I wondered what they called that shade. Probably something exotic like papaya.

Wishing I had her fashion sense and the body to carry off the peplum dress and killer heels, I welcomed her. "Hi, Lena. Thank you so much for coming."

She air-kissed my cheek. "We're happy to help."

Ty gave me a hug. "How you doing, sugar?"

"Okay," I lied. Looking over at Kelly, I asked, "Would you guys mind moving to the conference room while I chat with Lena and Ty?"

Kelly's eyes narrowed fractionally but he didn't argue. "Sure."

"Thanks." I gestured for Lena and Ty to join me at the table Sully and Winn were clearing. Kelly caught my hand

and dragged me toward my desk. I fought the urge to look at my computer monitor lest it draw his attention.

He cupped the back of my head and brushed his knuckles along my cheek. "Are you okay?"

"It's stress. I'll be fine once this whole thing is over."

"I'm taking you to see Jack this evening while I'm training. He's got a self-defense class with an opening." Kelly touched the tip of my nose. "It will be good for you to knock the crap out of some dummies tonight."

"I can't think of a better stress reliever than punching and kicking a dummy."

Lowering his face, he grazed his lips across mine. "I can."

Blushing, I let him give me a sweet kiss. His smoldering eyes warmed me right through to the core. I had a feeling tonight might finally be *the* night.

"Don't leave this office without calling for one of us."

"I won't."

Backing away, Kelly accepted an armload of files from Sully and left the room. I followed them out and shut the door. The sound of the lock engaging drew Ty's interested gaze. "Everything all right, sugar?"

With a sigh, I fell back against the door and rubbed my face. "How good are you two when it comes to blackmail?"

Ty actually chortled. "Sweetheart, how long have we known each other? I made my first million peddling gossip online. It's a very subtle line." His mood turned somber. He must have realized that the only thing I knew worth blackmailing were my brother's secret penchants—details Ty knew only too well. "This isn't about your business, is it? It's about Jeb."

We shared a private look as Lena asked, "What does that mean?"

Ty exhaled loudly and retrieved his phone from his pocket. "It means we need to clear our schedules for the afternoon." He started to dial a number, probably that of their receptionist. "It also means we might need help from some of those rather interesting contacts that Yuri has."

Lena didn't even bat an eyelash. "That bad, huh?"

Pushing off the door, I sank down into a chair across from them. "It's a really long story."

Lena settled into her seat. "Then let's start at the beginning..."

* * *

Kelly checked his watch and drummed his fingers on the steering wheel. Glancing around the parking lot of the bar where loan shark John Hagen operated the illicit side of his business, he wondered where the hell his brothers were. His agitation increased with every minute that passed. More than anything, he wanted to return to Bee.

Every time he left her, a knot formed in his stomach. Right now, it throbbed angrily and made his chest ache. He hated leaving her. Sure, she was safe with Sully and Winn, but he didn't like it.

Something else was eating at him. He couldn't prove it, but he felt certain she wasn't telling him everything. When Lena and Ty had arrived at Bee's office, she'd looked almost panicked. He'd squashed the instinct to confront her because he trusted her to confide in him. He hoped she wouldn't take too long to come to him. Standing on the sidelines while she was hurting wasn't easy for him. His urge to protect and help her was so strong.

Needing to get back to her, Kelly reached for his

phone, but spotted Jack's truck rolling onto the lot. Annoyed by their tardiness, he climbed out of his vehicle and gruffly greeted them as they spilled out of Jack's truck. "You're late."

"We had a run-in with Pop." Jack didn't elaborate but gestured to the bar. "Let's get this over with."

Kelly fell into step behind his older brothers. While he'd handled the Besian connection, Jack and Finn would deal with Hagen. The gym and the building were their livelihoods, after all.

Inside the bar, they were greeted by a couple of goons who escorted them to a back office. There were no chairs for guests in the small but tidy space. Shoulder to shoulder, they stood in front of the desk and waited for the behemoth loan shark to acknowledge them. Kelly had to wonder how much a bespoke suit like the one Hagen wore cost. It couldn't be easy to fit a giant like that.

"Gentlemen." Hagen leaned back in his chair and studied them. "Unless you're here to settle the debt your father owes in full, I'm not sure that we have much to discuss."

"Pop didn't have the right to use the building as collateral without my consent," Jack stated.

"He only used his half of the building as collateral," Hagen corrected. "So, when he defaults, you and I will be partners."

"I have a feeling we have different definitions of the word partner."

"You could always let me buy you out," Hagen offered.

"Like hell," Jack said. "We've put everything into that business. We're not going to lose it now."

"Then I would highly suggest you bet smart on the upcoming tournament," Hagen replied. "I hear Nikolai's man has good odds."

"We don't bet against our own."

Jack's remark seemed to soften up Hagen. The loan shark's gaze drifted to a picture frame on his desk. From Kelly's vantage point, he had a clear view of the pretty, smiling blonde. Whoever she was, she had a surprising effect on Hagen.

With a forceful breath, he sat forward. "Fifteenth of June, all of this," he motioned around him, "goes to Jackie Riccio's nephew. I'm out."

"Out?" Jack echoed Kelly's shock.

"It's been in the works for a while now. I'm tying up loose ends before I go totally legit."

For the blonde? Kelly's interest in her increased. She must be something special to make a man like Hagen walk away from the only life he'd ever known.

"Good for you, man, but what does that have to do with us?" Jack asked the question they were all thinking.

Hagen's mouth settled into an annoyed line. "If you don't close your account with me by the fourteenth of June, it's going to roll onto Jackie Boy's books—and you really don't want that."

"What do you propose?"

"Give me the building and we'll call it even. I'll take the hit and settle the balance out of my own pocket."

"What's so important about the building?" Jack asked. "You wouldn't take the hit unless you wanted it."

"It's not the building. It's the land."

"It's not for sale," Jack reminded him.

"You're not in a position to be making that decision, Jack."

"We have a few weeks to settle the debt, and we will. You're not getting our building or the land it sits on, Hagen."

The loan shark jotted something down on a notepad, ripped the sheet free and folded it in half. "Your balance."

Jack snatched it from his hand but didn't look at the amount written there. "You'll get your money."

"It's not personal, Jack. It's only business." Hagen sounded almost apologetic. Maybe he wasn't the cruel monster his dark reputation would have them believe.

Without another word, the three brothers left the bar and congregated between their two vehicles. Jack finally opened the sheet of paper and swore loudly. He slapped it against Finn's chest and stalked away from them. From the way Finn paled, Kelly could tell the number written there was much more than they had expected.

When Finn passed the paper to him, Kelly reluctantly glanced at the figure. "Jack's going to kill Pop over this."

"I gave Pop a couple hundred bucks and told him to lay low. We won't be seeing him for a while."

Crumpling up the paper, Kelly stuffed it into his pocket and fished out his keys. "If he knows what's good for him, he'll stay away."

Jamming his key into the ignition, Kelly hoped this was the last bit of shit news he would receive today. Of course, the way the week was going, he figured a damn plane was about to fall out of the sky and crush his truck. Only the knowledge that Bee waited for him kept him from marching right back into Hagen's bar for a stiff drink.

Thinking of his earlier quip about stress relief, Kelly couldn't wait for the day to end. Tonight, he was going to make love to Bee until she passed out from sheer exhaustion or his legs gave out.

CHAPTER NINE

"Okay, ladies, that's it for tonight." Jack Connolly clapped his hands together at the front of the room. "We'll meet up again on Wednesday. Y'all did great. If you have any questions, come find me on your way out."

Did Jack's compliment extend to me? I had a bad feeling Kelly's oldest brother wasn't very pleased with my performance in his self-defense class.

"Bee?" Jack crooked a finger at me. "Let's talk."

Biting my lip, I joined the sternest of the Connolly brothers in a corner of the room. Winn followed close behind and rubbed his still-red nose. I winced sympathetically at the reminder of my elbow accidentally jamming right into it as we practiced an evasive maneuver together.

Knuckles on his hips, Jack sighed. "Bee, what am I going to do with you?"

Wringing my hands, I tried to explain myself. "I'm sorry. I'm just really clumsy. I mean—seriously—I was, like, ten years old before Jeb and Mom took the training wheels off my bike."

Jack snorted with amusement. "After watching you trip over your own feet coming in here, I'm not surprised. What the hell was all that laughing when we were escaping holds?"

"He tickled me." I gestured to my bodyguard.

"I absolutely did not," Winn stridently defended himself. "I grabbed her around the waist."

"And it tickled," I countered. "Then you squeezed me tighter, and I couldn't stop laughing."

"Let's keep that to ourselves," Jack suggested. "As amped up as Kelly is after his training sessions, he'll blow a damn gasket at the thought of your bodyguard getting so hands-on." His gaze shifted to something just over my shoulder. He raised his hand as if to let someone know he was coming before dropping his gaze back to me. "Look, the first few classes are always the hardest. You'll get the hang of it."

Left with Winn, I glanced at my bodyguard and winced again. "You're bleeding, Winn."

He scowled and gingerly touched his nose. "Don't move. I'll be right back."

While Winn ducked into the nearest restroom, I grabbed my backpack, dug out my metal water bottle, and took a long sip. I was dabbing at the beads of sweat along my hairline when a woman from the class struck up a conversation with me.

"I'm Abby." Short like me, she smiled and held out her hand. "You're new in class."

"Yes. I'm Bee." I shook her hand. "Have you been in this class long?"

"A few weeks," Abby answered. Almost nervously, she glanced around the room. "We had an attempted break-in at our shop, so I decided I needed to learn to protect myself. What about you?"

I debated how much to tell her. "I've got a stalker."

"Seriously?" She peeled the hot pink elastic band from her sagging ponytail and combed her fingers through her black hair to gather it into a low bun. "That's crappy. Is it because of your company?" She must have seen the distrust in my eyes. "Sorry. I recognized you from that article in the paper last month. You created LookIt, right?"

"Yes. Do you use it?"

"All the time! It's one of my favorite places to hangout online and network with other artists."

"Oh! So you're an artist?"

"A photographer," Abby said. "Well—I'm trying, at least. Right now, I manage my family's pawn shop. I squeeze in classes whenever I can."

As we chatted about the Houston art scene, I noticed the way Jack kept glancing our way. He was talking with two other women in the class and seemed to be struggling with giving them his full, undivided attention. At first, I thought he was keeping an eye on me while Winn was dealing with his bloody nose, but then I realized his gaze was trained on Abby.

Like Kelly, he had a hard face to read. I suspected their abusive childhoods might have had something to do with that. Perhaps it was a coping technique or a defensive mechanism to keep their faces such expressionless masks.

The look in his eyes, however, was easy enough for me to decipher. It wasn't simple lust or attraction burning in his green eyes. No, Jack was staring at Abby with the same sort of protective desire often reflected in Kelly's gaze. Was she in trouble? Maybe the break-in?

"Anyways," she said, "I should really get going. It was nice to meet you. I'll see you on Wednesday?"

"Yes."

"Great. Bye."

"Bye." Sipping my water, I watched Jack gently disentangle himself from the two women he'd been chatting with so he could talk to Abby. He seemed completely oblivious to the fallen faces of the women or their irked expressions. The sweet smile he offered Abby reminded me of the one Kelly often had for me.

I couldn't tell if my new friend was even aware of Jack's interest in her. Unlike the preening duo who had done their best to get as close to him as possible while chatting, Abby kept a little distance between her body and Jack's. Judging by his gesture, he was offering to walk her out but she declined. He overrode her protest, and she reluctantly accepted his help.

Interesting...

"Where is Winn?"

Kelly's gruff, rumbling voice caught me by surprise. I whirled around to find him standing a few steps behind me. Wearing only shorts and sneakers, he wiped at his ridiculously sexy chest with a white gym towel before slinging it over his shoulder. The sight of his tanned, toned chest and the tattoos accentuating the rippling bulges of muscle left me momentarily speechless.

"Bee?"

Shaking myself from my lust-induced stupor, I said, "He's in the restroom. I sort of busted his nose."

He looked taken aback and then smiled proudly. "Way to go, sweetheart."

"Um...not exactly. It was an accident."

"An accident?"

"Well, it tickled and I started laughing—"

Eyes narrowed, he asked, "What tickled?"

"Winn's hold on me."

"I see." His lips twitched, and I knew he wasn't angry at all. Touching my cheek, he murmured, "I'll have to keep that in mind...for later."

At the mention of later, I trembled with anticipation. "Oh?"

"We'll practice some of the holds Jack showed you."

"Holds, huh?" I daringly traced his navel and delighted in the way he inhaled sharply. Thinking of the moves I had just learned, I considered whether or not I could take Kelly down. He was a foot taller than me and nearly twice as heavy. Could I catch him off-guard?

Deciding there was no time like the present, I hastily planned my attack. Kelly reached out to stroke my face, but I kicked out my leg to hook his knee. The expression on his face was comical as the realization that I was attacking him registered—but his lightning fast reflexes, honed by years at war, snapped into action.

I gasped as he snatched my ankle mid-air and jerked hard enough to pull me off my feet. The thick mat cushioned my fall. Kelly followed me down to the floor, attempting to trap me, but I twisted my hips and narrowly evaded him. My brief victory didn't last. He grabbed my wrists in one big paw and pinned them overhead before insinuating himself between my thighs.

Remembering Jack's lessons, I arched up onto my shoulders and tried to squeeze his ribs with my knees. Kelly shifted, and I ended up wrapping my legs around his waist. Our bodies locked together in such an intimate way. Suddenly my failed attack started to feel like foreplay.

Changing tactics, I hooked my ankles at the small of Kelly's back and rocked my body against his. His low groan sounded almost pained. Eyes flashing with need, he lowered his face and warningly growled, "Bee."

Breathless and shaking with desire, I whispered, "Kiss me."

He capitulated to my request and brushed his mouth against mine. Refusing to be denied what I wanted most, I thrust my aching breasts against his hot, hard chest and dipped my tongue between his lips. A rumbling noise emanated from his throat, vibrating against my lips and sending white-hot shivers through my core.

A loudly cleared throat interrupted our steamy kiss. Tearing away from each other, we glanced in the direction of the noise and discovered Jack standing a few feet away and watching us with amusement. The rest of the room was empty except for Winn, who seemed to have gotten his bloody nose under control.

Jack rubbed his jaw as if thinking. "You know, I'm pretty sure that's not a self-defense technique I teach."

Not the least bit embarrassed, I simply shrugged. "You'd have a hell of a lot more signups for your classes if you did."

Jack laughed and shook his head. "That's exactly the sort of reputation Connolly Fitness needs."

Kelly disentangled our limbs and pushed off the mat. He grasped my hand and hauled me to my feet. The swooping sensation in my belly strengthened when he captured my lips in a possessive kiss. His body heat drew me even closer. It was all I could do not to leap up onto him and beg him to take me home right now.

Kelly gently separated himself from me and grabbed the bag he'd dropped. Picking up my backpack and water bottle, I headed for the door but paused to playfully thump Jack's chest. "Maybe you could ask Abby to be your partner for demonstrating that move."

Jack's cheeks actually flushed. He hastily averted his gaze. "I don't think so."

Wondering at his strange response, I decided not to push it. The last thing I wanted to do was to cause him pain with my teasing. I tapped his chest and drew his gaze. "I'm sorry."

He waved his hand. "It's cool. It's...complicated."

Glancing back at Kelly, I reminded him, "I've been there."

Jack chuckled. "Sweetheart, you're still there."

Certain complicated was the best adjective to describe the relationship blossoming between us, I let Jack's remark slide. Kelly still hadn't bothered with a shirt as he placed his hand between my shoulder blades and escorted me out of the gym with Winn a few steps behind us.

"How did your training go?" I asked as we crossed the parking lot to his parked truck. The hour of his grueling session that I had been able to witness before my self-defense class started had been rough. His physical prowess inside the ring had awed me. I wasn't very fond of the aggressive, harsh way Alexei treated him, but I had reminded myself that he was only trying to prepare Kelly for the brutality that awaited him.

"I did decently." Even as he spoke, his gaze scanned the area. "Alexei is a brutal taskmaster, but he knows his stuff. I may not be as good as Sergei, but I'll be good enough to get to the final match."

"And then what? You hope to win enough from the earlier matches to settle the debts?" The Connolly brothers' plan didn't sit well with me. There were too many unknown variables and too much riding on Kelly winning to save them. Yuri's suggestion rattled around in my head. Was he right? Was it better to act now and simply ask forgiveness later?

"That's the general idea," Kelly muttered, his gaze fixed on a corner of the lot. Something must have put him on alert because he went rigid. I gasped when he unexpectedly grabbed the front of my shirt and flung me behind him. He backed me up against his truck and put his body between mine and whatever danger he had noticed.

Fully aware he needed to be able to move freely, I fought the panicked urge to grip his arms. "What's wrong?"

Before he could answer, the sounds of a scuffle met my ears. Winn's harsh voice echoed in the still night. "On the ground! Now!"

Holding my breath, I desperately prayed nothing bad would happen to my guard. Kelly pushed back against me, not quite crushing me, but making sure his wider, bigger body shielded me totally. Running footsteps pounded the paved lot. Soon, Finn and Jack's voices joined the fray.

"All clear!" Winn called out. "He's unarmed."

"Who is it?" Kelly still hadn't moved.

"ID says Richard Hawkins."

"Richard?" I pushed at Kelly's back, but he didn't budge an inch. "Kelly, please, let me see him."

Reluctantly, my hulk of a boyfriend eased over just a few inches. I peered around his bulging bicep to find Richard accepting Winn's help to stand again. Jack and Finn stood nearby, arms crossed and glaring at the man who had once been a major component of my fledgling tech firm.

Stepping around Kelly, I hiked my backpack higher on my shoulder and headed toward Richard. Kelly clasped my wrist to stop me, but I shrugged it off. Richard might be a corporate weasel, but he wasn't a killer.

Striding toward Richard, I held out my hands in a what-the-fuck gesture. "Richard, what are you doing?

Skulking around in the dark?"

"I had to see you." The middle-aged businessman ran a hand through his graying hair.

"You're supposed to talk to my lawyer. Because you're suing me, remember?"

He exhaled roughly. "Forget about the lawsuit."

"Forget about the lawsuit?" I repeated incredulously. "Do you have any idea how much that frivolous piece of crap has cost me?"

"It's just business, Bee. Our lawyers will hammer out a settlement, and we'll make nice in the press and life goes on—but I'm not here about that. I came here because of Trevor."

My heart stuttered. "What about Trevor?"

"We let him go four weeks ago, but he was in our building last night. He broke in and used his stolen credentials to launch his attack against LookIt from inside our offices." Stressed to the max, Richard massaged his temple. "I didn't have anything to do with this, but I know how it looks. We have some bad blood between us, but I'm not this petty—or criminal."

My eyebrows lifted at his continued insistence that he wasn't petty. "Why are you telling me this?"

"Because I know those sharks you've hired to work PR are going to slay us in the papers tomorrow," Richard said shrilly. "You have to call them off, Bee. They'll ruin us."

How in the hell had Lena and Ty already discovered Trevor's subterfuge? Their network of informers apparently knew no bounds. The bill I would soon receive would no doubt reflect their proficiency.

My lips parted and I started to assure Richard that I wouldn't drag him through the mud—but then I slammed them shut. What was Yuri always telling me about business? Hadn't he been counseling me to toughen up?

Actually, he'd rather indelicately phrased it another way, but his meaning was the same. My mentor had urged me to stop being so nice. Could I be a ballbreaker when it counted?

Pushing back my shoulders, I made myself as tall and stiff as possible. Looking Richard right in the eyes, I threw down my offer. "You drop the lawsuit, and I'll keep my PR team from running to the tech press with this."

Richard's mouth gaped, a puffing sound escaping his lips. "You can't do that."

Though my insides wobbled like JELL-O, I faked a calm shrug and presented my best poker face. "I can do whatever the hell I want. I'm not the one about to be linked to a vicious, blackmailing stalker, Richard."

Aghast, he sputtered, "Stalker? Blackmail?" He wiped a hand down his face. "Sweet Jesus. Look—I don't have anything to do with that. Whatever Trevor does on his own time has nothing to do with me or my company."

"By the time Ty is finished peddling his juicy tidbits to the tech blogs and press, no one is going to believe that."

Richard's panic quickly morphed to anger. His nostrils flared as he gritted his teeth. I watched his hands clench at his sides and wondered what he was thinking. Surely, he wasn't dumb enough to charge me, not with Kelly on my right and Winn on my left.

Exhaling noisily, he snapped, "Fine. We'll kill the lawsuit, but you have to bury this story." Swallowing hard, he admitted, "We need the Series B funding from the new venture capitalists or else we'll go bust. A whiff of this bullshit will kill us."

"Richard," I softly spoke his name. "I don't want you to go out of business. I don't want the people who work at your firm to lose their jobs, either. You have to remember that I'm not the one who started this fight. *You* sued *me*." Dashing a bit more salt on that wound, I added, "I warned you against hiring Trevor. I called you and emailed you, and I tried to tell you that he was a liability."

The older man glanced away from me. His eyes shone with such hardness, but I sensed his regret at the way things went down between us. Once, he'd thought he could push me over. He seemed to realize I'd finally grown a backbone.

Digging my phone out of my backpack, I scrolled through my contacts and found Ty's private number. He answered on the third ring. "Oh, sugar, wait until I tell you what I found out today!"

Hating to rain on his parade, I said, "I already know, Ty. I'm talking to Richard Hawkins right now."

He dramatically hissed. "Ooh, the enemy. Should we slay him now?"

"No, we're not going to slay him. We're going to bury the Trevor connection, and Richard is going to withdraw his lawsuit against me."

"My, my, my, sweet Bee, did we finally locate our spine?"

"It seems so."

"That big, sexy Russian of Lena's is going to be so proud of you." Sighing loudly, he said, "All right. I'll call off the hounds—but you better make sure Mr. Hawkins knows I won't hesitate to jerk off their leashes at the first hint of reneging on this deal."

Holding Richard's grateful gaze, I murmured, "He knows."

After ending the call and pocketing my phone, I stared at Richard. He finally nodded and reached for his cell. I waited while he contacted his lawyer and got the ball rolling. When he was finished, he asked, "Satisfied?"

"I will be when my lawyer confirms the suit has been

pulled." Before Richard could escape, I asked, "Where is Trevor?"

"I don't know. That's the truth," he added, eying Kelly warily. "If I knew, I would have had him arrested already for that stunt he pulled."

"I believe you."

With a stiff nod, Richard extricated himself from the tense situation. Kelly's strong hand settled against my nape. He gave the back of my neck a reassuring squeeze and drew my gaze. One corner of his mouth lifted with a smile. "Well played, Bee."

Indulging myself with a pleased grin, I admitted, "I bluffed my way through that. I kept thinking of everything Yuri taught me about business, about being strong and taking risks."

"We're taking a risk out here now," Winn interjected, his demeanor uneasy. "I suggest we get moving."

We quickly bid farewell to Jack and Finn. While Winn slipped behind the wheel of the SUV that belonged to LSG's fleet, Kelly helped me into the front seat of his truck and shut the door. After climbing in on his side, he leaned over and brushed his lips against my temple. "That was pretty amazing, Bee. You should be proud of yourself."

"For basically blackmailing Richard?" I wasn't so sure that what I'd just done was right.

"You used leverage to save your company. You protected the jobs of everyone who works for you. You're taking care of your people and everything you've built. That's what a good businesswoman does." He examined me more carefully. "What did you think owning a multi-billion dollar corporation would entail?"

Heaving a sigh, I admitted, "None of this. I suppose I was naïve to think it would be easier and cleaner. I just—I wanted to design cool things that other people find useful. The business stuff? It's not easy for me."

"Is that why you're thinking of selling LookIt to Insight?"

"Yes. I would retain some control over LookIt, and that would give me time and money to develop new products."

Kelly mulled it over. "Would it make you happier? Less stressed?"

"Yes."

"You're getting a good deal? I mean, they're not trying to cheat you or take money away from you?"

"I've had the tentative offer vetted by my legal team, and I ran it by Yuri. I counter-offered with my lines drawn in the sand. Once they're done crunching the numbers, they'll either make another offer or withdraw." I gripped his hand. "What do you think I should do?"

"I think you should do what's best for you, Bee. You're a brilliant woman. Deep down inside, you know what's right for you and your company." He kissed me so tenderly. "I believe in you."

Still reeling from his sweet encouragement, I held tightly to his hand while he drove us back to the penthouse. It felt so good to be able to talk to someone who didn't have a vested interest in my business decisions. Kelly truly only wanted me to be happy. He didn't have his hand in my pocket or a paycheck coming out of my coffers, or even an investment waiting to reap profits. The advice he gave came from a place of wanting to support me.

Once safely inside the penthouse, we separated. Kelly took my two guards into the kitchen to discuss the run-in with Richard and finding Trevor while I made my way to the master suite for a shower.

Like everything else in Yuri's penthouse, the master bathroom offered a sumptuous experience with the strikingly beautiful glass tile mosaics on the walls. I stripped down and stepped into the walk-in shower. The showerheads mounted flush with the ceiling provided a rainfall of warm water that spilled down my shoulders.

My ears perked to the whine of the door opening. Tensing, I glanced over my shoulder but instantly relaxed at the sight of Kelly. He leaned back against the door and watched me through the glass partition that separated the shower from the rest of the bathroom. "Mind if I join you?"

"Not at all." My cool answer in no way reflected the quake of anticipation rocking my belly. While the warm water pelted my skin, I watched Kelly shed his clothing. His sculpted, muscular body adorned with tattoos stole my breath. The memories of our unconventional tryst last night sent shivering rivers of white-hot delight through me. I still couldn't quite believe I'd done *that* with him—but it seemed there was nothing I could deny this man.

When Kelly entered the walk-in shower, I backed up until my back hit the wall. His wolfish grin warned me that this was going to be a shower—and a night—I would never   forget.

CHAPTER TEN

Without saying a word, Kelly reached for my body wash and squirted a dollop into his hand. He worked the cream into a foamy lather before placing his big hands on my naked body. Taking a page out of his playbook, I reached for the bar of soap he preferred and slicked up my hands.

Using our foamy fingers, we explored each other's bodies. Kelly lowered his head and captured my lips in a sensual kiss. My toes curled against the tile as his tongue delved into my mouth and tangled with mine. He backed me up against the wall and cupped my bottom before sucking gently on the tip of my tongue.

Shivering with pure, erotic delight, I surrendered to the gentle coaxing pressure of his seeking hand between my thighs. A freaking master of seduction, Kelly knew exactly how I wanted to be touched. His feather-light strokes primed me for the slow, easy swirl of his fingertips around my inflamed clit.

Wanting to make him feel just as good, I grasped his rock-hard cock with my soapy hands and stroked up and down his shaft. Kelly groaned against my mouth, the vibrations rattling down my throat and into my chest. As our tongues danced, we filled the shower with our soft sighs and low groans.

Just as I started to get close, Kelly stopped strumming my clit and cupped my pussy in his big hand. "Let's move this into the bedroom." His eyebrows arched in question. "If you're ready for that, I mean."

"Are you serious? If I wasn't afraid one of us would slip and end up in the emergency room, I would make you take me right here in the shower."

Kelly chuckled at my enthusiasm and nipped at my lower lip before giving my bottom a playful but stinging swat. "There are ways to make love here without slipping—but not for your first time." His expression turned more serious. "I'll make it special for you, Bee. I promise."

Hating that he had this added pressure on his performance, I caressed his face and lifted up on tiptoes to kiss him. "My expectations aren't that high. Please don't feel like you have to meet some crazy romance novel expectation of mine, okay?"

Narrowing his eyes, Kelly said, "Well, you've done it now, Bee."

"Done what?"

"Dared me to blow every romance novel sex scene right out of the damn water," he said matter-of-factly.

Thinking of some of the really smutty books I'd read, I playfully replied, "Well, maybe not *every* romance novel sex scene. Hot wax and anal beads might be a bit too much for this girl's first time."

"Jesus, Bee!" Kelly shot me a comical look. "What the hell kinds of books are you reading?" Leaning down to kiss me, he asked, "And where can I get my hands on copies of them?"

Giggling, I let him tug me under the closest water spray. He used his big mitts to rinse the suds from my body and then his. Out of the shower, we hastily toweled off and hurried into the bedroom. Kelly swept me up and deposited me on the bed.

Crawling over me, he kissed and nibbled his way from the very tips of my toes to my mouth. Stabbing his tongue against mine, Kelly caressed my bare breasts and petted my belly. On a similarly slow trek, he worked his way back down my body until he was flat on his stomach between my thighs.

Picking up my ankles, he draped my legs over his shoulders and nuzzled his face against my pussy. Remembering how amazing he made me feel last night, I clutched the sheet beneath me in both hands and held on for dear life as Kelly's tongue probed my pussy.

He made the naughtiest groaning noise as he traced my labia and dipped his tongue just inside my slick entrance. Already I was soaking wet for him and vibrating with desire. His tongue traveled right back to my clit and started swiping it with long, easy flicks.

One of his thick fingers carefully breached my virgin passage. The sensation of his thrusting finger and his fluttering tongue drove me higher and higher. That coil of bliss in my belly was already so damn tight. When Kelly gingerly worked a second finger into me and suckled my clit with slow tugs, I nearly passed out.

Digging my toes into his back, I squeezed my thighs and reveled in the dueling sensations of his stimulating tongue and probing fingers. Hovering right there on the edge of climax, I rose up on my elbows for a better view. The sight of Kelly between my thighs unleashed a torrid orgasm.

"Kelly!" I dropped back to the bed as wave after

powerful wave of bliss burst inside me like fireworks. He didn't let up one bit. Flicking and fluttering that wicked tongue of his, Kelly forced one climax into another. I cried out his name again and again as my body was wracked by the most intense spasms of ecstasy.

Letting me down easy, Kelly carefully removed his fingers and noisily kissed my clit. He dotted loud smooches along the curve of my hip and around my navel before concentrating on my breasts. He licked the buzzing peaks of my nipples and tweaked them between his fingertips until my hips were bucking off the bed.

Nipping at my neck, Kelly reached for the condom he had left on the bed before joining me in the shower. His heavy erection draped across my thigh, leaving a wet trail of pre-cum. The evidence of his excitement filled me with the most amazing sense of power. I'd never felt more desirable than in that moment.

When Kelly rolled onto his back, I thought he wanted me to go down on him. I started to move into position, but he grasped my hips and hauled me into a sitting position. "Not tonight, Bee."

"But—"

"If you put your mouth on me, I'm going to come. That was amazing last night, but right now I want to come inside you." Tangling his fingers in my hair, he dragged me down for a kiss, sharing the erotic musk of my own arousal with me. "I want to feel this tight cunt of yours milking me."

Gulping at the dirty word he had used to describe my pussy, I nevertheless found it incredibly exciting. Kelly pushed the condom into my hand. "Get me ready."

With trembling fingers, I ripped open the condom wrapper and carefully rolled the latex barrier down his steely shaft. I didn't miss that the brand was one designed for bigger men. I couldn't imagine the smaller condoms I'd used in my sex ed course fitting on Kelly's big cock.

Straddling his thighs, I stared at his erection with some concern. Last night, his penis had stretched my lips to their limit. I hadn't been able to take very much of his length into my mouth either. How the hell was I supposed to get his massive tool *inside* me?

As if reading my mind, Kelly said, "You'll be in charge tonight. I'm afraid that I'll lose control if I'm on top and go too hard or too deep. I don't want to hurt you."

"You would never hurt me."

"Not on purpose, Bee," he agreed. "But you're so small."

Worried he was about to change his mind, I hurriedly assured him, "I can take you."

"Sweetheart, I have no doubt of that." He ran a loving hand down my back. "If this position doesn't work, we'll try something else. You let me know what feels good and what doesn't, okay?"

I nodded. "Okay."

Grasping my hips, Kelly lifted me higher on his lap. My knees fell on either side of his hips and I braced my hands on his chest. Remembering that I was in control, I lifted my bottom and reached between my thighs to grasp his cock. I guided him into place, pulling him through the slippery folds of my pussy, and seating him right at the entrance of my passage.

Paralyzed by the discomfort I knew awaited me, I pleadingly gazed at Kelly. He understood my silent plea and gripped my hips. Planting his feet on the bed and curling his knees behind my backside, Kelly gave me only a fraction of a second's warning before he thrust up inside me.

I gasped as the thick crown of his cock entered me.

The quicksilver bite of pain knocked the air right out of my lungs. He didn't go any deeper than burying just the top of him inside my channel. Biting his lower lip, he held perfectly still, immobile like granite beneath me.

Inhaling a shuddery breath, I pressed down on his shaft. Aided by gravity and the slickness of my wet pussy, I managed to take him inch by deliciously slow inch. Yes, there was some continued discomfort, but it was nothing like I had been led to believe.

In fact, once I was fully seated and our bodies flush, I realized how fucking *good* it felt to have Kelly's huge cock buried inside me. My clitoris throbbed incessantly. Stretched and aware of every single nerve ending in my pussy, I rocked against Kelly in an experimental manner.

We both moaned loudly.

Gripping my hands, Kelly entwined our fingers and let me test a few different rhythms until I found one that worked for both of us. "There," I gasped. "Oh God! Right there!"

Kelly thrust up into me, and I cried out with sheer joy. Still holding one of my hands, he used the other to caress my front. He palmed my breast as I started to ride him and brushed his thumb across my nipple.

I had never felt so alive. A passionate fire engulfed me as I discovered all the wonders of womanhood. Rocking and swiveling my hips, I awakened that primal, sensual side of myself that had been waiting for this moment to be unleashed.

Kelly's thumb stopped stimulating my nipple and moved to another, even more tender, part of me. He rubbed my clitoris as I swayed back and forth atop him. My thighs started to shake as I grew wetter and wetter, and that vibrating ball of bliss began to throb in my core.

Throwing back my head, I shrieked his name. His cock

twitched inside me as my vaginal walls gripped his shaft. I lost myself in the throes of wild passion. The blazing streaks of ecstasy burned through me as I undulated atop Kelly, wringing every last ounce of joy from that orgasm.

When I sagged forward against him, Kelly gathered me in his brawny arms and gently flipped our position. Kneeling between my thighs, he slid home. Fingers interlaced with mine again, Kelly made love to me with wickedly deep and so very languid thrusts. There was no rush to completion. We had the whole night to enjoy and explore each other's bodies.

Kelly coaxed another orgasm from my body before finally succumbing to his own climax. He buried himself to the hilt before shuddering in my arms and jerking hard. Some primitive part of me was saddened to have that latex barrier between us. I wanted to feel all of him.

Forehead to forehead, we breathed each other's air and exchanged loving kisses. Kelly retreated from me with such gentleness. Reluctantly, he left my side to deal with the necessities but returned with a warm, damp cloth that he used to clean away the evidence of my lost virginity.

Climbing back into bed with me, Kelly hovered over me and peered down into my eyes. Staring up into his handsome face, I ran my fingertips along his strong jaw and chiseled nose. There was no stopping the hot tears that spilled onto my cheeks after sharing something so powerful with him.

"I need you to know this wasn't just sex to me, Bee." He wiped the tears from my face.

"I know."

"Do you know why it wasn't just sex?" He waited for me to answer, and when I didn't, he said the one thing I had always wanted to hear from him. "I love you, Bee."

"I love you," I murmured happily. "I have for so

long."

"Probably not as long as I've loved you," he said with a teasing smile.

"I doubt that very much."

Sliding down next to me, Kelly cradled me against his chest. "Did I hurt you badly?"

"No." I kissed his jaw. "It was perfect, Kelly."

"I'm glad you think so." Playfully tugging my hair, he said, "We'll get better with practice."

"Oh?"

"Yes. In fact," he reached over and killed the lamp, "you should get some rest. I intend to wake you up, bright and early, for another round of practice."

Snuggling close to Kelly, I decided that was one wake-up call I wouldn't mind. Of course, when the alarm went off just after three, I was less than thrilled. Apparently, I actually did mind that wake-up call.

Until Kelly's teasing fingers found their way between my thighs, that is.

CHAPTER ELEVEN

Later that afternoon, I stood in one of the firing stalls at the gun range that the LSG agents preferred and tried to hit the target downrange. After emptying the magazine, I performed the safety maneuvers Kelly had earlier drilled into my head and placed my unloaded pistol in the holding slot. The target slid toward me and I cringed at the sight of the nearly perfect slab of paper.

Stepping up next to me, Kelly tapped my shoulder before tugging the protective headphones off my head. "You're flinching before you fire, Bee."

"Well, it's really loud!" Immediately on the defensive, I puffed up and shot him an irritated look. Failing at new skills I attempted was not a feeling I enjoyed.

"Stop whining." Kelly gently censured me but made it clear he wasn't going to allow me to complain my way out of this one. "You can do this if you try harder."

"Why do I even have to learn this? Isn't this what I'm paying the three of you to do?"

Kelly's gorgeous green eyes narrowed. He invaded my personal space and lowered his face until our noses were close to touching. "What happens if the three of us get shot and you're left alone to defend yourself until the police arrive? What happens if you're kidnapped like Lena and all that stands between you and a crazy woman is your ability to defend yourself with a pistol? Or what if you're like Vivian and you get snatched out of a car and kidnapped because the man sworn to protect you gets beaten unconscious with a pipe?"

I gulped hard as Kelly described the very real attacks on two women he cared for deeply. He had a point that I couldn't argue. If the worst ever happened, I needed to know how to defend myself. Swallowing, I inhaled a steadying breath and reached for the unloaded weapon. "Will you show me again?"

Kelly relaxed and pecked my cheek. "Of course I will."

When he sidled up to my back and waited for me to load my pistol, I couldn't help but remember the way it felt to have his hot body pressed against mine. Squeezing my thighs together to quell the needful throb starting to ache there, I concentrated on the task at hand.

Once my weapon was loaded and a new target had been sent downrange, Kelly slipped my headphones back into place. He crouched a little so he could brace my arms with his. The sight of his strong arms flexing in that deliciously sexy way made me feel a bit faint, so I ignored them and focused only on the target. Though his voice was muffled by the headphones protecting my ears, Kelly gave clear instructions and coached me through another round of firing practice.

"Relax," he urged and gripped my hips. With a little pressure, he adjusted my stance. His hands moved to my arms and glided toward my elbows. "You're too stiff, sweetheart. Ease up on your grip."

Inhaling in a steady breath, I consciously relaxed my muscles and let the tension ease from my arms and legs. Kelly's huge hand spanned my belly, the searing heat of his touch penetrating the thin cotton of my tee to warm my skin. With his other hand, he pushed one side of my headphones clear so he could speak softer and communicate with me more clearly.

"You're gulping in air right before you fire. If we were training you for competition shooting, I'd make you practice all those breathing patterns Sully talked about, but we're not. We're training you to survive. You've got to learn how to shoot when you've got adrenaline pumping through your veins." His fingertips bit into my belly. "You'll only have a few seconds to react in a close quarters shooting, Bee. You have to learn to control your breathing and the shakiness in your limbs."

"I'm not a soldier, Kelly. I'm just a tech geek."

"You're not *just* anything. Women even younger than you are going through boot camp right now. If they can do it, so can you."

I glanced back at him. "Is this where you make me run fifty yard dashes and fire at moving targets?"

He snorted and kissed my cheek. "Don't give Winn any ideas, honey. He's chomping at the bit back there to get you into combat-ready shape."

Sliding my headphones back into place, Kelly gave my shoulder a double-tap as a signal that I was clear to fire again. Under his watchful eye and with the occasional comment from Sully and Winn, I shot my way through boxes and boxes of rounds and dozens of targets. My aim improved, but I hoped I never needed to use my new skills.

While Sully and Winn took turns firing off the last of the ammunition, I helped Kelly clean up our station. My cell phone started to ring in my backpack. Expecting a call from my lawyer to confirm Richard had withdrawn his lawsuit, I bent over to dig it out. Not one to pass up a chance to get his hands on me, Kelly swatted my bottom hard enough to make me yelp. When I glared at him, he rubbed the spot he'd smacked and gave my backside a squeeze.

Trying to figure out what it was about the gun range that got him so hot, I pressed back against him. He swept aside the long strands of hair from my ponytail to bare my neck to his ticklish kisses. Shivering, I answered the phone. "Hello?"

Heavy, deep breaths echoed in my ear. A chill crept down my spine. "Hello?"

The disgusting noises in my ear—the huffing and puffing and gross sounds—suddenly registered as a man masturbating. At almost the same moment I understood what was happening, Kelly ripped the phone from my hand. He had been close enough to me that he could hear everything.

Storming away from me, he snarled into the phone with a string of expletives. In all the many years I had known Kelly, I had never once seen him so furious. Rage turned his face red and made his jaw clench. I understood then how much control he exerted over himself to keep this feral beast locked away. The gentle tenderness he showed me stood in such extreme contrast to the fiercely protective warrior now growling into the phone.

"Enjoy yanking on your dick, you sick son of a bitch! You won't have fingers or a dick left once I'm done with you!"

Shaken by the gross call, I watched Kelly with a guarded eye as he spun back toward me. Winn and Sully had noticed the strange scene and were standing behind me now. As quickly as he had erupted with fury, Kelly grew shockingly calm. With a deep breath, he held out his hand, silently asking me to come to him.

There was no hesitation on my part. I needed Kelly to

know I didn't fear him, not even after witnessing him threaten my stalker. I understood that fierceness had originated from a deep need to protect and cocoon me from everything ugly in the world.

He embraced me tightly and kissed my cheek. "Are you all right?"

"I'm fine. It was gross, and I *never* want to hear some freak doing that again, but I'll live."

He actually growled again. "You shouldn't have to deal with this bullshit. We'll have that number and the phone call tracked. Maybe we'll get lucky and Spike will find something this time."

"Maybe," I said quietly, "but my stalker has been very careful."

Kelly rubbed my back and dropped a loving kiss to the top of my head. "We need to get you back to the penthouse."

Sadness gripped me as our interesting afternoon was interrupted by such ugliness. The three men hustled me out to the SUV and back to the penthouse. I stopped in at the office and touched base with Amita, who reassured me that the very last of the mop-up on the hack had been completed. Grateful for my small team's hard work, I made sure to thank each of them personally and started making plans to reward their tenacity and loyalty to the company.

Once upstairs in the penthouse, I kicked off my shoes, plopped down on the couch, and tugged my laptop out of my backpack. I finished the post I had started earlier that morning for our users. Under Lena and Ty's advice, I had been posting apologies and live updates on all my social media accounts since the hacking occurred, but now I had the time do a true heartfelt explanation of what was happening and the changes we were making to prevent another hack and to protect their blogs.

I cringed at some of the ugly messages from frustrated users. I didn't blame them and took their virtual blows on the chin. We could have done better. Hell, we *should* have done better. I accepted the full responsibility of this clusterfuck.

While I replied to comments and tweets, I remained vaguely aware of Kelly and my two bodyguards talking in hushed voices in the kitchen. Not wanting to recall the disgusting phone call, I tried to ignore them and concentrate only on cleaning up this awful PR situation. I had so much on my plate already and I trusted Kelly to do what was necessary to keep me safe.

Still slogging through the comments, I heard my phone's text message alert. With my stomach in knots from the earlier harassing call, I prayed this wasn't another sick message. I hoped it was Coby or Hadley sharing something funny or silly to make me laugh.

But I wasn't that lucky.

My stomach lurched when I took in the photo filling my screen. It was another picture of Jeb at one of the S&M clubs he had frequented. I followed the link in the message and was whisked away to a page with a countdown clock. The threat came through loud and clear so I quickly closed the window and the message.

Gripping my phone so hard my knuckles turned white, I refused to let my anger get the best of me. I wanted to throw my phone across the room and scream but that would only cause Kelly to come running in here—and then what? Could I tell him that his best friend since preschool had been lying to him for years?

"Bee?" Kelly strode into the living room.

Embracing my inner actress, I presented a calm face. "Yes?"

"I'm going to head out early for my training session. Is that all right?"

"Of course," I said with a smile. "I've got the Gruesome Twosome to watch my back."

Grinning, Kelly leaned across the back of the couch to kiss me. The spark of contact between our lips sent a delicious shiver through me. Thinking of the way he'd been teasing me with his touches all day, I gripped the front of his shirt and held him right there for a proper kiss. He groaned against my mouth but let me have the deep, soulful kiss I wanted.

"Don't stay out too late," I whispered.

"I want you naked and waiting for me when I get back." He spoke his order so quietly only I could hear him.

"I'll be here." My toes curled against the couch cushion as I imagined all the wicked ways he would keep me awake later. Now that I had gotten my first taste of lovemaking with Kelly, I craved it incessantly.

I waited until Kelly had been gone for a few minutes before picking up my phone and heading for the master bathroom. Locked inside, I paced the tiled floor and waited for Ty to answer my call. When he finally did, I rushed out my plea in one breath. "Ty, he sent me another message."

"Are you at the penthouse?"

"Yes."

"Lena has already left for the day but I'm still in my office. Would you like me to come up?"

"No, I'd rather come down to your office. It's more private."

"Have your minions escort you down."

Pocketing my phone, I combed my fingers through my hair and glanced at my reflection in the mirror. Something

Lena had mentioned during our meeting the day prior came to mind. She had gently suggested I consider changing up my wardrobe to include more conservative business attire. At the time, I'd bristled at her recommendation but staring at myself now I had to wonder if I shouldn't heed that advice.

Jeans, tees, hoodies, flip-flops, and sneakers had been my go-to uniform for so long I wasn't comfortable in anything else. I bought the occasional dress or skirt and nice heels for going out with friends, but I'd never gone into my office wearing anything like that.

What had Lena said? It was all about projecting an image of confidence. Did I project that image? I fit the stereotype of the programmer genius, but what about a businesswoman? I didn't think so.

Warring with my feelings of inadequacy, I left the master suite and sought out Sully. He had just cracked open a can of soda when I found him in the kitchen. "You need something?"

"Would you mind walking me down to see Ty Weston?"

"Not at all," he said.

Mouth agape, I watched him suck down the soda in four long tugs. "Dude, Sully, there was no rush. You could have asked me to wait."

He shrugged and tossed the can into the recycling bin. "I'm on your clock, Bee. The client's needs come first."

"*This* client isn't that demanding."

"Yeah, well, I don't want to get spoiled. Eventually this detail will end, and I'll be dreaming of the days I watched over you." He gestured around us. "A penthouse suite and a beautiful, brilliant protectee who lets me wear jeans on the job? It doesn't get much better than this."

At his mention of jeans, I asked, "Sully, do you think I

look like I should be in charge of a business as big as JBJ TechWorks?"

He tilted his head. "Where is this question coming from, Bee? You own the company. You built the company. It doesn't really matter what you look like, does it?"

"I guess not."

Shaking his head, Sully walked toward me. He squeezed my shoulder. "You're different and that's okay. It takes all kinds, right? You need to learn how to filter the information that comes at you. Use what works for you and your company, and discard the rest."

"What if I discard the wrong information?"

"You adjust your course and move forward," he said matter-of-factly. "Bee, you've built an empire on your instincts. Trust them."

As Sully escorted me down to Ty's office, I thought about his advice. Right now, my instincts told me I needed to come clean with Kelly before this whole mess blew right up in my face.

But the thought of betraying Jeb's secrets just killed me. I would do anything to protect Jeb's secret and the man he had loved so very much. I hadn't understood the nuances of their relationship, but I'd never doubted the love they shared. I refused to let that pig Trevor drag Jeb's memory or Peter's name through the mud.

I could only pray that it wouldn't cost me Kelly's trust.

* * *

Breathing hard, Kelly left the sparring ring and accepted the towel lobbed at him by Alexei. The Russian had the sleeves of his steel gray shirt rolled up to his elbows tonight. Wiping off his face and neck, Kelly didn't even try to hide his interest in the tattoos emblazoning the other man's skin. He'd seen that type of work on Vivian's husband and Yuri's friend Ivan. They were mob and prison markings, the type that only the hardest men earned.

If Alexei noticed him staring, he didn't acknowledge it. Instead, he barked, "Your defensive form is still shit."

"Thanks." Kelly took the water bottle Jack held out to him and swallowed a drink of the chilled fluid. "I'm doing my best."

"Bullshit." Alexei crossed his arms. "Maybe I should have that sweet little thing of yours come up here and climb in the ring with you. Something tells me you would learn to follow instructions better if it was your body between hers and the five animals I plan to throw in there with you."

Kelly's jaw clenched. "Leave Bee out of this."

"If you want to go home to your woman in one piece, I suggest you start paying attention to what I'm telling you and implementing that advice." Alexei picked up his jacket and stalked away from them. "Otherwise we're both wasting our time here. You'd be better off visiting a funeral home and picking out the fucking casket you're going to need."

When Alexei was out of earshot, Jack remarked, "He's right."

Kelly scowled at his oldest brother. "I thought you were supposed to be on my side?"

"This isn't about sides, Kelly. It's about you winning, or at the very least, surviving to the final match." Jack let loose a noisy breath and gestured to the ring. "You were sloppy as fuck on your takedowns. You seem to think the answer is faster and harder, but you're not *listening* to

169

Alexei. This is about stamina. You're going to gas out and then what?"

Kelly glanced away from Jack. Being wrong wasn't a feeling he enjoyed, but he knew that tonight Jack and Alexei had nailed him. "I'll try harder tomorrow."

"Kelly, this isn't a game. If you can't—"

"I said I would try harder," he interjected roughly. "I'm not a robot, Jack. You can't just reprogram me with the push of a button."

Jack's mouth slanted with amusement. "I bet Bee could reprogram you."

Kelly glared at his brother. "Funny."

Jack snatched the towel from his hand. "Get cleaned up and go home."

Rolling his eyes, Kelly saluted him but made sure to stick his middle finger way up in the air. Jack snorted and smacked him upside the head in that affectionate way only a big brother could master.

After showering and changing, Kelly helped Finn finish wiping down the equipment before following his brothers out of their gym. Out in the warm night, he caught sight of the dark SUV idling near his truck. He recognized the behemoth who stepped out of the front seat immediately.

"Jesus," Finn said with a breath of awe. "Is that who I think it is?"

Kelly nodded. "Yeah."

Sergei, the enforcer and underground fighting champion, walked to the middle passenger door. Arms crossed, he stared at Kelly and waited for him to make his move.

"What's going on here?" Jack asked, his voice laced with uncertainty.

"I think I've been summoned." Handing over his bag

to Finn, he said, "Hold this. I'll be right back."

Wondering what the hell was happening, Kelly crossed the parking lot. At the SUV, Sergei stared down at him with an expression of utter annoyance on his hard face. There weren't many men who could make Kelly feel small, but this beast managed it. Sergei didn't speak as he reached for the door, opened it, and stepped aside.

Realizing that was all the invitation he was going to receive, Kelly climbed into the SUV and settled into the empty seat. Once his eyes adjusted to the dimly lit interior, he spotted the most dangerous man in Houston sitting just to his left.

"Good evening, Kelly." Nikolai Kalasnikov fiddled with his cuff link. "You'll have to forgive this rather unorthodox meeting place, but I didn't think your brothers would appreciate me darkening their door."

He shifted for a better look at the reputed mob boss. "To what do I owe the pleasure?"

"Are you enjoying Alexei's brand of training?" Nikolai deftly avoided his question.

"That's one word for it." Though it felt awkward, he added, "Thank you for helping me. I appreciate it."

Nikolai sent one of those cold glances his way. "You should thank Vivian."

The Russian's unspoken words were the ones that left Kelly uneasy. Dimitri's comment from a few days earlier circled in his head. *Tread carefully.* "I will."

When Nikolai reached inside the jacket of his suit, Kelly instinctively tensed. He relaxed when the mob boss withdrew a folded slip of paper and held it out to him. Kelly didn't take it. "What is this?"

"Yuri told me about your little problem."

He blinked. "You mean Trevor Cohen?" When Nikolai nodded, he asked, "How did Yuri—"

"Lena," Nikolai answered. With a surprising smile, he added, "She'll use every asset at her disposal to help a client."

He stared at the paper, unwilling to take it just yet. "How did you find him?"

Nikolai actually chuckled. "Do you really want to know?"

"Yes."

"He likes strippers. One of my men owns a club that he frequents. He's there now." Nikolai waved the paper. "I've got my man keeping him...busy."

Ready to put an end to one of Bee's problems, he took the paper. "Thank you."

Nikolai shrugged. "One of these days, I'm sure you'll find a way to return this favor."

Of that, Kelly had no doubt. Hoping he hadn't just made a deal with the devil, Kelly reached for the door handle. A hand on his arm stopped him. Glancing back at Nikolai, he was surprised by the concern in the other man's eyes.

"Kelly, I won't try to stop you from fighting. I understand why you're doing it, and I respect that."

"But?"

"But you need to know that my aid to you ends with Alexei," Nikolai said, drawing back his hand. "I arranged that because Vee asked me to help you, but that's as far as I will go."

"I understand."

Nikolai considered him for a moment. "Good luck, Kelly."

Understanding that he had been dismissed, Kelly slipped out of the backseat and closed the door. Sergei had already turned his back and was heading back to the driver's seat. The coldness of the fighter he would soon face took Kelly aback. They had interacted on a social level a handful of times, especially when Sergei acted as Vivian's bodyguard, but it was clear that Sergei had labeled him the enemy.

He rejoined his brothers and unfolded the strip of paper. Seeing the name of the club, he waved the note. Grinning, he asked, "Either of you have some spare dollar bills?"

CHAPTER TWELVE

Like most men in their late twenties, Kelly had spent many nights drinking and watching half-naked woman shake their asses. Between deployments, there hadn't been much else to do with his fellow Marines. Without a girlfriend or a wife, he'd sought out visual stimulation to appease his pent-up frustration.

Those long nights of dropping tens and twenties on mirrored stages weren't nights he was particularly proud of or nights he ever wanted to talk about with Bee. The fact that Jeb had usually been right beside him would probably keep her from asking those sorts of questions. He doubted she wanted to talk about her brother's sex life any more than he did. Not that Jeb had ever gotten any action with strippers...

"This place isn't nearly as seedy as most clubs," Jack remarked as they stood just inside the main door. "I think you could actually sit on these chairs without having to whip out a wet wipe first."

Kelly snorted his agreement as Finn laughed. For a strip club, it was awfully nice inside. Nikolai's man clearly hadn't wasted any money on this place. Judging by the packed crowd, the investment was probably paying nice profits.

"What's this guy look like?" Finn asked.

Kelly dug out his phone and brought up the image. He

showed the screen to his brothers. "This is Trevor Cohen."

Always an officer, Jack took control. "Fan out. Find him. Take him out to the parking lot."

Once they had Trevor in the parking lot, Kelly would depend on his brothers to keep him in line. Trevor might not be the sicko making disgusting phone calls and sending Bee filthy photos, but he was trying to ruin everything she had worked so hard to build. Kelly refused to let that happen. He wanted this Trevor situation wrapped up neatly so he could focus on the real threat to Bee's safety.

A man Kelly recognized as one of Nikolai's inner circle caught his eye. Kostya, the purported mob *cleaner*, made a gesture before finishing his drink and weaving his way through the crowd to join Kelly. Without saying a word, he pointed to a closed-off corner where lap dances occurred and held up three fingers. Kelly understood and followed close on Kostya's heels.

Inside the lap dance section, Kelly tried not to pick up on the inappropriate sounds emanating from behind the curtains shielding each booth. While it was totally illegal for any sort of sexual activity to occur, the sight of high-heeled feet sticking out from under the drapes told him most of these men were on the receiving end of blowjobs.

At the third booth, Kelly listened more intently. He heard the murmur of a man's voice before a woman heaved an irritated sigh. "Look, honey, I can't make this work if you can't stay hard."

Kelly allowed a juvenile smirk to curve his mouth as Kostya stepped forward and rapped his knuckles against the frame of the booth. "Tasha, you're finished here. Get back out on the floor please."

Clothing rustled amid a man's frustrated grumbling. The curtain flicked back and a pretty redhead sauntered out of the booth. Kostya held out a handful of hundred dollar bills that the woman happily accepted for keeping Trevor occupied.

When the man in question stepped out of the booth, he took one look at Kelly and immediately retreated. Kelly reached in and grasped him by the front of the shirt. "You're coming with me."

"The hell I am!" The paunchy man slapped at Kelly's hand. "Security! Help!"

Kostya laughed and grabbed Trevor's arm. "Yell all you want. No one is coming."

Trevor's expression slackened with horror. He tried to fight, but Kelly and Kostya manhandled him out of the lap dance area and through a back exit. Jack and Finn were already waiting for them. No doubt one of Kostya's employees had send them.

"I'll leave this to you, Kelly." Kostya backed away from them. "I would appreciate it if you'd keep the blood spatter to a minimum. We're trying to maintain a certain atmosphere here."

Kelly grinned evilly. "We'll do our best."

Kostya shared a secret smile with him before returning to his club. The three Connolly brothers surrounded the weasel who had been threatening Bee and attacking her company. Kelly's hands fisted at his sides as he considered how best to get the point across that Bee was off-limits.

Trevor held up his hands and glared at them. "If you touch me, I swear to God I'll unleash every single picture I have. I'll fucking *ruin* her."

The mention of pictures stopped Kelly cold. His brothers shot concerned glances his way. Stepping toward

Trevor, he demanded, "What pictures?"

Trevor's malicious smiled chilled his blood. "She didn't tell you."

A stabbing pain speared Kelly's chest. What was Bee hiding from him? The realization that she hadn't trusted him with something this serious hurt badly.

What in the world had she done that would make her too afraid to come clean with him? Trevor said he had photographs. Had she taken nude selfies, or was it even worse? Had she been tricked by a former boyfriend into snapping provocative shots?

"Show me."

Trevor's smile faded at Kelly's growled command. He tried to back away but knocked right into Finn's chest. Recognizing that he was cornered, Trevor fished his phone from his pocket and tapped at the screen. He turned it toward Kelly who moved even closer for a better look.

At first, his brain refused to accept the image before him. It wasn't Bee. It was Jeb—but he was wearing women's lingerie and a leather collar and handcuffs and...

No. *No.*

"This is fake." Kelly batted away the phone. He knew Jeb. They'd been friends since preschool. If Jeb had been into that sort of thing, he would have known. "You've doctored these."

Trevor's acid laugh grated on his nerves. He swiped his screen before flashing it toward Kelly. "You think I doctored this one?"

He didn't even want to look but he couldn't stop himself. The sight of Jeb straddling some sort of leather and steel contraption twisted his gut. On closer inspection, Kelly realized the masked man beating Jeb's bare backside with a belt was also a Marine. The eagle, globe, and anchor tattoo marked him as a member of their brethren.

Swallowing hard, Kelly tried to make sense of it all. "Where did you get these?"

"That's none of your business." Trevor tried to pocket his phone, but Kelly snatched his wrist. Trevor yanked hard and warned, "I have copies of these stashed everywhere. Take my phone, and they'll be all over the internet by midnight."

Gritting his teeth, Kelly released the slimy bastard's wrist. "What do you want? Money?"

"Not from you," Trevor remarked. "I doubt you could scrape together enough change to buy me a cup of coffee."

The reminder of his relative poverty compared to Bee wasn't a welcome one, but he let that dig slide. Refusing to let this asshole hurt Bee, he insisted, "She won't give in over a couple of pictures. She's tougher than that."

"I have more than pictures." Trevor's self-satisfied grin gnawed at Kelly. "I have *names*."

Something told Kelly that the names of the men Jeb had done those things with were worth a lot of money. "Why are you doing this?"

Trevor shrugged. "She shouldn't have killed my baby."

Kelly's eyes widened fractionally. "Your baby? Oh. You mean that stupid program that never even worked?"

Trevor's nostrils flared. "It worked beautifully before she got her hands on it. That bitch doesn't know the first damn thing about coding."

"Watch your mouth," Kelly ground out between clenched jaws. "You'll need a bigger set of balls to call Bee names in front of me."

"Oh, I see how it is. You know, when I first found those pictures of her pervert brother, I thought for sure you'd be right there next to him, on your knees and sucking some other guy's dick. I wondered if there wasn't some special Marine brigade of fag—"

That was all that disgusting asshole got out before Kelly punched him square in the nose. The impact knocked Trevor right off his feet. He fell to the pavement hard and grunted. Kelly's fighter instincts kicked in, and he leapt atop the downed man. Seeing red, he planted his fist right into Trevor's jaw and reared back for a third blow that never happened.

"Kelly! Stop!" Jack wrapped both arms around Kelly's chest and hauled him off Trevor. "You'll kill him."

"Maybe I should," Kelly spat out angrily. Jerking out of Jack's grasp, he kicked at Trevor's leg. "If you publish one fucking picture or one word about my best friend, I'll hunt you down and slit your fucking throat myself. He was a hero who died for his country, you cowardly fucking prick."

Spotting Trevor's phone on the ground, Kelly stomped it three times, delighting in the crunching snap of plastic and metal cracking under the weight and force of his shoe. Overwhelmed by a jumble of emotions, Kelly stormed out of the alley and headed right for his truck.

Finn raced after him. "Kelly! *Kelly!* Stop."

Fumbling in his pocket for his keys, he refused to turn around and look at his brother. Finn caught up to him, grasped his shoulder, and whirled him around. "What are you going to do?"

Kelly didn't know. Waves of betrayal and anger and pain crashed over him, threatening to suffocate him. "How the fuck could he keep something like *that* from me?"

Finn shrugged one shoulder. "Kelly, bro, it was a different time. Even now that Don't Ask, Don't Tell is gone, you know how hard it is for men to come out." He shifted his glance to the ground as if uncomfortable. "To come out as a man who likes to do those things?"

The images he had seen of his best friend allowing himself to be degraded and humiliated confused Kelly. Who the hell was *that* man? Did he ever even know the real Jeb?

There was only one person who could answer those questions.

And she had a hell of a lot to explain.

* * *

Primping in front of the mirror and trembling with anticipation for Kelly's return, I heard my phone ringing in the master bedroom. I hurried in to answer but didn't recognize the number. Wary after the onslaught of weird phone calls I'd been receiving, I hesitantly answered, "Hello?"

"Bee, it's Finn."

"Oh." Surprised that Kelly's brother would call me, I instantly went into panic mode. "Oh my God. What's happened? Did Kelly get hurt at training?"

"No, sweetheart. He's fine. Look—we had a run-in with Trevor Cohen."

My heart skipped a few beats. "What?"

"Kelly will explain. Listen, Bee, he's pretty pissed off but not with you. He's mad at Jeb."

"Jeb? Why would he...?" My voice trailed off as the horrid realization hit. *He knows.* "How long until he reaches the penthouse?"

"Ten minutes?" Finn guessed. "Maybe fifteen if he hits bad traffic."

"Thanks for the heads-up." I dropped my phone on the bed and rushed to get dressed. The argument we were about to have wasn't one I wanted to have stark naked.

Dressed in yoga pants and a camisole, I rushed out of the master suite and into the living room, where I hoped to intercept Kelly. Winn leveled a curious stare at me and switched off the television. "Everything all right?"

I started to lie and say yes, but then I decided I'd had just about enough of keeping secrets. "Kelly is on his way, and we're going to have an argument over my brother."

"I see." Winn pushed off the sofa. "I suppose I'll make myself busy in the kitchen then." As he passed, he gave my shoulder a squeeze. "Whatever it is, you two will work it out."

I wished I had a tenth of Winn's confidence in us right now. I honestly didn't know how Kelly would react once it was all out. I cringed at the thought of what Trevor must have told him or showed him. To see Jeb in those sordid photos? It sickened and saddened me to think Kelly's memories of my brother and his best friend were now tainted with doubt and confusion.

When Kelly stepped through the front door a few minutes later, he froze and simply stared at me. The pained expression on his face made me ache. Regret twisted my gut. I thought of all the times I could have come clean about Jeb. If I'd only been brave enough to say something, we could have avoided this.

Squeezing my hands together, I whispered, "I'm so sorry, Kelly."

His tense expression went lax. "*You're* sorry?"

Holding my breath, I watched him cross the distance between us. His unreadable face left my stomach in knots. Was he upset with me for lying?

He tossed his gym bag onto the couch before cupping

my face in his big hands. He gazed down into my eyes and brushed his thumbs across my cheeks. "Don't apologize for protecting your brother."

I gulped nervously at his unexpectedly gentle voice. "You're not mad at me?"

"I'm not mad at you. I'm angry at the situation, and I'm pissed off at Jeb for keeping something like that from me." He nuzzled his mouth against mine, rubbing our noses together as he sought a sweet kiss. "But I'm not mad at you, Bee."

Closing my eyes, I murmured, "We need to talk but not here. Let's go to the master suite. There's a lot that I need to explain."

"Yes, there is," he agreed. "I need to—"

The shrill ring of the main penthouse phone interrupted us. Someone picked it up in another room. I assumed it was Winn.

"It's probably just maintenance," Kelly guessed. He made a face and rubbed at his knuckles. The movement drew my gaze and I gasped. Grabbing his hand, I tugged it closer for a better look. Blood stained his skin. Because I'd seen him wearing sparring gloves when training, I knew this wasn't from the gym. "Kelly, did you hit someone?"

Before he could answer, Winn came into the living room with a stormy expression on his handsome face. "The police are on their way up."

"The police?" I repeated, shocked. "Why are the police here?"

"They've come to arrest Kelly."

"What?" I jerked on Kelly's hand and forced him to meet my questioning gaze. "What did you do?"

Somewhat reluctantly, he admitted, "I hit Trevor. Twice."

Aghast, I dropped his hand and backed up a few steps. "Why would you do that?"

"He said awful things about—"

"So what?" I hated that my voice had climbed an octave as panic gripped me. "People say awful things all the time. That doesn't mean you hit them, Kelly. You sure as hell don't hit them when they're threatening to unleash photos and video of your brother and his married lover who is now a high-ranking officer in the damn Marine Corps!"

Kelly's head snapped back as if I'd struck him. "The man in the photos is an officer?"

"Yes."

"And he's married?"

"Yes." I didn't want to get into the specifics of the arrangement Peter had with his wife right now, not with Winn watching us. "It's not just that man either. There are other men in those photos that could be identified."

"Why didn't you destroy them?" Kelly demanded angrily. "We could have avoided this entire mess if you'd just been more careful!"

"Don't you dare try to turn this around on me!"

A knock at the door interrupted our argument. My stomach dropped when Winn welcomed two Houston police officers into the penthouse. One of the cops stepped forward and asked, "Kelly Connolly?"

"That's me."

The officer pulled out his cuffs. I instantly put my hand on Kelly's chest. Brows furrowed, he peered down at me. "What?"

"Don't say a word, Kelly. I'll have a lawyer meet us at the police station. He'll take care of you."

Hardness glinted in his bright green eyes. "I don't need you to rescue me, Bee."

Annoyed at his refusal of my help, I simply remarked, "I wasn't asking your permission."

Though he clearly didn't enjoy being the one who needed protection, Kelly didn't argue with me. He bent down and kissed me lovingly before allowing the police officers to cuff and read him his rights. Watching the cops perp-walk him out of the penthouse cut deeply, but there was nothing I could do right now.

Spurred into action, I rushed into the bedroom to change. While I tugged on jeans, I called the law firm I kept on retainer. They immediately promised to send someone from their criminal defense division over. As I slipped on socks and shoes, I dialed Finn and quickly filled him in on the situation.

By the time I returned to the living room, Sully had joined Winn. Both wore grim expressions, but neither said anything derisive about Kelly. Something told me they, too, would have punched Trevor if they had been in Kelly's position.

On the ride to the police station, I stared out the window and tried to figure out what the hell I was supposed to do now. The carefully planned overture toward Trevor that I had strategized with Ty no longer seemed possible. After Kelly humiliated him by crunching his face, Trevor would never accept the modest sum I'd been willing to offer.

So what to do?

It occurred to me that this was one of those moments in my life where I had to make hard decisions, but I needed to be smart about them. Remembering the way I had bluffed my way through my interaction with Richard Hawkins in that parking lot, I wondered if I had it in me to do it again—but this time with Trevor.

When we reached the police station, I was a bit taken

aback to see Lena and Yuri already waiting for me. Judging by the way they were dressed, they had been enjoying a night out together. I hurriedly apologized for dragging them out for something so sordid. "I'm so, so sorry about this."

"Hush," Lena said gently and gave me a hug. "I'm not here because you're paying me to manage the crisis with your firm. I'm here because I care about you and Kelly." She glanced over at Yuri, who looked very troubled. "We both care about you."

"What happened, Bee?" Yuri seemed totally stunned by Kelly's arrest.

I explained the situation as we entered the police station and waited in line at the reception area. Yuri sighed heavily but kept his opinions to himself. I was pretty sure Kelly would be getting an earful later from his former client.

The lawyer finally arrived and was taken back to the area where Kelly was being held and questioned. Lena guided me to a corner of the waiting room while Yuri went in search of coffee. As Lena tried to reassure me, I spotted Trevor exiting the main area of the station. His bruised and battered face made me wince. He ducked into the men's restroom, and I popped out of my seat.

Lena grasped my hand. "What are you doing?"

"I don't know," I admitted, shaking off her hand. "But I have a feeling it's going to get me into trouble."

With Sully shadowing me and shooting me incredulous looks, I crossed the waiting area and entered the men's restroom without hesitation. A quick glance confirmed Trevor was the only man in there. He stood at the sink, washing his hands and inspecting his broken face. Shooting only a cursory glance my way, he said, "I'm pretty sure this is sexual harassment."

"Well, you are the expert on that."

He frowned at me. "I've never come on to you. Anyway, you can't intimidate me."

"Maybe I should take a page out of your playbook and try extortion," I retorted tightly. "Of course, I hear that's a federal crime, especially when you use the internet to do it."

Trevor turned away from the mirror to look at me. "It seems we've reached an impasse, Bee."

"Drop the charges against Kelly."

"In exchange for?"

"Come to my office in the morning. Let's say ten o'clock. We'll finish this."

Trevor looked almost relieved that I was backing down and agreeing to pay him off. He tossed the sodden, dirty paper towels he'd been using to dab at his face into the trash. "Let's make it eleven. I'm going to need my beauty sleep."

As he strode by me, I gripped the front of his shirt. His dark eyes narrowed but he didn't try to tug free from my grip. "Trevor, I'll only tell you this once. Don't try to fuck me over again. I screwed up with Jeb's email accounts, and I'll pay for that—but I'll only pay for it one time. I will not allow you to drag the other people in his photos through the mud."

"And how the hell do you plan to stop me?"

I released his shirt. "You really shouldn't underestimate me, Trevor. I have friends in some very low places."

My connections to anything even remotely related to the underbelly of Houston ended with Kelly and Yuri, but Trevor didn't know that. I watched his Adam's apple slide up and down. Was he finally understanding how far I would go to protect the innocent people he wanted to harm?

I followed Trevor out of the bathroom—and collided with Jack Connolly. Kelly's oldest brother steadied me. His brow creased as he glanced between my face, the back of Trevor's head, and the bathroom. Finally, he asked, "Do I even want to know?"

"Probably not," I said softly. "Is there any news?"

"The lawyer popped out to let us know that Kelly will have his bail set and be out of here in a few hours."

Totally at a loss in this situation, I asked, "Where do I go to pay his bail?"

Jack seemed taken aback. "I'll take care of it."

I shook my head. "This is my fault. I'm responsible for this."

"Your fault?" Jack scoffed. "Kelly is a grown man. No one made him assault Trevor. He did that on his own."

"But he did it because I lied to him and allowed Trevor to blindside him," I insisted. "If I'd only—"

"If you'd only done what, Bee? Spilled your brother's deepest, darkest secrets after his death?" Jack shook his head. "I know what it's like. I've been there. Kelly has been there. He knows why you did this."

"I just wish I had been able to explain everything before the police arrived."

"There's plenty of time for that." He gave my shoulder a reassuring squeeze. "That hardheaded brother of mine is lucky to have you in his corner."

But as Jack led me back to Lena and Yuri, I couldn't help but wonder if that was true. The consequences of dragging Kelly into my personal disaster were staring me right in the face, and I highly suspected the blowback from this mess was far from over for him.

CHAPTER THIRTEEN

Sitting at my desk a few hours later, I rested my aching head in both hands and massaged my temples. I had sneaked in a quick nap after we had gotten Kelly home, but I'd actually woken up feeling more tired. How that was possible I didn't even know.

The tension between Kelly and me hadn't eased any since paying his bail and getting him out of police custody. The moment we'd stepped inside the penthouse he had locked himself inside the office to return phone calls to Dimitri and Lev. When he had finally sought me out, he had rather coldly informed me that he had been suspended from the Lone Star Group until further notice.

The guilt of Kelly losing his job gnawed at my gut. I grimaced as my empty stomach pitched painfully. I didn't know what to do anymore. Feeling lost and adrift, I suddenly wished that Jeb was still alive. He'd always steered me straight. Today I needed him more than anything.

"You look like you could use two of these."

The sound of Ron's voice drew my gaze toward the door of my office. He smiled warmly and held up a huge cup of my favorite coffee. Waving one of those slices of his shop's coffee cake in a plastic container, he asked, "May I come in?"

I gestured to the chairs in front of my desk. "Please."

He handed over the coffee and cake before sinking down into one of the chairs. He regarded me for a moment. "So—I heard about your friend."

"What did you hear?" I sipped the soothingly hot coffee and leaned back in my chair.

"That he got into a fistfight with one of your former employees," Ron said. Rubbing his thumb, he remarked, "After seeing how tightly wound the guy is, I'm not surprised."

"You don't know anything about Kelly." My cheeks grew hot after I snapped at my friend. Sitting forward, I hastily apologized. "I'm sorry, Ron. I didn't mean to be so rude to you. I'm running on no sleep, and there is a lot of stuff going on behind the scenes that has me stressed to the max."

Reminding me why he'd always been such a good friend, Ron happily accepted my apology. "It's okay, Bee. I've been there myself a time or two. Is there anything I can do to help?"

I sipped my coffee. "Unless you sell some sort of special coffee that makes stalkers and blackmailers go away, I think I'm on my own on this one."

"You're not alone, Bee." Ron's expression seemed so sad. "Please don't ever think that you're in this alone. You have so many friends who want to help and protect you. You've got Kelly and Coby and Hadley—"

"And you," I added with a smile. "Who would have thought that getting lost downtown and stumbling into a coffee shop because of the free Wi-Fi sign would have led me to such a great friend?"

Ron laughed. "Maybe it was fate."

"Maybe," I agreed, grinning at him. As I sipped my coffee, I spotted Trevor and his lawyers stepping off the elevator.

Ron must have noticed the grim set to my mouth. He immediately stood up and spun toward the door. "What's wrong? Is it your stalker?"

With a heavy sigh, I pushed out of my chair and came around to stand beside him. "No, Ron, that's my blackmailer."

"What's he doing here?"

"He's getting what he always wanted."

"And what about what you want?"

"I'm trying to protect my family. That's all I want."

Ron hesitated before patting my shoulder. "I wish you didn't have to go through this, Bee."

I clapped my hand over his. "Thanks."

The elevator opened again but this time it held Yuri and my team of legal counsel. He'd promised to be here with me while I negotiated the end to the hostilities with Trevor. The Russian billionaire was proving to be the greatest mentor in the whole wide world. Sometimes I wondered how I'd been so damn lucky to gain him as a supporter.

"I need to go, Ron. Thanks for coming by this morning."

"It was my pleasure. Good luck, Bee."

With Ron's smile of encouragement, I gathered up my notepad and pen and made the trek across the office space to the conference room. Along the way, my employees and friends rose up out of their chairs to watch me, most of them curious but some of them saddened. Though the exact details of my problems with Trevor weren't public knowledge, the gossip mill was running full steam and had filled in many of the blanks.

Yuri waited for me outside the closed door of the conference room. The devastatingly handsome Russian narrowed his pale eyes and asked, "Why are we here,

Beatrice?"

Certain he wasn't asking about the legal team waiting to draw up papers that would silence Trevor, I answered honestly, "We're here because I made a mistake."

"Yes, you did. What has this mistake taught us?"

I considered all the questions and what-ifs that had been tormenting me all night and morning. "It's taught me that I can't survive in business if I'm soft and sentimental. I have to…I have to be more decisive. I have to always be aware that others will exploit my weaknesses."

Yuri didn't look happy to be leading me through this lesson. "There's a time for being soft and sentimental, Bee, but it's not here in the boardroom. Leave that to Kelly, and to your friends and your family. Here? In this place? You have to be a shark. You have to be willing to do whatever it takes to protect what you've built and the people who rely on you for their paychecks."

"I understand."

Yuri touched my face in a gentle, almost fatherly way. "Yes, I think you do." Glancing toward the conference room, he said, "I want you to go in there and slay this man. Do you understand me? If he refuses to give you what you want, you get up, and you walk out."

"But what about Kelly and Jeb and—"

"Trevor knows what pain feels like now. He's going to take one look at me and think about my ties with certain people. I'm sure that taste of discomfort Kelly caused him last night was enough for him."

Though it felt dirty to exploit Trevor's pain, I wasn't about to toss out the option. After what he'd put me through, he didn't deserve any kindness from me.

I entered the conference room with Yuri and took a seat across from Trevor. All the irritation and anguish he had caused hit me like a ton of bricks. Sick of the whole thing, I tossed my notepad across the table. "This is the deal I'm offering. Take it or leave it, Trevor."

Trevor's cheek twitched as he picked up the notepad and scanned my terms. His gaze flitted to Yuri who sat on my left and then back down to the notepad in front of him. "I want more—"

"No," I cut him off and rose from my chair. "We're done." With a shrug, I stepped away from my chair and headed toward the door. Looking back at him, I remarked, "Maybe we'll find another way to settle this out of court."

"Fine. *Fine*!" Anger filled his shaky voice. "I'll take it. I'll take this deal."

Relief washed over me. Keeping my expression hard, I returned to my seat and placed my hands on the table. "Then let's finish this..."

* * *

Upstairs in the penthouse, Kelly paced the living room like a caged animal. The restraining order Trevor and his lawyer had filed required him to stay away from the bastard. Just thinking of Bee sitting across from that asshole and paying him her hard-earned money to keep him quiet sickened Kelly.

He rubbed both hands over his head and scratched at his scalp. How the hell had he let this happen? He had sworn to protect her, but it was his fault she was in this mess. Knowing that she had paid his bail made it even worse. Having the damsel in distress ride to his rescue? That wasn't the way this was supposed to work.

The doorbell chime surprised him. With Winn and

Sully down in the JBJ TechWorks offices, he was all alone up here and not expecting any company. At the door, he glanced at the monitor attached to the wall. The sight of Ty Weston was a further surprise.

"May I come in, Kelly?" Ty asked after he'd opened the door. Looking uncomfortable, he nervously explained, "It's about Jeb."

The mention of his best friend's name caused his chest to constrict. Stepping aside, he gestured to the living area. "Come in, Ty."

The reformed gossip blogger turned public relations expert found a spot on one end of the white sectional. Kelly sat across from him and watched as Ty placed his leather satchel on the coffee table. He unbuckled the latches and retrieved a couple of worn diaries and stacks of letters that he slid across the glass surface.

Putting a cleanly manicured hand to his perfectly styled hair, Ty said, "I can only imagine what sort of things Trevor showed you, but you need to know that was simply one very small side of Jeb." He placed his hands on the small books with reverent affection. "This was the heart of Jeb. This was everything wonderful and sweet and tender about him. This was the boy you called your best friend and the man who died in your arms over there."

Kelly's throat clogged with the heavy emotions that Jeb's memory always spurred. Voice husky, he asked, "Were you his lover?"

Ty's eyes were suspiciously watery. "I'm not sure lover is the right word for what we shared. We were both so young and innocent. All of this was so new to us. I don't think we ever understood where that summer of experimentation was going to lead us."

"How long...I mean...when did Jeb realize he was

gay?"

"I think he always knew."

Kelly cringed as he considered all the times he had teased Jeb or pushed women toward his shy friend. Why hadn't Jeb said something? Why hadn't he been honest? "I can't believe I didn't know."

"Jeb was very skilled at hiding it. He'd always wanted to be a Marine. He knew what that entailed. When you two signed up after 9-11, Jeb shoved that part of him into a box and locked it away somewhere deep inside him."

Thinking of the photos Trevor had shown him, he hesitantly asked, "What about the S&M? The women's clothing?"

Ty didn't answer immediately. "That came after me, Kelly. I don't know if he always had those desires or if they were borne of his experiences at war."

"I went to war, and I didn't come back wanting to wear panties or a dog collar."

Ty's eyes narrowed to slits. "You shouldn't judge the things you don't understand. It's not my cup of tea either, but I know many people who find a great deal of freedom in submission and embracing their kinks."

Duly chastised, Kelly said, "You're probably right."

"There's no probably to it." His voice took on a faraway quality as he recalled, "I ran into Jeb again after that second deployment, the one that took you both to Fallujah. I was way, *way* too young to be in the leather club where he found me. Jeb took care of me and got me into a safe spot. That was the first time I had ever seen him like *that*. He seemed so at peace and so...free."

Smiling, Ty continued, "I understood then that I never could have made him happy. What we shared when we were teenagers was beautiful and sweet, but it wasn't what he needed. At the same time, Jeb could never have been the man I needed either."

Kelly thought of the Russian bodyguard Ty had been seeing for some time now. "And Vasya? Is he the man for you?"

Ty's mouth curved into a loving, happy smile. "He's the closest damn thing I've ever found to perfection."

"I'm glad. You two seem good together."

"And what about you and Bee? Are you two still good together?"

"Sure."

Ty's eyebrow arched. "She didn't look so good when I saw her earlier this morning in her office."

Guilt speared his heart at the thought of her waiting for him at the police station and then going in to work so early. "I'll make sure she gets some rest today."

"Maybe rest isn't what she needs, Kelly." Holding up his hands to show that he didn't want argue, Ty offered a little advice. "If there's one thing I know better than anyone on this earth, Kelly, it's that secrets kill beautiful things. Don't let secrets kill the thing you two are trying to build before it's even had a chance to draw a full breath."

Taking Ty's advice to heart, Kelly walked the other man out of the penthouse before returning to the couch. He stared at the piles of letters and diaries a long time before finally working up the courage to pick them up and sort through them. An anxious sensation settled over him as he trespassed across Jeb's secret life.

He was still trying to mesh together the younger man who had written these things with the battle-hardened warrior he'd known when the front door opened and Bee entered the penthouse alone. Instantly alert, he tossed aside the letters and asked, "Where are Sully and Winn?"

"They're out in the hall. I wanted some time alone

with you." She dropped her backpack on the nearest chair and came to sit next to him. Her gaze moved over the letters and diaries. "I see Ty has been here."

"Yeah." Though it felt awkward to ask, he couldn't help it. "Did you know that he and Jeb were together?"

"Yes, but not when it happened. I mean, I was only, like, eleven when Ty and Jeb were secretly dating."

Kelly did the mental calculations. "So Jeb was a senior in high school?"

She nodded. "Ty was a freshman. That was the summer Jeb worked at the country club Ty's parents frequented. I don't know the specifics of how they got together but I do know it was...um...a summer of firsts, if you will."

"I see." Kelly couldn't help but picture a teenaged Jeb kissing a teenaged Ty. The image didn't bother him in the least, of course. "Did Jeb think that I was homophobic?"

"No!" Bee took his hand in her two smaller ones and interlaced their fingers. She seemed to be choosing her words carefully. "He never once thought that you would stop loving him as a friend if he told you the truth. No, Kelly, he kept this a secret because he wanted to protect you."

"Protect *me*?"

"He knew that you would try to shield him from the hazing and bullying—or worse—that he might endure if people knew he was gay. Once you two decided that you were going to skip college and go straight into the Marines, Jeb understood what that meant. He was practical about it, Kelly. A gay Marine?" She shook her head. "He never wanted you to be drawn into that battle. He feared what it would mean for your safety."

Deflated with shock, Kelly sat back against the cushion and simply stared at the stacks of letters and books. He started to insist that no single man in their unit ever would have treated Jeb differently if they had known he was gay, but stopped himself because it wasn't true. As much as he would have liked to paint all his brothers in arms as loving and accepting of all orientations, it wasn't reality.

"You know," he said with a sigh, "during that last deployment, I thought he was pulling away from me because he had seen the way I was falling for you or because he was so torn up over your mom's cancer. Every time I tried to reach him, he pushed me away even harder."

"He was in a rough place emotionally, Kelly. Mom was dying. I was over here alone, trying to hold it all together. He was so in love with Peter, but Peter wasn't willing to end his sham marriage to keep Jeb in his life."

Kelly's gaze snapped to her face. "Peter? Major Peter Carillo?"

She reluctantly nodded. "Yes."

"How the hell...? When did that happen?"

"Jeb had been in the Marines maybe a year when he went to a private club in San Diego. Apparently Peter took him under his wing that night." She fidgeted and wouldn't meet his gaze. "Peter started, you know, training him or whatever, and soon they were a couple."

"A couple?"

Bee finally met his searching gaze. "Look, I don't really understand *why* Jeb needed those things, but I do accept that he needed them. Jeb loved Peter, and I know, without a doubt, that Peter loved Jeb."

"But not enough to leave his wife," Kelly grumbled.

"It was complicated. There was an arrangement in place. The scandal would have hurt Peter and Jeb both." Sadness tugged the corners of her mouth down into a frown. "I don't think that Jeb and Peter had a real future together. Jeb wanted a man who could stand by his side and build something real. Peter wanted a man who was content to stay in the shadows."

"Maybe Jeb was finally tired of hiding," Kelly commented quietly.

"Maybe." Bee picked up some of the teenage love letters Ty and her brother had shared. "Have you finished reading all these?"

"No, and I'm not going to," he decided.

"No?"

"Jeb was my best friend. We were attached at the hip for nearly twenty-one years. This?" He gestured to the letters and diaries. "It doesn't change anything. I wish he had told me who he was." Kelly reached out and brushed his fingertips along her jaw. "I wish we could have been honest about the people we loved."

She clasped his hand and brought it to her mouth where she proceeded to kiss his bruised knuckles. "I think he would have been very happy about us."

Kelly laughed sharply. "After he planted his boot in my ass!"

She grinned. "Probably."

He leaned forward to claim her lips. After their tender kiss ended, he asked, "How did it go?"

"It's finished. Trevor will get his money after he signs a non-disclosure agreement. He's agreed not to press charges against you, and my lawyer thinks the DA won't come after you. If he does, they'll find a way to plea you down to probation." She pressed her lips to his cheek. "He can't hurt us anymore. That's all that matters."

It wasn't all that mattered, but he sensed she didn't want to dig into the details right now. Later, he would coax them from her.

Combing his fingers through the silky waves of her hair, he murmured, "I'm sorry I wasn't there for you."

"And I'm sorry that I got you embroiled in this mess," she whispered. Her eyes shone with unshed tears. "I never meant for you to get arrested or hurt or lose your job."

"Bee." He touched their foreheads together. "I've been arrested before, and I've lost jobs. Whatever happens with this mess, I'll come out all right on the other end."

"I hope so, Kelly."

"Well, if Dimitri cans me, maybe your friend Ron will hire me at his coffee shop. I'll finally learn how to pour those milk foam hearts," Kelly joked.

"Or," she said while playfully walking her fingers up his arm, "maybe I could hire you to be my full-time bodyguard."

"Hmmm," he hummed uncertainly. "What are the working conditions?"

"They're very, *very* hands-on," she said, taking his hand and sliding it under her shirt.

Gliding his palm along her soft belly, he asked, "What about your benefits package?"

Taking his hand, she rose to her feet and tugged him to his feet. "Why don't you follow me into the bedroom? We'll take a peek at the full package..."

CHAPTER FOURTEEN

"Are you sure you want to do this?" Sully's displeasure with my plan came through loud and clear. We sat in an idling SUV parked outside the art studio of Vivian Valero Kalasnikov, but neither Sully nor Winn would let me get out of the backseat just yet.

"Yes, I'm sure. You can take me inside or sit out here. Either way, I'm doing this."

From the seat next to me, Winn sighed heavily. "I'll take her inside. You watch the front."

Sully grumbled before exiting the SUV. With Winn guarding me, I made my way to the front entrance of the studio. We were greeted by a tall, dark-haired man with the brightest blue eyes I had ever seen. "Can I help you?"

Judging by his thick Russian accent, I assumed he was one of Nikolai Kalasnikov's men. It made sense that his wife would be guarded around-the-clock, especially if the rumors about him were true.

"Hi." I extended my hand but the man didn't shake it. "My name is Bee Langston, and I'm here to see Vivian."

"Is she expecting you?"

"No."

"Well—"

"We have a friend in common. His name is Kelly Connolly."

The guard's eyes glinted with recognition. "Let me see

if she's taking visitors today. When she paints, she prefers not to be disturbed. In your case, she might make an exception."

I waited patiently as the guard made a phone call and traded a few short Russian phrases with someone else. The only words I understood were Kelly's name.

"She'll see you. Take the stairs."

Winn followed me up to the second floor where yet another guard awaited us. This one took my freaking breath away. I had never seen a man that big in my entire life. Leaning back, I craned my neck to take in what had to be seven feet of this giant. "Um...hi?"

The giant didn't say a word. He simply opened the door behind him and stepped aside to let me enter. When Winn tried to follow, the giant held out his hand and shook his head. "Only the girl."

Winn didn't like it. "I go where she goes."

"You don't go in there."

"Look, I understand that you're trying to do your job. Let me do mine. After I clear the space and ensure there is no danger to Miss Langston, I'll happily wait out here."

The giant considered it and finally nodded. "Okay."

Certain Winn was overreacting, I nonetheless appreciated his concern. We entered the spacious studio to the sounds of electronic music that I instantly recognized as one of Coby's latest remixes. Floor to ceiling windows on the left permitted natural light to bathe the space. My gaze traveled across the selection of paintings propped up on easels along the right wall.

"They're part of my upcoming show." Wiping her hands on a towel, Vivian strode toward me. Bare legs and feet peeked out from behind the paint-splattered apron that protected her flirty sundress. "It's nice to finally meet you, Beatrice."

"Bee," I corrected gently and held out my hand.

"Everyone calls me Vivi," she said as we shook. A playful smile lit up her face. "Well—everyone except for my husband." She glanced at Winn. "And this is?"

"Michael Winchester, ma'am. I'm a private security specialist with the Lone Star Group."

"Oh. You're one of Dimitri's men. I'll be sure to let him know how incredibly thorough you were."

"Thank you, ma'am." Touching my arm, he said, "I'll be outside when you're ready."

When we were alone, Vivian gestured to the long work table littered with art supplies. "So what can I do for you? Danny said you were here about Kelly. Is this about the upcoming fight tournament?"

"In a roundabout way, yes." I picked up a tube of paint and played with it. "If I had my way, Kelly wouldn't fight at all. I would settle the debts and wipe the slate clean, but he refuses to let me help him."

Vivian rolled her eyes. "Men! If the tables were turned, and you were the one who needed money, he would be tripping over himself to save you."

"Right? At this point, I've accepted that he's going to fight. It's about honor to him now." I hesitated. "I need to make sure that his family is protected if he loses."

"Some people might accuse you of being unsupportive for planning ahead for a loss."

"Are you one of those people?"

"No. I think it's smart of you to be practical at a time like this." She pointed to the door with a paintbrush. "Did you see that man guarding the door?"

"Sure."

"His name is Sergei. He's Nikolai's champion for a reason. As much as I like and care about Kelly, I'm realistic. He can't beat Sergei."

Glancing back at the closed door, I thought of the man-beast standing out there. Though Kelly was big and sexy and so strong, he was no match for the freaking grizzly bear standing out there.

"What can I do to help you?"

"Do you know the men who hold the loans against Kelly's dad and the gym?"

"I don't know them personally. I know of them. Why?"

"I want to meet them."

Vivian fiddled with the clean, damp brushes she was letting air dry on a towel. "You really don't want to tangle with Besian and his crew, Bee. You don't approach men like that with an open purse. Nikolai would blow a pupil if I took you to that social club."

Trusting Vivian's judgment, I dropped the possibility of meeting with the Albanian mobsters. "What about the other guy?"

"John Hagen? He's got a certain reputation, but he's a stand-up guy as far as I know. He would probably negotiate with you." Vivian started untying her apron. "I'll take you to see him."

My eyes widened. "You?"

She nodded. "No one will dare hassle you if I'm there. Who knows? Maybe Hagen will cut you a better deal."

If anyone had a shot at helping me, I figured it was Vivian. "Thank you. I really appreciate this."

"It's no problem." She walked me to the door and rolled her eyes. "Just a quick heads-up. My shadow is going to hate this plan of ours."

Sure enough, Sergei argued with her. I couldn't understand a word they said as they snapped back and forth in Russian. Vivian won the battle, but Sergei's clenched jaw made it clear he wasn't pleased with this development. Considering Vivian's husband had probably entrusted her safety to Sergei, I didn't blame the man. That must have been a hell of a weight to carry on those broad shoulders. I sure wouldn't want a man like Nikolai pissed off at me.

Back in our SUV, Sully and Winn exchanged looks as I asked them to follow Vivian's vehicle. They didn't fight my request to visit the loan shark, but they didn't hide their displeasure with it, either. When we reached the seedy bar a short time later, Winn made an annoyed, growling sound. He made sure to sigh loudly as he escorted me into the bar behind Vivian and Sergei.

As we waited for Hagen to receive us, Vivian leaned over and asked, "How long have you had the bodyguards?"

"About a week," I said. "I'm still not used to it."

"It can be difficult to adjust," she agreed. "Sergei and Danny are normally very good about giving me space. They've become a bit more protective now that..." Her voice drifted off as her hand brushed against her flat belly.

Was she pregnant? Before I could ask whether congratulations were in order, a broad-shouldered man tall enough to look Sergei in the eye stepped out of an office and into the hallway. There was no mistaking the surprise on his face. "Mrs. Kalasnikov, to what do I owe this honor?"

Smiling, Vivian stepped forward. "I'm sorry to drop in unannounced, Mr. Hagen, but my friend would like to discuss some business with you."

Hagen's gaze settled on me. His eyebrows lifted even higher as he seemed to recognize me. "Beatrice Langston?"

"Bee," I said and held out my hand.

He hesitated before finally shaking my hand. "Knowing what I know of your business, I don't think my pockets are deep enough for the sort of loan a woman in your financial position might require."

"I'm not here to borrow money. I'm here to pay it back."

"You're not on my books."

"No, but Nick Connolly is."

"And his debt is a concern of yours because...?"

"Because I say it is," I replied matter-of-factly. "I know that you want the land that sits beneath Connolly Fitness, but I'd like to make you a better offer."

Uncertainty flashed in his eyes. After a moment of indecision, he stepped aside and gestured to his office. "Step inside, ladies. Let's talk..."

* * *

"*Da!* Good, Kelly!" Alexei called out from the sidelines. "That's the way!"

Finally, Kelly thought as he wound his legs around his sparring opponent and applied a chokehold to force him into submission. The man tapped three times, signaling his surrender, and Kelly instantly released his grip. After checking to be sure his opponent was okay, Kelly helped the man stand and knocked gloves with him as a sign of sportsmanship.

Alexei strode toward him and gripped his shoulders. "Tonight you fought beautifully. You fight like this at the tournament, and you might actually survive to the final round."

Kelly spit out his mouth guard and smiled at the

harsh-talking Russian. "Gee, Alexei, I'm starting to think you like me."

Alexei smacked his arm. "Like is a strong word. Let's go with tolerate, okay?"

Kelly snorted. "Yeah. Okay."

"That's it for tonight. Go home and get some rest. Try to stay out of jail," the Russian added, the sting of censure burning his tongue.

Taking it on the chin, Kelly nodded. "I will."

After Alexei left his side, Finn crossed the gym. The anxious expression on his face made Kelly's gut clench. "What is it, Finn?"

"Pop is outside. He says he needs to speak with you."

Kelly snatched a clean towel from the chair where his gym bag sat and wiped at his face and neck. "I don't care what he needs."

"Kelly, he said it's about Bee."

Infuriated that their old man would try to manipulate him through Bee, Kelly slapped his towel against Finn's chest and grabbed his bag. He stalked across the gym and out into humid night. His father leaned against the door of Kelly's truck while he smoked a cigarette. The sight of his dirty, wrinkled clothing only further irritated Kelly.

Stopping a few feet from his old man, Kelly pointed a finger in his face. "You leave Bee alone."

He took a long drag on the cigarette, burning it right down to the filter before dropping it to the ground and smashing it with the toe of his shoe. Exhaling long streams of smoke, he said, "I'm trying to help you."

"Help me?" He guffawed. "Yeah, Pop, you've been such a help to me. I'll be sure to send a thank you card while I'm recuperating in the hospital."

The tiny twitch around his father's eye told Kelly he'd hit his mark. "I didn't ask you to settle this debt."

"What the hell else am I supposed to do? Let those mobsters kill you?"

His father scoffed. "They aren't going to kill me."

"You don't know that." Kelly's fingers curled at his sides. "It's not just about you anymore. You risked everything that Jack and Finn have built. I won't stand here and let them lose it all because you're a miserable gambling drunk."

The old man flinched but didn't argue with Kelly's characterization of him. Instead, he said, "Jack and Finn aren't at risk anymore, so you can drop that hammer and stop beating me over the head with it."

Confused by his father's remark, he asked, "How's that? Did you finally hit a hot streak and settle up with Hagen?"

"No, but I watched Bee walk into Hagen's bar earlier this evening with that Russian girl you used to pant over."

Ignoring the comment about Vivian, he demanded, "What do you mean you watched Bee walk into Hagen's bar?"

"I mean what I said. I watched her go into that bar. She was in there for half an hour. I assumed you sent her there to settle the debt."

Kelly's teeth clenched together so tightly he feared his jaw would break. "No, I didn't."

Incensed that she had gone behind his back and against his wishes, Kelly jerked open the door of his truck and tossed his bag inside. His father followed and tried to stop him. "Wait. Kelly, I need to tell you about—"

"I don't care." Kelly shook off his father's hand and climbed behind the wheel. "Just leave me the hell alone!"

He slammed the door, jammed the key in the ignition, and peeled out of the parking lot. As he raced across Houston, Kelly couldn't decide what had pissed him off the most about this fucked up situation. Even as he rode the elevator up to the penthouse suite, he wondered at the anger he experienced. Was he mad at Bee? Was he mad at himself? His father? He worried the answer was a tangled mess of all three.

When he stepped into the penthouse, Bee popped right up off the couch and started to wring her hands. Even if he hadn't known what she had done, her anxious behavior would have tipped him off. Seeing her so nervous made his gut twist. Did she honestly fear his reaction? Was she afraid of him after he'd lost control and hit Trevor?

Winn made his presence known by moving into the doorway between the living area and kitchen. Kelly's anger erupted at the guard. "You're getting paid to protect her, Winn. Why the hell would you let her visit a damn loan shark?"

Winn crossed his arms and didn't immediately reply. When he did, his voice was unnaturally calm. "Mate, I'm paid to protect her, and I did. She's a grown woman fully capable of making her own choices. She wanted to go, so we went. Without incident, I might add."

Bee stepped in front of him and held out her hand in a silent plea for understanding. "Winn, give us a minute, please." When the guard disappeared into the kitchen, she turned her worried eyes on him. "Don't be upset with Winn and Sully. You know how I can be when I want something."

"They're supposed to keep you out of trouble. Not only did they allow you to expose yourself to a damn mobbed-up loan shark, but they also let you drag Vivian into this mess."

"She's married to a mob boss, Kelly. She's already in *this* mess."

Surprised by the coldness of Bee's reply, he asked, "So what? She's disposable? She's someone you can use and discard without concern?"

"I didn't say that! I can't believe you would even think—"

"I can't believe you went against my wishes, Bee. I specifically asked you to stay the hell out of this."

"You expect me to just stand on the sidelines and watch you get your head knocked in by a bunch of bloodthirsty animals, and do nothing? Kelly, I *love* you. I'm not going to let you risk everything on the slim chance you'll win this thing."

Hearing her voice how little faith she had in him cut Kelly more than he would ever admit. He didn't dare believe that he could win and had gotten used to the doubt from Alexei, Jack, and Finn, but Bee? He'd needed her to believe in him, to believe that he could do anything if he tried hard enough.

"Look," Bee said softly, "it's not a big deal, okay? I gave Hagen my building and he agreed—"

"You did *what?*" His snarled question startled her, and she bit her lower lip. He reined in his outrage, because the last thing he wanted to do was scare her. "You gave him your building?"

She gulped before answering his question. "It's just a building, Kelly. It's bricks and rebar. It's easily replaced."

"It's not *just* anything, Bee. That building is worth so much more than the loan Pop owes Hagen. Do you realize how badly you got taken? How could you agree to something like that?"

"I did it to protect you."

"I don't need protecting."

She sadly shook her head. "You just don't get it, Kelly. You do need protecting. You need my help. It's just money, Kelly. I'll make more of it."

The reminder of their vastly different financial situations made him so uneasy. "So that's your new answer for everything? Spread around some money and make it all go away. You made Jeb's secrets go away. You made Trevor go away. You made Hagen go away. What's next, Bee? What else is your money going to buy you?"

As if on cue, Bee's backpack started ringing. He glanced at the offending sound before glancing back to her. His brain finally caught up with what he had just seen, and his gaze snapped to her backpack again. Her cell phone sat on the couch next to her bag, but it wasn't ringing. It was another phone buried in her backpack that was making that noise.

Wondering what the hell was going on, he stalked to the couch, unzipped her backpack and dumped the contents onto the couch. Bee rushed to his side and gripped his arm. "Hey! What are you doing? That's my stuff!"

Kelly ignored her protests and swept his hands through the books, pens, notepads and makeup to find two old school cell phones. One was ringing while the other was actively making a call. A cold ball of dread settled in the pit of his stomach as he answered the call and heard the unmistakable sounds of a man panting on the other end. It was a recording.

Gripping the phone in his hand, he pressed the buttons until he found the text messages. All of the messages in the phone's history had been sent to Bee's cell phone. They were the messages from her stalker.

The stalker he started to doubt even existed.

He switched to the other disposable cell phone and found the same thing. The ball of dread in his gut knotted and throbbed as anger and betrayal took hold. "What the hell is this, Bee?"

"How should I know? I've never seen them in my life."

Taken aback by the easy way she lied to him, Kelly narrowed his gaze until his eyes were mere slits. "The truth, Beatrice. What the hell are these phones doing in your backpack?"

"I. Don't. Know."

"What's wrong?" Winn cautiously entered the living area with Sully only a few steps behind him.

"You tell me," Kelly said and thrust the phones into the other guards' hands. When he glanced at the pile of crap he'd dumped out of her backpack, he noticed the sheets of photo paper. He picked them up and rubbed them between his fingers, mentally comparing them to the photos she had supposedly received from her stalker.

Kelly's mind reeled as he pieced together the damning evidence. Something she had said the other day ricocheted around his brain. *I wondered what it was going to take for you to see me.*

His heart gripped in an icy vise, he held her gaze. "Did you set this up, Bee? To make me take care of you?"

Her brown eyes widened. "Are you *insane*? You think I would fake a stalker just to get close to you?"

Before he could answer, Sully interjected his opinion. "It wouldn't be the first time a woman has done that."

Bee gawked at them. "You're all crazy if you think I would fake something like this."

"Then how do you explain having these phones and the photo paper?" Winn asked. "We've had you on a tight leash since taking over your detail. You're only alone in the shower or bathroom—and even then Kelly is usually with you. We haven't let you out of our sight once, and that backpack is always with you. No one could have gotten to it but you."

She took a step back and frantically searched their faces. "I did not fake this. I wouldn't even know where to start!"

"Bullshit," Sully rudely retorted. "You're a genius. You could easily figure out how to make this happen."

"Oh, and I suppose I stole my own panties and jacked off on them, right?"

"You're rich," Sully answered matter-of-factly. "In the last couple of days, I've watched you reach into your deep pockets to fix a whole lot of problems. It wouldn't be that difficult to pay someone to dirty up some panties in a box."

"You guys are unbelievable!" She rubbed her face. "Do I look like a freaking criminal mastermind?"

"You look like a young woman who never lets anything get in her way," Sully replied honestly. "When you want something, you go after it. Like today with the loan shark." His gaze drifted to Kelly. "And now with him."

"Other than the phone call at the gun range and that business with Trevor, you haven't received any other messages or photos since we came onto the scene," Winn added.

"Because you're protecting me, and my stalker is too afraid to try to get close to me!"

"If we're protecting you that well, how do you explain these phones and paper finding their way into your bag?" Sully turned the scenario on its head. "You can't explain it because it didn't happen. Kelly's right. You stalked yourself."

Bee's lower lip wobbled as she pinned him with a desperate stare. "Kelly, please, you have to believe me."

He wanted to believe her. He wanted to deny that she

would stoop so low to drag him back into her life after that disastrous New Year's Eve kiss.

But he couldn't refute the proof before him. "I believe what I see, Bee."

A tear dripped down her face. "You believe I'm a liar?"

A painful ball clogged his throat. "You lied to me about Jeb for years, Bee. If you could hide that—"

"Get out." She sobbed the words and pointed to the door. "All three of you. Get your shit, and get the fuck out." When they didn't move, she screamed, "*Now!*"

Sully and Winn gave her a wide berth as they headed for their bedrooms to gather up their suitcases and equipment. Kelly didn't make a single move. He simply held her furious gaze. "I'm not leaving."

"I wasn't asking." She swallowed hard and wiped at her wet, shiny cheeks. "Get your things and go—or I'll call the police. This time you'll have to pay for your own lawyer. If you can afford one," she added nastily.

Her ugly remark flayed his already wounded pride. "Fine."

She moved to the far side of the room, refusing to even look at him as he stormed toward the master suite. As he stuffed his clothing and toiletries into his suitcase, Kelly hurt so badly he could hardly breathe. The painful pressure squeezing his chest had to be worse than a heart attack. The knife-like ache twisting his gut was even worse.

How could he have been so stupid and easily fooled? He'd fallen for Bee's damsel in distress routine hook, line, and sinker. That Lev and Dimitri had believed her softened the blow some. Glancing at the bed they had shared, he was reminded of her remark about useful minions. Clearly, there was nothing Bee couldn't buy.

He wondered at the guilt she had expressed over

embroiling him in that drama with Trevor. That guilt had been as sincere as the threat the man had presented to her. Kelly couldn't understand why she had manufactured this fake stalker when a real problem like Trevor had already existed.

Unless she wanted to be assured he would stick around...

Was that it? Had she feared the Trevor issue would be easily and quickly cleaned up, and he would take off again? Was she trying to keep him close by inventing this other fake stalker who would never be caught?

He heard two sets of footsteps in the hall. A few moments later, the door closed loudly. No doubt Bee had slammed it shut behind Winn and Sully. The thought of leaving her alone here in the penthouse didn't sit well with him. She had majorly screwed up, but he could forgive her. God only knew he'd forgiven much worse from others.

Leaving the suitcase on the bed, he returned to the living room and found her waiting by the door. Her reddened eyes and the tears leaving slick paths on her face saddened him. How the hell had things gotten this bad between them?

Bee took one look at him and shoved off the wall. She marched by him and right back to the master suite. Seconds later, she emerged with his suitcase in hand. She stormed right to the door, flung it open, and tossed his suitcase into the hall. "Get. Out."

Shocked by her rage, Kelly decided there was no way they could have an adult discussion tonight. He strode out into the hall and turned to speak to her. "Bee, I think we—"

"Goodbye, Kelly." She pushed the door closed. "And good luck with your fights."

With a thud of finality, the door slid into place. A second later, the locks engaged, sealing him in the hallway. He stared at the reinforced steel slab between them. His damned heart felt like it was being ripped out of his chest. He raised his hand to knock, but his knuckles never touched the metal.

Lowering his hand, he spun on his heel, picked up his suitcase, and walked away from the only woman he had ever loved.

CHAPTER FIFTEEN

The incessant ringing of the doorbell dragged me from my fitful sleep. Sitting up, I rubbed my face and tired eyes and glanced around the living room of the penthouse. Before all the awful memories of my night penetrated the foggy haze of my hangover, I heard the front door open. Panicked, I shoved to my feet and grabbed the closest weapon, an empty wine bottle.

It wasn't my crazed stalker who walked into the place like he owned it. It was Yuri—who actually did own it. His eyebrows lifted quizzically at the sight of the wine bottle in my hand. "Rough night?"

Groaning, I put the bottle on the table and flopped down on the couch. "You have no idea."

"Actually, I do." Yuri sat down on the table and cautiously touched my knee. "Are you all right?" Reaching over, he picked up the empty wine bottle. "It must have been one hell of a fight if you had to drown your sorrows in a seven-thousand-dollar bottle of wine."

I cringed and croaked, "I'll reimburse you."

"Nonsense," he murmured. 'What's the point of having a wine cellar if my friends can't make use of it?" Sitting up straight, he exhaled loudly. "Well—tell me what happened."

I massaged my aching head. "Something tells me you already know."

"Dimitri called me this morning. He told me that your guards reported you had fired them and thrown them out of the penthouse last night. He said you later called and left a rambling, drunken message with the night dispatcher."

I didn't remember calling the Lone Star Group, but after glugging down that entire bottle of wine anything was possible. "Well, that's embarrassing."

"Why did you fire the guards? And where the hell is Kelly?"

"He's gone. They're all gone."

"But your stalker—"

"Isn't real," I lied. Last night, alone in the penthouse, I'd come to a decision. My stalker, whoever the hell he was, had played me for a fool. He'd gotten close enough to frame me to prove a point. I wasn't safe anywhere. Now my only choice was to face him—alone.

"What are you saying? You made him up?"

I looked at Yuri and nodded. "Yes."

His eyes narrowed to slits. "I don't believe that."

"Kelly did."

The billionaire allowed a hint of shock to show on his face. "Then he's not the man I thought he was."

Though I shared Yuri's sentiment, I didn't voice it aloud. Instead, I peeled the black hair elastic from my wrist and gathered my messy locks into a bun. "I'll be out of here by lunch."

"No," Yuri said quickly. "I don't think that's a very good idea."

"I wasn't asking, Yuri. I need to get out of here. I need to get back out on my own."

"I don't like it. Your building isn't safe."

"It's not my building anymore."

"What?"

"I sold it to John Hagen."

"The loan shark?" he practically gasped. "Why would you...?" Realization dawned. "For Kelly?"

I nodded. "For Kelly."

Swearing in Russian, Yuri shot to his feet and sifted his fingers through his hair. After a few seconds of intense thought, he turned back to me. "You will hire new guards and stay here at the penthouse."

"No."

"Beatrice—"

"No, Yuri. I don't need guards, and I don't need to stay here. I'll couch surf or find a hotel room. Hell, maybe I'll finally go on vacation."

"I don't think you should travel alone."

Not wanting to argue with him, I said, "You're probably right."

"And yet I doubt you're actually going to listen to me."

"I'll try."

He harrumphed and changed the subject. "Have you heard from Trevor or his lawyer?"

I shook my head. "I expect him to contact me today."

"The sooner that situation is neatly tied up, the better."

"Agreed."

"Why don't you take a shower and get dressed? I'll take you out for breakfast."

"To talk business? Yuri, I don't have it in me this morning. Frankly, the whole damn company could implode, and I wouldn't give a shit."

"I know." He gave my shoulder a squeeze. "That's why it's good to be the boss. You can't get fired for skipping a day of work."

I laughed. "So what? We're playing hooky? And do what?"

"Do you like miniature golf?"

218

"Are you serious?" I honestly couldn't tell.

"Get dressed, and you'll find out."

Befuddled by the strange turn my morning had taken, I trudged back to the master suite. It wasn't until I stepped into the bathroom and spotted Kelly's forgotten toothbrush on the counter next to mine that a fresh wave of agonizing heartache engulfed me. Turning on the shower to mask my ragged sobs, I hastily stripped and stepped under the hot blast of water.

Even there, in the confines of the shower, I couldn't escape the memories of my fleeting relationship with Kelly. With tears running down my face, I remembered the feel of his rough, strong hands gliding over my naked skin. The things we had done in this shower!

And I would never experience them with him again.

I hadn't been kidding when I said goodbye. Standing there in that living room and realizing that he didn't have any faith in me was too much. In that moment, I had known what it truly felt like to be alone.

I could already feel my heart hardening toward him and any other man. To go from the utter joy of love to this despondent ache of heartbreak was a sensation I never again wanted to experience. In time, I hoped to teach myself that I didn't need anyone. I had built a multi-billion dollar company on my own. I could build a life on my own too.

But as I combed my wet hair and gazed upon my reflection in the mirror, I understood that my angry vows were empty. I could no more live the rest of my life alone than I could go without breathing.

And I missed Kelly. I missed him terribly.

* * *

Kelly missed Bee so damn much. The knotted, throbbing ball of pain in his gut hadn't eased once in the week since he had walked out of the penthouse. So many times he had picked up his phone or driven by the downtown skyscraper. Some cowardly impulse stopped him from following through on his desire to contact her. He didn't know what to say to her.

The very real possibility that they couldn't move beyond this goat-rope of a situation paralyzed him from acting. The smallest bit of hope that someday, somehow, he could figure out how to fix this prevented him from tracking her down and confirming that their relationship was broken beyond repair.

As he hopped from foot to foot inside the sparring ring, he couldn't stop thinking about her. Unable to concentrate on his opponent, he missed a signal and took a nasty hit to the jaw. Blinking hard, he stumbled backward. His opponent hooked Kelly's ankle and tripped him.

Dazed, Kelly was vaguely aware of Alexei shouting for the other guy to stop. The Russian trainer stalked across the ring and crouched down next to him. He pried Kelly's mouth guard off his teeth and stared down at him. "You okay?"

"Yeah." Kelly pushed up onto his palms and waited for his vision to clear. "I'm fine."

"You're a bad liar." Alexei dropped his mouth guard onto his shorts. "We're done for tonight."

"We don't need to stop. I just need to clear my head."

"I suspect it's going to take more than a few minutes to clear your head."

He stared up at his coach. "What's that supposed to mean?"

"It means you're thinking about your girl—and that's

dangerous." Alexei held up four fingers. "You fight in four nights. You need to get your shit straight or else you're going to get hurt."

He didn't tell Alexei that he was already hurting.

"You want my advice?"

"Not really," Kelly grumbled.

Alexei chuckled and lightly kicked Kelly's foot. "Let it go until after the fight."

He glanced up at his trainer. "Let it go?"

"You love this woman, yes?"

Even after everything she had done, he still loved her. "Yes."

"And she loves you?"

"I don't know."

Alexei studied him. "If she does, she'll forgive you for whatever mistake you've made."

Kelly frowned up at him. "Whatever mistake *I* made?"

The Russian shrugged. "Call it a hunch."

"*She* lied to *me*."

"So?"

Kelly blinked. "So she lied. She made up this whole story about a stalker and—"

"And you came running to save her, yes?"

"Yes," he groused.

"And this made you feel good? It made you feel like a man? It made you realize how much you love her?"

Kelly swallowed hard. "Yeah."

"So what's the problem, Kelly?"

Alexei's line of question shook him right up. "Take my advice, Kelly. Let it go for a few days. Finish the tournament, and then go find her. Once she sees that someone else already beat the shit out of you, she'll forget how mad she is and forgive you."

Kelly wasn't so sure that taking romantic advice from

Alexei was a smart idea. Of course, he'd already fucked things up so badly himself he was grasping at straws here.

"I've already spoken to Jack about your morning workout. We'll start weaning you down every morning until the fight, okay? I want you limber and conditioned but not tired. Tonight was the last sparring session." Alexei bent down and clapped Kelly's back. "Get a good night's sleep."

"He's right, you know," Finn said as he helped Kelly out of his gloves and helmet a short time later. "Whatever mistakes Bee made, they aren't important. You two have loved each other for years. Forgiveness is a powerful thing, Kelly."

"Jesus," Kelly said gruffly, "don't start on that Twelve Steps forgiveness bullshit, Finn. I can't take it tonight."

Finn slapped the sparring gloves against his chest hard enough that Kelly winced. "I understand why Bee threw you out on your ass now. You can be such an asshole sometimes." Walking away with his slight limp, Finn called over his shoulder, "It must be nice to be so fucking perfect, Kelly."

Feeling lower than mud, Kelly watched his brother disappear into the office he shared with Jack. The quip about Twelve Steps was way out of line, especially after everything Finn had overcome to find sobriety and peace after losing his leg.

"Man, you are on a roll this week," Jack announced with a bit of sadness in his voice. "You better watch it, brother. You're going to wake up one of these days and have no one left in your corner." Taking the sparring gloves and helmet from him, Jack quietly added, "Take it from me, Kelly. It's a lonely place to be."

Alone in the gym, Kelly felt like a boat lost and adrift at sea. There was no course correction he could make that would fix things.

The sudden yearning to speak to Jeb knocked the breath right out of him. How long had it been since he'd wanted to hear his best friend's voice this badly? In those months following Jeb's death, Kelly had secretly listened to a saved voicemail a thousand times at least. It was nothing more than Jeb chastising him for being late to a pickup football game, but it had brought him such peace.

He'd finally let that recording go almost two years earlier. Now, more than ever, he wished he had kept it. The comforting sound of Jeb's voice would have been priceless tonight.

Thinking of Bee's older brother, he wondered if this was why that unspoken rule about dating little sisters of friends existed. Bee had counted on him to be her support, to be her rock, after Jeb had died. After tempting fate and crossing that line, Kelly had taken away her last remaining tie to Jeb.

Berating himself for not being stronger when it came to Bee, Kelly gathered up his things and left the gym without stopping in to say goodnight to his brothers. He would see them in the morning, over breakfast, and make his apologies then. As for Bee?

He decided to go with the Russian on that one. Alexei had made one point very clear to Kelly. If he went into this tournament all torn up inside, he was going to make an even worse mistake than the one he had made sparring earlier. Except there wouldn't be padded gloves and a helmet to protect him on Friday night.

If he went to her tonight, and she rejected him or refused to let him try to make things right, he didn't know if he could get his head right again before that first fight. He could get hurt—seriously hurt—if his head was all messed up with Bee.

Deciding it was time to go into survival mode, Kelly started to compartmentalize his emotions. He stowed away all the troubling, painful thoughts of Bee. As the numbness spread through his belly and filtered through his chest, Kelly prayed she wouldn't give up on him before Saturday night.

Because once he had settled his father's debts, broken bones, black eyes, and a concussion wouldn't be enough to stop him from seeing her.

CHAPTER SIXTEEN

Perched on a crate behind the hastily arranged DJ station inside the airplane hangar, I watched the wild crowd dancing to Coby's music. To reward my team and celebrate the offer for LookIt I had accepted earlier that morning from Insight, I had rented out the empty hangar and arranged the sort of party that could only be described as epic. It was nice to see my hardworking employees cutting loose with their friends. They all deserved it.

As I sipped some tequila sweetened with a bit of pineapple juice, I caught sight of Ty Weston weaving his way toward me. He indicated that he wanted to chat, so I hopped off the crate. Before I left Coby's side, I made sure to replace her empty can of that caffeine crazy energy drink she loved so much with a new, cold one. She bumped my hip in a sign of thanks.

Out on the makeshift dance floor, I let Ty drag me into a dance. The slight buzz from the tequila lowered my inhibitions enough that I didn't feel as self-conscious as I normally did when dancing. Unlike some of the couples around us who were rubbing together in ways that were absolutely scandalous, we managed to dance without being trashy.

Laughing and breathing hard, Ty gripped my hand and dragged me off the dance floor to a quieter spot in a corner. "I'm so happy for you, sugar. Really. I'm *thrilled* this deal went through for you."

Teasing him, I smacked his arm. "You're just excited about the big fat bonus check your firm is about to receive for helping me through that crisis with Trevor."

He didn't even try to pretend that wasn't the case. "So maybe I went window shopping for a private jet earlier..."

I rolled my eyes. "Your bonus is going to be nice, but it's not *that* nice."

When his laughter died, he more seriously asked, "Did Trevor's lawyer call you today?"

"He did."

"And?"

"And he said the contract and the hard copies of the emails and photos Trevor had managed to salvage from Jeb's account showed up at his office via a courier. He's tried calling him, but Trevor doesn't answer. He's basically vanished."

"But you hadn't paid him yet, right?"

"Right," I confirmed. An uneasy feeling invaded my chest. "It's weird, right?"

"Very," Ty agreed. "Maybe he finally grew a conscience."

"Doubtful," I replied dryly.

"So," Ty said carefully and rubbed my bare upper arm, "how are you doing?"

"I'm doing okay." I figured okay was the best way to describe my current state. I hadn't had a crying jag in nearly two days, and I considered that a huge improvement.

"He still hasn't tried to contact you?"

"No." The reminder of the way Kelly had so easily cut ties with me was like splashing acid on an open wound. "I don't think he's going to, either."

"I'm really sorry, Bee. I thought...well. I guess it doesn't matter what I thought."

I shrugged as if I didn't care and pasted a smile on my face. "That's life, I guess."

"First love is a bitch," Ty said sagely. "It's always the hardest one to get over too. Give it some time. You'll wake up one day and realize he no longer has any hold over you."

I didn't think that was possible. I had been head-over-heels crazy for Kelly for so long that the fleeting taste of love with him was enough to crush my freaking soul.

Desperate to change the subject, I asked, "Where's that Russian bear of yours?"

"Oh, Big Poppa is hanging out with his people tonight."

Ty's nickname for Vasya made me giggle. "His people, huh?"

Ty hesitated before admitting, "He's watching the fights."

"Oh." My stomach clenched with dread. "Has he said anything?"

Ty shook his head. "He knows I don't approve of them." He paused. "I could text him and see how it's going."

"No, that's okay. I'm actually in touch with Finn. He promised to let me know how it goes later tonight."

"Good." Ty tugged on my hand. "Come on. You need to dance more."

"Why? Is that part of a cure for a broken heart?"

"Well—that and tequila, sugar."

The rest of the night passed in a blur of dancing and tequila. When I finally managed to extricate myself from Ty's clutches to sneak behind the DJ station with Coby, I ducked down under her table of equipment to grab my cell phone from my purse. I had a message waiting for me from Finn. All that tequila sloshed around in my stomach as I tapped at my screen. Even though Kelly had broken my heart, I prayed he was safe.

Two wins. One K.O. One tap-out.

Relieved, I noted the time stamp on the text. It had arrived on my phone half an hour earlier so I went ahead and replied to Finn.

Glad to hear he won. Is he okay?

While I waited for Finn to answer, I swiped one of the bottles of water from Coby's stash and took a long drink of the cold, refreshing fluid. Wearing a crop top and skirt had been a good choice. With the summer heat and the bodies packed into the hangar, the temp was getting uncomfortable in the huge metal building even with the air conditioner blasting.

My phone vibrated in my hand.

He's good. Bruised but nothing broken. Except his heart—the hardheaded bastard.

Smiling at Finn's reply, I allowed the tiniest glimmer of hope to spark in my chest. Maybe, in time, Kelly and I could get back to the way it was. Forgiving him for doubting me wasn't going to be easy. I mean—he was going to have to do some *serious* groveling.

But I wanted to try. I really, really did.

My phone buzzed again. Thinking it was Finn, I glanced at the screen and noticed it was from a different phone number. I tapped the screen and waited for the message to load. My fingers tightened around my phone, and I glanced around anxiously.

My stalker was somewhere in the crowd surrounding me. The photo on my screen had been taken only a few seconds earlier. He had captured me taking a drink of water while standing close to Coby.

You look so hot, baby. I'd love to help you cool off.

Gulping nervously, I let my finger hover above the keyboard before finally working up the courage to make the next move. Sick and tired of being hunted like prey, I thought of the loaded handgun in my purse. I didn't want to take it *that* far, but I wanted this to end. I wanted to vindicate myself. I wanted my life back.

Certain I could protect myself, I decided it was time for a face-to-face with this creep. *I want to meet you.*

You pick a time and place. I'll be there.

The safest place I could imagine popped into my head. After I sent the time and place, I dropped my phone back into my backpack and joined Coby behind her equipment. She shot me a questioning glance, but I smiled at her to set her at ease.

Looking out over the dancing crowd, I wondered if my stalker was staring right back at me. Was he watching from the shadows?

A chill raced down my spine. What the hell had I done?

* * *

Trying to think about anything but the low, throbbing ache permeating every single cell in his already bruised and battered body, Kelly mentally psyched himself up for his third fight. He had been insanely lucky on Friday night. The two fighters he had drawn were damn good, but they were sloppy.

Facing off against them, he had been incredibly grateful for every minute of the agony Alexei had put him through during the preceding three weeks. The first man he had managed to put down within the first minute. One perfectly placed punch had dropped the paunchy man to the concrete floor and saved Kelly from the punishment of a full five rounds.

The second man, one of those lightning bolt tattooed freaks from the white supremacist camp, had taken considerably more effort to beat. They'd gone three brutal rounds in the cage before Kelly had seized upon an opening and taken him down to the ground. A submission hold that put extreme pressure on the man's leg had been enough to make him surrender.

"Shit!" Kelly hissed as Jack massaged the knotted muscle running between his shoulders.

"Sorry, bro." Jack didn't stop working the tender spot. After his warm-up, Kelly still struggled with tightness there. "You'll thank me later."

"I doubt it." Kelly watched Finn check and recheck their bag of supplies before he filled the sinks with even more ice to chill his body between matches. If he won against his next opponent, he would end up fighting Sergei—and he needed to be in the best shape possible if he had any chance of winning.

An uproarious cry from the crowd exploded in the abandoned meatpacking plant. Kelly's gaze drifted to the open door of the room where they had been stashed by the organizers. Right now, Sergei was in the ring. That sound could only mean one thing.

"Forget about it," Jack urged and gave the back of Kelly's neck a squeeze. "Focus on your fight."

Alexei came into the room, but his face remained an unreadable mask of calmness. He shut the door behind him, dampening the excited roar of the crowd. Coming over to the bench where Kelly sat, Alexei crouched down in front of him. "Okay. Here's the deal. Midnight, the guy you're fighting, he has a nasty injury to his right arm and shoulder."

"Are you suggesting I go out there and wail on his arm?"

"Do you want to step into the cage against Sergei with half your energy burned up?"

"No."

"Then get the fuck in that cage and break Midnight's arm," Alexei growled. "You have to win this match fast. You need to conserve your energy and protect your body."

Kelly didn't like it, but he understood Alexei spoke the truth. Out on the main floor of the factory, another chilling roar erupted from the crowd. A few seconds later, someone raced down the hallway outside their room, shouting for an ambulance.

"No." Alexei lightly smacked his face. "We don't care what happens to anyone else. We only care about what happens to you. Yes?"

Kelly nodded. "Yes."

"Good."

The door opened and a man poked his head inside. "Five minutes, Alexei."

With Alexei leading the way and his brothers flanking him, Kelly left the safety of the warm-up room. Out in the hallway, he flattened against the wall as two men with a backboard rushed the downed fighter into the night. Kelly couldn't help but wonder if the man would end up in an ambulance—or simply dumped in the parking lot of the closest emergency room.

Tonight the crowd of spectators was much heavier and thicker than the Friday night fights. He spotted some familiar faces in the crowd—Dimitri, Winn, Sully, Lev, Yuri, and even Hagen. Besian and his crew had a prominent place directly across from the spot Nikolai and his men had taken. He shuddered to think how much money was on the books tonight. There were going to be some very flush men walking out of this empty warehouse.

Kelly wouldn't be one of them. His brothers had some action on his fights, but every penny they might win would go toward settling their debt with Besian. They had agreed that anything left over would go to Bee to repay her for settling the loan against the gym.

As he watched Midnight enter the ring, Kelly couldn't help himself. He pictured Bee's sweet, smiling face. Earlier that morning, he had seen news of her successful sale to Insight pop up on the tech blogs. From what he had gleaned from the articles, she had gotten everything she had wanted. He was so happy for her.

But—God help him—he missed her so much. He couldn't wait for these damn fights to be over so he could seek her out and try to make amends for everything that had gone badly between them.

Remembering Alexei's tip about Midnight, Kelly carefully eyed his opponent. The tall, dark man was trying to project a cool, relaxed façade but Kelly wasn't fooled. He easily read the tightness in the man's face as a sign of pain. His right shoulder sat a bit lower than the left and he kept the fingers of that hand loosely curled.

Tapping fists with Midnight, Kelly inhaled a steadying breath. Even though it felt like shit, he made up his mind right then and there that he was going after that injured arm. Midnight seemed to instinctively know that was Kelly's tactic, because he came out kicking.

Kelly blocked the first couple of kicks but took a graze to his ribs. He sucked in a sharp breath but ignored the burst of pain. He slammed his fist into Midnight's temple and followed with another blow to his jaw. When

Midnight stumbled backward, Kelly wrapped his arms around the man's waist, used his brute strength to lift him up and slammed him down onto the pavement, making sure to put the force of the take-down on that right shoulder.

Midnight screamed out in pain but didn't tap-out. He knocked his knuckles into Kelly's temple twice. Deciding he had taken just about enough of this bullshit, Kelly swiveled his hips and kicked his legs into the perfect position. With his calf against Midnight's neck, Kelly trapped the man's wounded arm between his thighs and jerked hard. Midnight shouted again but wouldn't surrender, so Kelly applied even more pressure.

Only when the man's shoulder started to slip from its socket did Midnight finally tap-out. The second the referee ended the match, Kelly released the big man's arm and tried to help him stand. Midnight refused his help, smacking Kelly in the face and spitting at him.

Sucking in a shuddery breath, the big man rolled to his knees and shot Kelly the finger. "Fuck you."

Kelly let the insult roll of his back. The guy was in pain, and he'd probably just lost a shit-ton of money for his sponsors.

Turning away from his opponent, Kelly rejoined his brothers and trainer, and returned to their room. Finn iced Kelly's hands while Jack pushed fluids and applied a frigid enswell to the bruises forming on his cheeks. The shocking cold metal square pressed to his skin made Kelly wince.

"You've got to remember to set the pace with Sergei," Jack instructed. "You let him control the fight, and you're fucked."

"Jack is right," Alexei agreed. "Listen, his last fight was a tough one. Sergei is tired. You need to wear him down even more, and then strike."

Before he was ready, Kelly was summoned to the cage for the final round. He jogged in place and swung his arms back and forth to loosen up his muscles. The burning ache along his already swollen knuckles was only going to get worse, so he decided to pretend his hands didn't exist.

Back out in the cage, Kelly shifted his weight and sized up his opponent. The giant Russian looked unnaturally calm. Considering how many times he fought in this cage every year, Kelly wasn't surprised. A rush of adrenaline surged through Kelly's veins. His fingertips buzzed as his heart rate ticked up a few notches, and his breaths grew shallow and fast.

Alexei massaged his shoulders while giving him some final pointers. Across the cage, Ivan Markovic did the same thing for Sergei. Kelly didn't miss the similar tattoos both trainers shared. What was it like for two old friends to stand across the ring from each other now?

"Work your kicks, Kelly." Alexei stepped in front of him and forced a shared gaze. "For the love of God, watch those legs. Sergei has a kick that will break you if you aren't careful. *Da*?"

"Yeah. I hear you."

Alexei affectionately rubbed the back of Kelly's head. "Good luck."

The referee summoned the two fighters to the center of the cage. Standing in front of Sergei, Kelly was forced to stare up at the man. He bristled at the unwelcome sensation of smallness Sergei inspired. The Russian looked unhappy to be there and reluctantly knocked fists with Kelly.

"I'm sorry for what I'm about to do to you."

It had been a long fucking time since Kelly had

experienced a quiver of fear. Normally, it took the snap and whiz of bullets flying past his head to force that sensation. Tonight, the look in Sergei's eyes was enough.

The bell clanged—and the brutal battle began.

The two men danced around in a circle, shifting their weight from foot to foot while waiting for a perfect opening. Kelly struck first, catching Sergei on the chin, and managing to knock the Russian's head back. His brief victory was short-lived. Sergei returned the blow, punching Kelly right in the mouth.

The bastard hit like a fucking truck. Dazed by the blow, Kelly shook off the blast of pain and hastily side-stepped another wicked punch. He crashed his fist into Sergei's ribs twice and slammed his knee into the Russian's stomach, earning a deep *oof* from the giant man.

When Kelly tried to shove his knee into Sergei's gut a second time, the Russian fighter grabbed his leg and jerked hard. Yanked off balance, Kelly fell backward and hit the concrete hard. He caught the brunt of his fall on his ass, sparing his head from the worst of it.

Sergei tried to pin him to the ground but Kelly kicked his feet and rolled his hips to evade the other man. He narrowly escaped a hold and clambered to his feet. Before Sergei could stand, Kelly buried his foot in the man's side. Sergei growled and snatched Kelly's leg. Only the blast of the air horn saved Kelly from another ugly fall.

Seated on a stool in the corner of the cage, Kelly tried to catch his breath while Jack wiped his bloody face and tended his injuries. Alexei barked commands. "Good! Good! Keep trading punches with him. Wear him down. In and out, Kelly. Shoot on him, yes?"

Kelly couldn't speak. He simply nodded.

Too soon, he was called back to the center of the cage. The second round proved to be even more brutal and bloody than the first. He traded punches and kicks with the other man. One of Sergei's kicks caught Kelly's thigh. The force behind it probably would have cracked a tree trunk, and it left Kelly limping as they entered their third round.

Judging by the look on Sergei's face, the Russian fighter couldn't believe Kelly had lasted this long. Nikolai's champion breathed heavily but seemed far from worn out. Kelly didn't know how much more fight he had in him. Somehow, he would dig deep and find the energy, but he didn't know if he had enough steam left to take Sergei down.

As the men traded hits, Kelly landed a good kick that sent Sergei stumbling backward. Kelly pounced on the opening and enveloped Sergei in a bear hug. He drove the other man into the wall of the cage, the noisy metallic clatter swallowed by the din of the crown.

Using his brute strength, Sergei peeled one of Kelly's hands from his body. The Russian jammed his elbow into Kelly's ribs, the blow so painful that Kelly's lungs deflated and he tottered on his feet. Sergei seized the opening and hooked his foot behind Kelly's, knocking him off balance and taking him down to the concrete.

They grappled on the ground, both men going for blood now. Kelly rocked his hips and slammed his fist into Sergei's temple. He stunned the bigger man with a few well-placed blows. Sergei's grip slackened just enough for Kelly to kick out his legs and escape the hold.

Both men scrambled to their feet. Sergei spit blood to the side of the cage while Kelly wiped the back of his hand across his sweaty, bloody face. They charged one another. Sergei got in one good punch, slamming his meaty fist into Kelly's jaw. The powerful blow left Kelly seeing spots.

Staggering on his feet, Kelly missed the incoming kick. Sergei connected with his ribs and Kelly felt the sickening crunch of bone. Unable to breathe, he gulped in air, the swell of oxygen within his lungs causing an excruciating pain along his right side.

Something in the Russian's eyes changed as he watched Kelly struggling to breathe. Sergei flew at Kelly, catching him off guard with another punch to the head before wrapping his arms around Kelly's neck and taking him to the ground. As Kelly felt the life being choked right out of him, Sergei's harsh whisper hissed in his ear. "Tap out, or I'll kill you."

It wasn't a threat but a desperate plea. Sergei seemed to recognize that Kelly would keep fighting until the very end—and Sergei was telling Kelly in the frankest terms that he would beat the life right out of him.

"Tap out!"

His vision darkened as his oxygen starved brain began to misfire. Jack slid down to the floor across the cage and shouted something at him. He couldn't make out the words, but the look on his eldest brother's face was easy to read. He wanted Kelly to surrender before it was too late.

With a shaking hand, Kelly smacked Sergei's burly forearm twice. His arm started to fall as he lost muscle control. Digging deep, he found a last burst of energy and smacked Sergei's arm a final time.

His opponent let loose immediately. The rush of blood that pounded through Kelly's brain caused him to gasp. His misfiring neurons projected strange images before him. The sight of Bee in the crowd couldn't be real, but that didn't stop his hand from reaching out to touch her phantom form.

"Bee." Her name came out on a raspy whisper.

Overwhelmed by his love for her, he sucked in a long breath—and passed out cold.

CHAPTER SEVENTEEN

My cell phone chirped and rattled on the tabletop. Taking a sip of coffee, I reached for the device and prayed it was news from Finn. My prayer was answered.

He lost, but he's alive. He passed out, but he's okay. We're at the ER getting him patched up.

I quickly typed back a reply.

Is he badly hurt?

Finn's answer came swiftly.

A few broken ribs and some cuts but nothing serious.

A few seconds later another reply landed in my inbox.

He was asking for you when he woke up.

I wasn't sure what to say to that. I didn't want to pin my hopes on anything Kelly had said after regaining consciousness. Even so, hope flared to life within me.

"You okay, Bee? You're looking a little pale."

Shifting aside my phone, I glanced up at Ron and smiled. "I'm good."

He glanced around his coffee shop. "Are you waiting for someone? It's just that you never sit here. I noticed that you keep looking at the door. Is everything okay?"

"Everything is perfectly fine," I lied.

He seemed unconvinced. "Are you sure?" Lowering his voice, he asked, "What about your stalker?"

Shaking my head, I reached for my coffee and tried to appear nonchalant. "I was mistaken, Ron. I don't have a stalker."

"Really?" His brow furrowed. "You're sure?"

"I'm positive."

"Well..." He looked toward the door again. "I would still prefer it if you let me take you home. It's not safe for you to ride your bike this late at night."

"I'm not on my bike. I took a cab."

"Let me drive you, Bee. Some of these cab guys are real weirdos."

Smiling up at him, I relented with a little nod. "All right, Ron."

"Give me twenty minutes so I can chat with my night manager and then I'll take you home."

"Great." Feeling rather lucky to have a friend like Ron, I finished off my coffee and cleaned up the table where I had set up shop earlier that evening. I sneaked a glance around the place but still didn't see anyone who fit the bill for a stalker.

A few times during the evening, I had spotted lone men who seemed a bit shifty, but none of them had tried to approach me. My phone hadn't received one single weird message or phone call. I wondered if my stalker was simply waiting for me to leave the shop so he could accost me, but the gun in my backpack and the fact that Ron was giving me a ride left me feeling mostly secure.

"Ready?" Ron gestured toward the back exit.

"Yep." With my backpack dangling from my hand, I followed him outside and across the street to the parking garage. He led me to his mid-sized SUV and opened the passenger door for me. "Thanks."

"No problem."

I tucked my backpack between my feet and fastened my seatbelt. Ron climbed into the driver's seat and started his vehicle. "Where are we going?"

"To my building," I said. "Well...it's mine for a few more weeks, at least."

Ron glanced at me with surprise. "You sold it?"

"Yes." Not wanting to get into the specifics, I said, "I decided I wanted a more downtown location."

"Do you have a new spot picked out yet?"

"No, but I have a realtor looking for suitable properties."

"I hope you find something quickly. After that Insight deal, I imagine you're ready to move into your own space and expand JBJ."

"You have no idea."

He chuckled and reached out to fiddle with the stereo controls. When he adjusted the volume, I heard the opening bars of a song I'd had on repeat for most of the day. "Hey! That's my favorite song. You know, right now."

Ron laughed and switched lanes. "Yeah, I know. Every time I swing by your table, I hear it blaring out of those ear buds of yours." He shot a look my way. "You really should turn down the volume before you damage your ear drums."

"You sound like Hadley. She's always on Coby's case and mine about the volume of our music."

As we idled at a red light a few blocks down, the song I loved faded off and a new song began. It surprised me to hear another song from my current playlist. Deciding it was a coincidence, I didn't mention it to him. The song was high enough on the charts that lots of people had it on their playlists right now.

Saddened by how paranoid I had become, I glanced at Ron. He looked like his usual calm, cool self as he tapped his fingers against the steering wheel. Hating the effect my stalker had on me, I wished he had been gutsy enough to come see me at the coffee shop. It would have been empowering to look him in the eyes and tell him to go fuck himself.

When we reached my building, Ron offered to walk me upstairs. I'd switched security companies and had the locks changed on my apartment so I was reasonably assured of my safety. Still, it felt nice to have Ron escort me inside. He even went so far as to check the rooms and closets, just in case.

"Okay. I think you're good, Bee."

"Thanks again, Ron."

"I'm happy to do it."

When he stepped toward me and awkwardly opened his arms, I was momentarily taken aback. Ron had never initiated any sort of touch with me. Pleased by his progress with this quirk, I was more than happy to let him hug me.

But he held the embrace a bit too long. I wasn't certain if it was because he seemed to be new to this whole hugging thing or if maybe I'd read the situation wrong somewhere along the line. Was Ron attracted to me? Because the hand gently rubbing my back didn't feel strictly platonic.

Not wanting to hurt his feelings in case I was wrong, I let him end the embrace and stepped back to smile at him. Rather than ask him if our wires had crossed somewhere, I decided to let it slide. From now on, I would be more careful around him so he wouldn't get the wrong idea about our friendship.

"Night, Ron." I stood in the doorway and bid him farewell.

"Good night, Bee."

Closing the door, I made my way to the bathroom. I wanted a nice, hot shower before bed, so I started to strip. While I stood under the pounding spray, I began making mental lists of all the packing that needed to be done. The movers I had used were fantastic, so I would definitely hire them again. Of course, I still needed to find a place, even if it was temporary. Coby and Hadley had offered my old bedroom back, but I felt like I needed to stay on my own for a while.

Wearing only a towel, I left the bathroom—and froze stiff at the shockingly unexpected sight before me.

Lit candles had been placed all around my bedroom. The flickering flames spilled a glowing warmth around the room. Soft music played in the background and blush pink rose petals had been scattered over my sheets and the hardwood floors.

Panic squeezed my heart. What. The. Fuck.

And then I saw him.

Stripped down to his boxers, Ron stepped out of the shadows. "Good evening, Beatrice."

Clenching the front of my towel, I swallowed hard. "Ron, what are you doing?"

The question sounded so stupid to me. It was painfully obvious what he was doing—and what he was.

His eyes seemed different as he strode toward me. They had lost their usual warmth and friendliness to morph into such chilling, cold orbs. In one hand, he held some sort of lacy lingerie. In the other, he grasped my gun, the gun I knew for a fact was loaded.

"I waited so long for you to give me a sign." His creepy smile made the hairs on my arms stand straight up. "So long, baby."

Baby? I bit back the urge to call him a fucking nutcase because he had that gun in his hand. "You sent me those photos and the text messages."

"Yes."

"You put them in my backpack and on my car."

"I did."

Thinking of my housewarming party, I said, "You stole my panties during my party, didn't you?"

"Yes."

Remembering the mornings he had delivered coffee to my office, I inwardly groaned. "You put those phones in my backpack to get my guards to leave."

"They were standing between us. It was time for them to go."

Wondering how the hell I had missed what a total freak he was, I asked, "Why didn't you simply tell me how you felt about me, Ron? Why all the subterfuge?"

"I wanted to speak to you in the way you spoke to me," he said, as if I were the dumbest woman on the planet. "Your photos and your blogs," he added. "I knew you were speaking to me. I wanted to show you that I understand you, that I know what you need. I wanted our courtship to be a true courtship of the 21st century."

He was a straight-up psycho—with a gun. It occurred to me that if I wanted to survive, I had to do whatever I could to keep him calm and happy.

"Take off your towel, Busy Bee."

Clenching the damp fabric even tighter, I asked anxiously, "Why?"

"Because I want to see you," he said matter-of-factly.

The muzzle of the gun inched higher. I didn't dare refuse him. With trembling fingers, I tugged on the front of the towel and let it fall around my feet. Ron's hungry gaze raked my naked curves. I'd never felt so uncomfortable or so frightened. When I spotted the growing bulge in the front of his boxers, I wanted to puke.

Ron moved even closer. Wrapping the lingerie around

his fingertips, he used the silk and lace to caress my bare breast. Somewhat breathlessly, he whispered, "You're so beautiful, Bee. More beautiful than I had imagined."

Even though his touch sickened me, I desperately wanted to keep him happy, especially with that gun so close. "Thank you."

His cloth covered fingertips glided toward my nipple. He brushed the puckered peek gently at first but then pinched it hard enough to make me gasp with pain. "You shouldn't have defiled your body with that Marine."

A tear slid down my cheek as the stabbing pain of having my nipple twisted amplified the terror I felt. He released my aching flesh and caressed the bright red splotch he'd created. "What's wrong, sweetness?"

Realizing I had to play along with his fantasy to stay alive, I said, "I'm just sad that you weren't my first."

He looked absolutely touched by my statement. "Oh, my love, that's all right. You didn't know I was waiting for you. That's my fault. I should have been clearer."

Leaning forward, he pressed his lips to mine. I forced myself not to recoil from his unwanted kiss. He seemed to buy my interest in him and petted my cheek. "Once I'm finished with you tonight, you'll never want another man."

He couldn't have been more wrong. As he took my hand and led me toward the bed, I had never, ever wanted Kelly more.

* * *

Smarting from the epic loss to Sergei and aching with discomfort, Kelly shifted in the front passenger seat of Jack's truck. He winced as the drive-thru attendant shouted through the speaker to confirm his brothers' order. His own stomach wouldn't allow him to eat anything right now, but Jack shoved a cup of coffee at him anyway.

Scratching numbers on a piece of paper, Finn finally piped up from the backseat. "We should have maybe twenty thousand left over to put toward the debt to Bee. It's not much, but it's a start."

At the mention of her name, Kelly experienced the deepest pang of longing. "Take me to the penthouse, Jack."

His oldest brother glanced at him as they passed through an intersection. "You think this is a good time to see Bee? You can barely walk, Kelly."

"I need to see her."

Finn leaned forward and cautiously touched his shoulder. "She's not at the penthouse."

"What?" Kelly tried to twist in his seat for a better look at his brother, but the movement caused him to grimace with pain. "Where is she?"

"Back in her apartment," Finn said. "Hagen agreed to give her a few weeks to find a new place before he takes it over."

"And you know this how?" Jealousy raced through him at the idea that Bee had contacted Finn but not him.

"We've been keeping in touch," Finn admitted. "She was worried about you."

Gingerly rubbing his throbbing forehead, Kelly murmured, "I'm worried about her."

Without a word, Jack switched lanes. Grateful for his brothers' support, Kelly brought the cup of coffee to his lips and tried to figure out what the hell he was going to say to Bee. He didn't even know where to start. She had screwed up massively, but he wasn't blameless in this situation.

The first sip of the scalding hot coffee made him gag. Pushing the cup into the nearest holder, he shuddered as he swallowed the bitter mouthful. "I've gotten spoiled by Ron's coffee. That shit tastes like swill."

"Who?" Jack asked as he turned at an intersection.

"Bee's friend," Kelly explained. "He owns her favorite coffee shop. She likes to go there to work in the evenings." Stretching his cramping fingers, he added, "He made deliveries to her office. Best damn coffee I've ever had."

As Jack and Finn debated the best place to get a late night breakfast in Houston, Kelly stared out the windshield. His fuzzy brain jumbled his thoughts together. Memories of the last three weeks flashed before him, melding together into a bizarre and incoherent stream of conscious.

Something about that first morning at Bee's building stuck in his mind. An image of that residue on the door raced before his eyes. Winn's voice rattled through his brain. *Spike says it's a mix of cocoa, powdered sugar and coffee. Maybe it's someone who works in a bakery or restaurant...*

"Or a coffee shop."

"What?" Jack looked at him like he'd lost his damn mind. "Are you okay?"

Kelly wasn't sure. He braced his head between his hands and tried to make sense of his thoughts. "There was a stain on Bee's door from that break-in."

"That wasn't a break-in," Jack reminded him. "She faked it, remember?"

"Did she?" Kelly's stomach soured as he considered that maybe it wasn't Bee who had played them. "There was brown residue on her door, just a smudge. Spike couldn't get a fingerprint but he said it was a mixture of cocoa, powdered sugar and coffee. We thought maybe it was from someone who worked in a restaurant until we found those phones in Bee's backpack. After that, we assumed she had left the smudge after eating some of that coffee cake she loves so much."

"And now?" Finn sat forward again. "What are you thinking?"

The memories of the night he had discovered the phones blasted his brain. "No one got close to her that wasn't vetted. She wasn't ever out of our sight. When we found the phones, we assumed she was setting up the stalker thing—but what if it was someone we had already been vetted."

"Like who?" Jack asked, his voice tight.

"Ron," Kelly said, as the pieces fell into place. "He had access to her office every morning. He could have easily dropped them into her backpack." Cringing at his stupidity, Kelly added, "She would never have noticed him putting things in her bag while she was at the coffee shop either. He's her friend. She trusts him."

A blue glow lit up the backseat as Finn tapped at his phone's screen. "Shit. She was at the coffee shop earlier tonight. She tagged it in an update of hers."

Kelly swore under his breath. "I told her to stop doing that. It's not safe."

"What if she was trying to draw her stalker out?" Jack shot him a worried glance as he punched the gas.

Kelly's heart raced. "She wouldn't do that. She's way too smart to do something so risky."

"Normally, I'd agree with you." Jack swiftly maneuvered around a car slowing their pace. "But she's backed into a corner, Kelly. You didn't believe her. She has no bodyguards. She's on her own."

"And you gave her a gun," Finn interjected. "It might

give her a false sense of security. Sure, she knows how to shoot it, but that's only a small part of self-defense."

Panic clutched Kelly's heart. What the fuck had he done? If something happened to her, he'd never forgive himself. He had sworn to Jeb he would look after her, but he'd abandoned her. *Some hero you are*, he thought angrily.

When Jack squealed around the corner and Bee's building came into view, Kelly immediately spotted their father's silver clunker parked down the road.

"What the hell is Pop doing here?" Finn asked, incredulous.

"I think he's been following Bee." Kelly flicked off his seatbelt as Jack slowed to a stop. "How else would he have known Bee visited Hagen?"

"Hopefully, the old man finagled his way inside and is babysitting her," Jack muttered as he slid out of the front seat.

Out on the sidewalk, they hustled to the side entrance of Bee's building. The sight of the door propped open with a rock made them break into a sprint. Without a word, they rushed into the building and headed straight for the elevator.

Realizing it was malfunctioning, Kelly hurried to the stairs. The prospect of climbing eight flights after the beating he'd taken wasn't one that thrilled him, but he had to get to Bee. Thinking of his brother's prosthesis, Kelly glanced back at Finn who waved them on.

"Go," he urged. "I'll call the police and catch up with you."

Ignoring the agonizing pain that accompanied every single breath and every single step, Kelly mounted the stairs as if the fires of hell nipped at his heels. He thought only of reaching Bee and whisking her away to safety.

Just as they cleared the fifth floor, a gunshot cracked

upstairs. A soul chilling shriek tore through the building. A few seconds later, another gunshot blasted their eardrums. There was another scream, this one longer and even more frightened.

Sheer fucking terror clutched his heart. It was Bee. Someone was hurting *his* Bee.

And someone was about to die.

CHAPTER EIGHTEEN

Nervously eying the bed, I clutched Ron's hand and offered him my most flirtatious smile. "Ron, there's no need to rush this."

He dropped the lingerie onto the mattress and cupped my face. "You don't need to be nervous, sweetness. I'll be gentle with you."

The cold metal muzzle of the gun nipped at my hip. I tried to suppress the panic threatening to overwhelm me. I couldn't fake interest or attraction to him if he started to touch me intimately. He would know that I was lying, and then what? Would he react violently?

"Close your eyes, baby." Ron's fingertips touched my eyelid. "Let me make you feel good."

Not daring to deny him any request, I clenched my eyes tightly shut and choked back the sob threatening to erupt from my throat. When his lips touched my neck, I flinched and bit my lower lip. He misinterpreted my flinch as excitement and flicked his tongue against my skin. The sensation sent shivers of absolute disgust through my core.

My eyes fluttered open—and I nearly fainted at the sight of a man's shadowy figure in the doorway of my bedroom. The man stepped forward and revealed himself to me.

My God! It was Nick Connolly!

251

Kelly's father gripped a baseball bat in one hand and brought a finger to his lips, urging me to be silent. I didn't know how the hell Nick Connolly had gotten into my building but I really didn't care. He was my only chance to escape being raped and murdered by Ron.

I mouthed one word of warning to him—*gun*. He nodded his understanding and started to slowly stalk toward us. Desperate to buy him some time, I slid my arms around Ron. Though it made me sick to encourage him, I surrendered to my survival instincts. I would do anything to walk out of here alive.

"Kiss me," I whispered with faked need.

"Oh, Bee," he murmured against my lips. I managed not to stiffen when his tongue touched the seam of my mouth. Eyes wide open as he kissed me, I watched Nick inching closer and closer. I shut my eyes and shifted just to the side, clearing my body from the danger zone of that gun.

Ron suddenly went rigid in my arms. Had he felt Nick's approach? Or was it the subtle pulse of air as the bat swung toward his head?

It didn't matter. My stalker had no time to react or evade the oncoming assault. As the bat connected with his head, Ron's finger jerked against the trigger. The weapon fired into the wall behind me as Ron sagged forward against me. Shrieking like a teenager in a horror flick, I jumped back and let Ron hit the ground.

"Come on! Move!" Nick Connolly grabbed my wrist and hauled me forward roughly.

Not caring that I was bare-ass naked, I raced out of my bedroom. Clothing seemed like such a trivial thing when a gun-wielding psycho had just tried to rape me. I had just cleared the edge of the kitchen when I heard Ron snarling at us.

Glancing back over my shoulder, I could barely make out his silhouette against the flickering backdrop of candles in the bedroom. The boom of the gunshot and the muzzle flash registered at the same time. Behind me, Nick gasped and crumpled forward, slamming into my back as he fell.

With another scream, I dropped to my knees and tried to help Kelly's wounded father. Blood gushed from a hole in his belly and spilled onto my hands and the floor. I pressed hard against the wound, desperate to slow the bleeding, but Nick shoved me away. "Run!"

Torn between saving myself and saving Kelly's father, I hesitated a moment too long. Ron stumbled into the living area and pointed his gun at me. Blood poured down the side of his face and onto his chest. "You bitch! I thought you loved me!"

"You shot at me! How can I love someone who shot at me?" I hated how hysterical I sounded and tried to rein in my panic. Pressing one hand to Nick's gut wound, I held up the other and begged my stalker for help. "Ron, please, put down the gun. Let me call an ambulance for Kelly's dad before he bleeds to death."

"Screw Kelly, and screw his father!" Ron waved the gun at me, and I flinched. "Why him, Bee?"

"I don't understand."

"What does Kelly have that I don't?"

Was he really going to ask me that now? Fully aware that no answer would truly appease Ron, I said the first thing that came to mind. "My brother's love."

Ron's face slackened for a fraction of a moment before hardening toward me. "Your brother's love wasn't worth much if he kept all those secrets."

"You don't know what you're talking about, Ron."

"Don't I?" He gestured toward us with the gun. "I saw

253

the photos and emails Trevor had recovered. I know exactly what your brother was."

Taken aback, I asked, "When did Trevor show you that information?"

"After I broke into his house and killed him," Ron coldly replied.

My heart stuttered in my chest. "Trevor is dead? But the paperwork for our deal arrived—"

"Consider that his last will and testament," Ron said with a frightening smile. "He promised to leave you alone if I would just stop torturing him. You have no idea how good it felt to make him pay for all the pain he caused you over the years. I tried to make him understand that sabotaging ReadIt was his warning but—"

"*You* sabotaged ReadIt?" I gawked at Ron. Who the hell was this man?

"Sweetness, I was writing code before you were out of braces." He puffed up a little. "I had my first hacking arrest at seventeen. Breaking through your company's layers of security to tamper with Trevor's project wasn't that hard. He deserved to be hurt for causing you so much trouble after you hired him."

Reeling with shock, I could only stare mutely at Ron and wonder what else this crazy man had done to interfere with my life and my business. Now I understood why Spike had been unable to find any evidence of my stalker entering or leaving my building on the security cameras and logs. Ron would have easily manipulated the security protocols.

"Ron, put down the gun."

Staggered by the sound of Kelly's voice, I snapped my attention to the front door of my apartment. Looking like absolute hell, Kelly filled the open frame with his battered body. He held up both hands in surrender but wouldn't meet my desperate gaze.

Locking eyes with Ron, he took a cautious step forward. "I know you love Bee. You don't want to hurt her like this."

"You've got a lot of fucking nerve coming in here and lecturing me about hurting her." Ron pointed the gun at Kelly's chest. I choked on a sob of fear but kept my hands pressed hard against Nick's oozing abdomen. He was still alive and conscious, but I could feel the life spilling out of him as quickly as the blood now pooling around my knees.

"You're right, Ron." Kelly took two slow steps toward us. "I hurt Bee. I broke her heart and her trust in me." His anguished gaze flitted to me ever so briefly before returning to my gun-wielding stalker. "Don't be like me, Ron. Don't ruin what you have with her."

When I glanced at Ron, I noticed the vaguest outline of legs dangling over the glass doors leading out to the balcony behind him. Stunned by the sight, it took me a few seconds to realize a man—Jack—was lowering himself down from the roof onto the small balcony. Praying the glass door was unlocked, I hastily averted my gaze lest Ron be tipped off to the Connolly brothers' plan of attack.

"I don't have anything with her anymore." Ron actually sounded like he might start crying. "You just had to come riding to her rescue like some damn white knight."

"I'm no white knight." Kelly tilted his head as if studying Ron. "Were you trying to scare her with the pictures and calls?"

"I was trying to help her see how easily I could protect her." Ron's gaze dropped to me, and he sneered. "But you had to go running to him."

"I was terrified! Kelly is the only man in the world I trusted to save me."

"Yeah—and how well did that work out for you?" Ron glared at me. "At the first sign of trouble, he ran. He abandoned you and turned his back. How does that make you feel?"

After the trauma I had just survived, my emotions were too close to the surface. I couldn't hold back the sob that burst from my lips. "Bad," I finally admitted. "Really bad."

Kelly exhaled roughly next to me. Nick gently patted my hand, almost as if to console me.

"But you still love him," Ron harshly spat. "After years of pushing you aside and ignoring you, and even abandoning you when you needed him most, you still fucking love him."

I didn't even try to deny it. Owning everything I felt for Kelly, I lifted my gaze to Ron's enraged face. "Yes, I love him."

"I hear death is a good cure for that."

Ron lifted his gun but didn't get a chance to fire. Something heavy slammed into the back of his head and exploded in shards of glass. I felt the spatter of oil on my skin and realized Jack had hurled the citronella lamp from the bistro table at Ron's head.

Kelly charged Ron, taking advantage of my stalker's momentary slump to bat the gun out of his hands. Wrapping his hands around the back of Ron's neck, Kelly jerked the man's face forward and slammed his knee into Ron's nose and mouth. The sickening crunch and explosion of blood left me lightheaded.

Rendered unconscious, Ron dropped like a sack of rocks. Jack raced across the apartment and kicked aside the gun, sending it far out of reach of Ron if he regained consciousness before the police arrived. The wail of approaching sirens wafted in through the open balcony door.

Jack dropped to his knees on the other side of his father and replaced my bloody hands with his. "Pop? You're going to be all right. Just hang on!"

When the lights suddenly popped on, Jack looked just over my shoulder and shouted, "Finn, grab some towels!"

Shaking myself from the stupor of the horror I'd just survived, I pointed to the kitchen with a shaking finger. "Top drawer in the corner, Finn."

Kelly's brother streaked by me, his prosthesis hardly slowing him down. "The police are here. An ambulance is right behind them."

Strong hands gripped my shoulders. At the first spark of contact, I knew it was Kelly now touching me. Despite his obvious injuries, he scooped me right up off the floor and carried me to the couch where he carefully deposited me on a cushion. He dragged the fringed throw blanket from the back of the seat and draped it around my naked shoulders.

Cradling my face in his busted hands, he peered intently at my face. "I'm sorry, Bee. I'm so damn sorry."

"Stop. Please." I couldn't handle listening to him apologize right now. Mindful of his father's blood on my palms, I kept my hands clenched together on my lap. "You didn't do this to me."

"It's my fault it happened." Swallowing hard, he drew slow circles on my neck with the pads of his thumbs. His voice was hardly a whisper as he asked, "Did he rape you, Bee?"

My lower lip wobbled, and I shook my head. "He tried, but your dad saved me."

Kelly looked like he was going to start apologizing

again, but he stopped himself. The eye that wasn't swollen shut blinked rapidly. A couple of tears dripped onto his bruised cheeks. Seeing so much emotion from him shocked me. When he carefully pressed his forehead to mine, his ragged breaths buffeted my skin. I could feel the guilt and regret and anguish radiating from his body, the waves so powerful they burned right through me.

"I love you so much, Bee. So much," he murmured. "I don't deserve you. I never deserved you."

Hearing him say that finally helped me understand how he had so easily believed the evidence planted by Ron. I was reminded of the way he had berated himself as being a nobody and unworthy of me. No wonder he had jumped on the first chance at bailing on our relationship. Maybe some part of him believed it was the easiest way to avoid the inevitability of me finding someone better and dumping him.

Except I wasn't going to find anyone better. I'd always known Kelly was the only man for me—much as I suspected he understood that I was the only woman for him. Our lives had been intertwined for so many years. We simply belonged together.

Forgiving him for doubting me wasn't going to be easy. Rebuilding our trust wouldn't come quickly. It was going to take some hard work from both of us, but preserving our love was worth it.

As paramedics and police rushed into the apartment, I nuzzled my mouth against his, seeking a chaste but loving kiss that he gladly returned. It was the simplest of things—but it was a good start.

CHAPTER NINETEEN
EIGHT WEEKS LATER

Awash in the warm rays of sunlight, I sighed contentedly and rolled onto my tummy to get some of that sun on my back. The soft blanket beneath me protected my body from the hot sand. Eyes closed, I enjoyed the lulling sound of waves lapping at the shore.

People liked to say that money couldn't buy happiness, but this sure felt pretty happy to me. The peace and tranquility of this long stretch of private beach couldn't be matched. As I let the sun warm my legs, I decided this excursion was worth every single penny required to rent the island for two weeks.

The first two days, I had suffered extreme withdrawal from my cell phone and the internet. The staff lodge for this secluded retreat provided internet access, but I had purposely forced myself to unplug from the rest of the world. Amita, the new COO of JBJ TechWorks, had promised to contact the island's caretaker if anything required my attention, but I doubted there was anything she couldn't handle. After all, I wouldn't have asked her to take a step up in the company if I didn't trust her.

The splashing sound from the shoreline heralded Kelly's arrival on the beach. My belly trembled with anticipation as I waited for him to rejoin me on the blanket. I craved his touch so much and counted down the seconds until he was close to me again.

After that horrific night at my apartment, we had agreed to reset the clock on our relationship. Taking leave from the Lone Star Group, Kelly had focused on aiding his father's recovery from that gunshot while I focused on cleaning up the deluge of crap that had invaded my personal and professional lives.

With Ron in jail awaiting trial, I finally felt safe. He would be going to jail for the rest of his life, or he would get the death penalty. Either way, I would never have to worry about him bothering me again.

The evidence against him in Trevor's death was irrefutable and overwhelming. The police had recovered the programmer's body from a freezer in Ron's garage. Along with hours of video the crazed stalker had shot during his attack on Trevor, Ron had also converted a room in his house into a creepy shrine-like space dedicated to me.

The thought of how close I had been to my own stalker still made me shiver with fear. I doubted I would ever again trust friends the way I had prior to my harrowing experience with Ron. I had also changed the way I used social media. In fact, before leaving on vacation, I had hosted a webinar about my experiences being stalked and what I could have—and should have— done to protect myself online.

When the truth about Ron had come into the light, Dimitri had personally visited me with Sully and Winn in tow to apologize. I didn't hold the tall, blond Russian in any way responsible, but I couldn't deny that I had enjoyed watching the two bodyguards grovel. Because they were good guys who had made an honest mistake against a dastardly foe, I had forgiven them easily. Something told me the two men would never make that type of mistake again, and that their future protectees would benefit from their misjudgment of my case.

Cool droplets of water rained down on me as Kelly stepped onto the blanket. I expected him to drop down beside me, but he surprised me by crawling over me. Sweeping aside the long strands of my hair, he peppered soft kisses along the patch of skin between my shoulders. Shivering with delight, I asked, "How was your swim?"

"Lonely." His lips followed the curve of my spine. "I missed you."

"I told you I don't like swimming."

"Then why are we vacationing on a beach?"

"Because you offered to take me skinny dipping," I said with a little laugh.

"Tonight," he promised. Those big, rough hands of his gently rolled me onto my back. With his knees planted on either side of my thighs, Kelly grasped my hands and dragged them high above my head. Holding my wrists in one big paw, he nuzzled the side of my neck before kissing his way up the side of my jaw.

Eyes closed, I relished the intimacy we now shared. Because we wanted to take things slow and rebuild the trust between us, we had decided to draw the line at kissing for a few weeks. Though it had been harder than anything to deny my desire for Kelly, I had accepted that we needed to take the physical side of our relationship out of the equation for a while. Without the safety net of lovemaking to smooth over the bumps along the way, we had been forced to work hard on fixing our relationship.

Kelly used his free hand to give the loose knot of my halter bikini top a tug. "So I was thinking that maybe today is the day."

"Oh?" Wrapping my thighs around his waist, I pulled in him a little tighter. The coolness of his body felt so good against my sun-kissed skin. "Do you think we're ready?"

He shot me one of those boyish grins that made my heart do crazy flip-flops in my chest. "Do you think we can hold out a minute longer?"

"Well," I rocked against him and felt the hard outline of his cock against my inner thigh, "maybe a few more minutes."

Capturing my mouth, Kelly caressed my naked breast. His tongue teased against mine before he deepened the kiss in the most erotic way. Surrendering to his sensual onslaught, I relaxed into him and reveled in the wondrous feelings he evoked. Still holding my wrists in place, Kelly drove me wild by flicking his tongue at my nipples and suckling me. The stiff, dusky peaks throbbed by the time he was done with them.

The ache between my thighs begged for attention. Bucking against him, I pleaded, "Touch me, Kelly."

"After two months of abstinence, I plan to do so much more than touch you, Bee."

His promise left me quivering inside. When he released my wrists, I closed my eyes and ran my greedy hands over his bulky biceps and broad shoulders. I giggled as he dotted ticklish kisses down the slope of my belly. He easily divested me of the skimpy bikini bottoms. My breath caught in my throat when his mouth continued its downward trek.

Flat on his stomach, Kelly clasped my inner thighs and gently parted them. He brushed his mouth up and down the seam of my pussy, the slight stubble on his cheeks rasping my tender skin. His tongue delved between my labia, seeking out and finding my pulsing clitoris, and fluttering over the swollen nub.

"Kelly!" I moaned his name and scratched my fingers

through his short, dark hair. He groaned against my sex, the sound so hungry, and lapped at me like a man starving for sustenance. His skilled tongue circled and flicked in the way that I loved most, pushing me closer and closer to the edge.

My hips rose up off the blanket, pressing my pussy against his tormenting mouth. I clutched at his shoulder with one hand and clawed at the fabric beneath me with the other. Kelly's hand slid under me to grip my bottom as he feasted between my thighs.

When he sucked hard on my clit, I lost it. Exploding with weeks of pent-up desire, I came so hard I couldn't even cry out. Mouth wide open, I jerked atop the blanket as Kelly's tongue fluttered over my pink kernel and gave me an orgasm so good it left me trembling and gasping for air.

I was still rocked by the aftershocks of my climax as Kelly shoved his shorts down and freed his massive cock. Reaching between us, I stroked his shaft with both hands and cupped his heavy sac. He bit back a curse word before claiming my mouth in a punishing kiss.

"I can't wait, Bee." He stabbed his tongue between my lips, fucking my mouth with it in the same way he planned to use his cock. "I need you."

Widening my thighs, I welcomed him closer. Clasping his erection, I guided the weeping head of him between my folds. I drew a slow circle around my clit with the blunt tip of him before dragging it down to my entrance. Sliding my arm around his shoulders, I pulled him down for another kiss.

Kelly surged forward as our mouths mated, sheathing every last inch of his huge cock inside my slick channel. I groaned against his lips and curled my legs around his waist. He rocked against me, slow and easy at first, but gathering his speed and force with each passing minute.

Tangling his fingers in my hair, Kelly pumped his hips and found a rhythm that set us both on fire. He brought the fingers of my left hand to his mouth and wet them with his tongue before bringing them down to my clit. With one smoldering look, he told me exactly what he wanted.

Strumming my clit, I exalted in the wickedly exciting thrill of our coupling. Clutching and groaning, we chased that shuddering, panicky sensation invading our cores and arcing into our chests. Crying out his name, I fell over the cliff's edge first, tumbling into that abyss of pure ecstasy. Kelly followed a moment later, his body seizing up as he slammed deep inside me and filled me with the jets of hot seed bursting from his cock.

Locked together so intimately, we gazed into each other's eyes. Kelly kissed me with such love and tenderness that tears prickled in my eyes and soaked my lashes. We shared a secret, knowing smile before he carefully dropped onto his side and dragged me onto his chest.

With the sounds of the ocean filling my ears, I relaxed in Kelly's arms. Too soon we would have to get dressed and return to our cabana, but for now we were content to let the sun warm our nakedness.

"So I thought we might pick through that vacation folder of yours tonight and choose our next destination," Kelly said as he combed his fingers through my hair.

Taken aback by his suggestion, I lifted up so I could gaze down into his face. "Are you seriously considering my request to travel for a year?"

Kelly traced my lower lip. "I am."

"What about your job?"

He'd been talking about leaving the Lone Star Group,

but I didn't know if he could stand to cut ties with Dimitri or the friends he'd made there.

Kelly traced my lower lip. "There's only one person in the whole wide world I want to protect."

"Oh yeah?" Drawing my initials on his chest, I said, "I hear she's on the lookout for a new bodyguard."

"Is that so?"

"Yep."

"Maybe I should submit my resume," he murmured before capturing my mouth in a sweet kiss.

"I have an even better idea." Sitting up, I clasped both his hands and dragged him into an upright position. "Why don't you chase me back to the cabana and show me all those wicked bodyguard skills of yours?"

Popping my backside with a playful swat, Kelly laughed. "I'll give you a ten second head start."

Giggling, I shoved to my feet and streaked across the sand as Kelly counted out loud. The rotten cheater was rushing after me before he'd even reached the number five. He easily caught up with me and swung me up into his arms.

Like a damned caveman, he dropped me over his shoulder and strode toward the luxury cabana. Once inside, he dropped me on the bed and leapt on top of me. Smiling against my mouth, he teasingly whispered, "Sweetheart, prepare to be amazed."

Laughing, I closed my eyes and relished the wondrous sensation of his mouth on my skin. "Oh, Kelly, I think you're about to earn a Christmas bonus."

Snorting with amusement, he nipped at my breast. "I'm a very hands-on bodyguard, Miss Langston."

And I hoped those wicked, masterful hands of his never left my body again...

Roxie Rivera

AUTHOR'S NOTE

Thanks so much for reading In Kelly's Corner! I hope you enjoyed Kelly and Bee's story. Big brother Jack is up next in January 2014 with In Jack's Arms. You can check out my website, Facebook page or sign up for my newsletter for updates and notices on upcoming releases.

If you haven't read the *Her Russian Protector* series and are wondering about Yuri, Dimitri, Nikolai, Sergei, Lena, Vivian or Ty, you should definitely check it out! The fifth book in that series features Sergei and is available now.

ABOUT THE AUTHOR

When I'm not chasing after my wild preschooler, I like to write super sexy romances and scorching hot erotica. I live in Texas with a husband who could easily snag a job as an extra on History Channel's new *Viking* series and a sweet but rowdy four-year-old.

I also have another dirty-book writing alter ego, Lolita Lopez, who writes deliciously steamy tales for Ellora's Cave, Forever Yours/Grand Central, Mischief/Harper Collins UK, Siren Publishing and Cleis Press.

You can find me online at www.roxierivera.com.

ROXIE'S BACKLIST

<u>Her Russian Protector Series</u>
Ivan (Her Russian Protector #1)
Dimitri (Her Russian Protector #2)
Yuri (Her Russian Protector #3)
Nikolai (Her Russian Protector #4)
Sergei (Her Russian Protector #5
Nikolai Volume 2 (Coming 2014)
Sergei Volume 2 (Coming 2014)
Kostya (Coming 2014)
Alexei (Coming 2014)

<u>The Fighting Connollys Series</u>
In Kelly's Corner (Fighting Connollys #1)
In Jack's Arms (Fighting Connollys #2)—Coming January 2014!
In Finn's Heart (Fighting Connollys #3)—Coming April 2014!

<u>Seduced By...</u>
Seduced by the Loan Shark
Seduced by the Loan Shark 2—Coming Soon!
Seduced by the Congressman
Seduced by the Congressman 2

<u>Erotica</u>
Chance's Bad, Bad Girl
Halftime With Craig
Tease
Eddie's Cuffs 1
Eddie's Cuffs 2
Eddie's Cuffs 3
Disturbing the Peace
Quid Pro Quo
Search and Seizure

Made in the USA
Lexington, KY
07 June 2015